The Watcher

Nicholas P. Oakley

See Sharp Press ～ Tucson, Arizona

For information contact

    See Sharp Press
    P.O. Box 1731
    Tucson, AZ 85702-1731

    www.seesharppress.com

Oakley, Nicholas P.
    The watcher / Nicholas P. Oakley – Tucson, Ariz. : See Sharp Press,
2013.

ISBN 978-1-937276-45-4

    1. Social change - Fiction. 2. Culture conflict – Fiction.
3. Utopias — Fiction. 4. Science fiction.

              823.92

The Watcher

Part I
Chapter 1

The Watcher was huge, far taller than Tian had ever dreamt. The monster climbed down from the tree above where Tian had strung her hammock for the night, its long legs unfurling, revealing strong, sinewy limbs covered in coarse black skin. The Watcher must have been at least three meters from head to toe. And it was heading right for her.

Tian lay unmoving and unblinking as the monster slowly emerged from the darkness and came to a halt a few meters above where she lay, helpless. She was petrified. She struggled to stifle a scream. Her heart thumped, and her breath came in quick shallow gasps that she tried, poorly, to conceal. She remained as still as she could. In the moons' pale light bathing the grove, though, it was clear that the Watcher, dangling precariously above her from a branch by one extraordinarily lank arm, was looking directly at her.

"You have no reason to fear me," said the creature, breaking the silence. Tian started violently. The voice was strange but clear. "I need your help, Tian.

* * *

Tian was four days away from the village, camping in a grove she often visited. This was the place where, five seasons before, she had killed one of the largest boars that her tribe had ever seen. The memory of that triumph was one of her fondest. She could recall the details with vivid clarity, even now. The tracking, the quick kill, the long journey home with the burden, and the smiles that greeted her arrival, all were unforgettable.

Ever since that day, she had returned often to this place, especially when she needed some time alone. To escape her thoughts, her fears, or vent her anger aloud to the glittering, star-encrusted sky above. The trees here were much sparser than in the surrounding woods, and Tian often lay down on the spongy ground looking up, watching for hours the moons trace their paths overhead. There was an aura around the place, the hint of something special that kept her coming back here, something that made her feel safe.

Tian had come to the grove after fighting with Grashin in the circle again. She had left the village several nightfalls before, wandering for days downriver before at last turning back and making camp here, the soft moss underfoot reassuringly familiar. She strung her hammock between two trunks and let her fingertips trail idly across the floor. The horse, Nimsha'h, was tired, and, in her haste to leave after the argument, Tian had forgotten most of the hunting and sleeping gear she normally carried with her on expeditions into the deep forest. Still, even as unprepared as she was, Tian had resolved to stay at least a couple more nights before returning, even though the nights were becoming cooler and she missed her warm autumn clothing. Though she wouldn't admit it to herself, she missed Erkan a little, too.

But she didn't want to go back. Not yet. The argument with Grashin had turned violent. Just the thought of it brought tears of shame and rage to her eyes. She couldn't bear to face the tribe yet. She was unsure whether she would be allowed back at all, or if she even wanted to go back.

Over the past few seasons she'd had a string of confrontations with Grashin. Their latest had come at a bad time for both her and the rest of their tribe. Early autumnal rains had swept down from the mountains, causing a flood as unexpected as it was devastating. Tian recalled the horror on the faces of her brothers and sisters. She remembered the panic as they led the horses to safety, and the shrieks of the younger children as the brown torrent cascaded through the trees and into the village. What the flood waters didn't carry off was ruined. The flood waters left the village decimated. The bedding was covered in a slimy, smelly sludge, the sleeping huts that were still standing were uninhabitable and, worst of all, the food stores had either been spoiled or swept away.

It was a disaster. Not only would the tribe have to start all over again, it was facing starvation.

The morning after the flood Tian had set out into the forest with a few others, determined not to return until they had some game to bring back with them. Those less proficient at hunting and trapping made preparations to travel to the silo, around twenty days trek away, to fetch supplies. They would be forced to take most of the surviving food with them on their long journey.

That meant Tian and a few other hunters had the formidable task of feeding those too old or young to go, nearly half the village, while the others went to the silo. It would be tough. Most of the big game in the area had already moved on or been killed by the village's hunting parties, and Tian knew it might be several days before any of them came across anything worth bringing back. There would be a lot of growling stomachs before she saw her tribe's faces again.

They had been in this area for many months, and the tribe had been preparing to move to the warmer, drier north when the flood hit, ruining their stores and plunging them into their current desperate state. Tian had suggested that the tribe move north early, a week before the flood. She'd seen how little game remained in the forest around the village, the empty traps, and the days without spotting, let alone killing, any game big enough to feed all those mouths. The forest seemed to have made the decision for them of when they should leave, and she'd said as much in the circle.

That was one of the reasons she left the village early that morning, before the others had even set out for the silo. She knew she wouldn't have been able to hold her tongue if she had seen Grashin before she left—his cronies had blocked her proposal to move the villages early. To Tian, the man's stubbornness made him at least partially responsible for the tribe's predicament.

Tian often hunted with a small group, usually four or five others. Although she was a good shot, she wasn't as agile as most of the others, and she found it difficult to find or follow tracks on the forest floor. She had her head in the clouds and not on the ground, one of the elders used to tell her when she was younger. Perhaps it was true. Either way, Tian relied on the others to locate prey. When they did, though, she usually took the first shot. She rarely missed.

They'd been out in the forest for two days after the flood when Tian found herself alone with Erkan, a youth several seasons younger than her. The others had peeled off gradually, following different trails, and now just the two of them crept through the undergrowth, the sounds of the forest around them their only company. Erkan was an excellent tracker, and as nimble as anyone in the village. They made a good hunting pair. She watched him ahead of her, stopping occasionally to listen to some distant twig snap, head tilted, looking intently at the ground. He was quiet and, unlike most of the other young men in the tribe, thoughtful, contemplative. Tian enjoyed his company, and they often hunted together.

Although the nights were getting colder, the middays were still very hot, and sweat trickled down her back. She missed Nimsha'h, her favorite horse.

"You should climb up sister," Erkan said, from a branch

above, where he'd paused for a break and a better view of the forest ahead. "It's much cooler up here." She unslung the bow from her back and passed it to him before scrambling up. Erkan was right. Just a few meters above the floor, the temperature and humidity dropped noticeably. They sat in silence for a while and took big draughts from their water carriers. The noise of the forest around them, the midday heat, and their tired legs soon lulled them both to sleep in their aerial perch, limbs and hair entwined.

Tian awoke at Erkan's soft tap on her forehead. He was crouched, listening intently, motionless. The heat had dropped off considerably, and the beads of sweat on her neck and chest made her shiver. Erkan's head turned sharply to the left, eyes squinting, focusing on a particularly dense area of undergrowth fifty meters upwind. He pointed toward the area with two extended fingers, glancing sideways at Tian.

Tian peered into the thick undergrowth trying to get a glimpse of whatever Erkan had spotted, but she could see nothing, so she climbed down, holding the bow loosely at her side, and crept forward as silently as possible. Apart from bird calls and the wind, the forest was quiet.

She stopped about thirty meters away from the area that Erkan continued to observe from his perch. She could see him fully now. The tree bark camouflaged his dark brown skin well. She had hunted with him for many seasons, and shared a blanket with him for two, but in that moment—poised, alert, ready to pounce like a leopard—she realized that Erkan was more man than boy, now. He was as tall as she was, and his shoulders were becoming broad and powerful. He glanced down at her as she stared. She nodded almost imperceptibly, adrenaline heightening her perceptions of her surroundings. A big boyish grin spread across Erkan's face. His anticipation was infectious. A small smile crept across Tian's lips, her first in many days.

Erkan made a number of small hand gestures—quick, precise. Tian nodded again, bringing the bow up. Her grip was light, practiced. She drew the string back until her knuckles just grazed her ochre-colored cheek. She still could not see the prey in the bushes, a young deer, according to Erkan's gestures. Seeing that she was ready, Erkan dropped down from the tree. It was a good two meters, but he didn't hesitate for a moment. He landed softly, but birds took flight above them, squawking angrily. Tian saw movement, the hint of pale fur, a bundle of nervous energy.

She released her grip on the taut bow-string. The arrow flew straight.

The deer stumbled and fell, and Erkan was upon it, grunting as he slit the fallen animal's throat.

They returned to the village before nightfall, a drizzle soaking them and muddying their path. The other members of the hunting party had killed several monkeys, and the tribe welcomed them back warmly, the worry on some of the older faces easing. The cooks quickly stripped the carcasses of their meat, which they placed in a broth simmering on the open fire in the center of the village. It was the first proper meal since the flood.

Their hunger satiated temporarily, Tian and Erkan lay near the fire listening to the songs and birds in the forest around them. Erkan ran his rough fingers across her back, and felt the stress that had gripped her fall away under his caress. She drifted off to sleep, her stomach full and her legs tired from the day's hunt.

A short while later she sensed Erkan leaving her side. She smiled without opening her eyes, basking in the fire's heat. She listened to the snatches of conversation that bubbled around her over the crackle of burning wood. The fears that had been allayed by the food were already beginning to creep back, but the warmth of the fire kept her worries at bay, for the moment.

Tian was just dozing off again when she heard her name spoken softly in the distance. She cracked her eyes open, looking towards the washing area. Erkan was speaking to someone. A

bent figure in the shadows. She opened her eyes a fraction wid
er for a better look. The faint orange glow of a pipe revealed a
familiar face: Grashin's. She scowled, closing her eyes, pretending not to have seen. After a while, Erkan returned to her side,
touching her on the shoulder as he lay back down next to her.
"What did he want?" Tian asked. Erkan jerked in surprise.
"Who? Oh, nothing," he said. Tian remained silent, trying
to compose herself. "Just congratulating me—us—on the kill,
that's all."
"Playing his games again," she said.
Erkan only shrugged.

Tian knew Grashin, and knew his methods. He was an old
man, too old to do any hard labor in the community, but appreciated as a scribe and historian. He often traded tales with
visitors from the other tribes, recording them on fragile parchments he kept stored in the deep mountain caves where they
spent the winter. Everyone in the village liked him—a nice old
man, who spoke quietly yet pleasantly, barely above a whisper.
Tian was convinced it was just an act. She'd had first-hand
experience of his more manipulative side when she first started
asking questions about the way things were done. At first, she
didn"t realize what was going on, but gradually she worked out
the pattern, and told her friends about it.
Then Grishin had some quiet talks with her friends in the
tribe, and they grew distant. Some of them began to shun her,
and she hunted alone more often She started spending a lot of
her time alone in the forest. The benches around her in the Circle emptied over the weeks.
When she called out Grashin in one of the meetings, accus-
ing him of manipulating her friends with promises or whispered threats, they shouted her downs, called her an egoist, a
troublemaker. Exasperated, lonely, she lost her temper. That
was the first time she was removed from the Circle for refusing to relinquish the floor, for refusing to let one of Grashin's

cronies block another of her ideas without consideration. She"d glared at Grashin as she left the Circle. He sat on his bench, his bony legs crossed, pulling serenely on his pipe, a small grin on his face. His eyes glistened, mocking her.

She knew then that he'd played her, that she'd fallen into a trap. She saw plainly in that moment the manner of his power, and choked back tears. She felt sick with helplessness in the face of this old man who, with a whisper in an ear or a casual remark, held more sway in the tribe than she ever possibly could.

Tian had spoken to Erkan about Grashin on several occasions out in the woods. He had been sympathetic, but refused to believe her. He found it inconceivable that the old man could have as much influence as she said he did.

"That's absurd, Tian," he said to her as they made camp one night after an exhausting day of hunting, and after Tian had loosed another diatribe about Grashin. "You know no one can rule us like that. Even I could block his proposals. We have the Circle, after all. The Circle stops all of that, all the things you accuse Grashin of doing. He just can't do it; we wouldn"t allow it."

Tian grunted.

"I don't understand why you're so fixated on Grashin, anyway," he continued. "I don't even remember the last time he blocked one of your proposals, or even said anything about them."

"No, of course not. That's exactly my point. He doesn't need to say anything in the meetings. Things are already decided days, weeks before. He insinuates, he suggests... talks about the old days, about the ways things were before. I've seen him do it. The others, get the hint. He gets his way, and he stays as this nice little old man who spends too much time with his papers." Tian couldn't help the bitterness in her voice.

Erkan was silent, thoughtful for a few minutes as he undressed. "You make it sound like he controls us—like, he's a leader, or something." Erkan's voice lowered as he uttered the profanity. "We would kick him out of the community if he ever tried to pull that here. But he never makes any proposals. I can't see how he could have control when we have the Circle, when we have the Way."

"The Circle doesn't do anything. You know Grashin never makes any proposals, except to do with his stupid histories that he's so protective of, that nobody else even cares about. He doesn't *need* to do anything. Everything is the way he likes it, the way it's always been. His power is *outside* of the Circle. Don't you see that? He protects the old ways. The old ways protect him!"

"Because the old ways work, Tian."

"Not always."

***

The long benches in the Circle seemed empty. With half the tribe away, there were many empty spaces on the long benches. Several other hunting and scavenging groups had arrived since Erkan's and Tian's group returned, some bringing meat, but most bringing sacks of roots and berries. The tribe was not at immediate risk of starvation. Ulgha roots were prevalent throughout the forest; when boiled and mashed with water, they made a barely edible paste that was at least minimally nutritious, for both for humans and the horses. The tribe could, and had in the past, lived on ulgha for weeks, but it was a food that tasted of hardship, of failure. So the tribe was reluctant to resort to ulgha yet, and the game and berries were welcome.

Tian could see a few of the hunters slumbering in the huts, the canvas doors pegged open. The summer villages were usually spare and unelaborate, because the tribe sometimes moved three or four times during the long season depending on the game, water supply, and weather. Despite the regular upheaval, it was Tian's favorite season. Summer meant game, warmth, hunting trips, long days and short nights.

This season had been easy until the flooding. They had only had moved twice that summer, and had been scheduled to leave just a quarter-moon after the flood struck to escape the approaching fall and the heavy rains. The flood could not have come at a worse time. It had ravaged the stocks of food they had amassed in preparation for their relocation, stores they could ill afford to lose so close to their move. They now had to hope for good hunting and that those traveling to the silo would bring back enough to keep them going until they could resettle in the warmer north.

Most of the younger villagers had volunteered to go to the silo, taking with them most of the horses and all of the dogs. The morning bustle of the village was muted without them.

The tribe always held Circles at night, after the final meal, before the nightly recreation. Tian couldn't remember the last time they'd held one in daylight, let alone before midday. The grey dawn was on the cusp of turning into bright sunshine, the unseasonably rainy weather apparently behind them now.

She chose an empty bench in the Circle and readied herself. Erkan came across the grassy communal area to the benches, sat down next to her.

"Feeling better?"

"Not really."

She hadn't seen Grashin yet this morning, but she was still furious with him. "None of this would have happened if he had given my proposals a fair chance in the Circle."

"Please, don't start anything today." He knew exactly who she was talking about.

He reached out for her hand, and she let him take it. The benches around them began filling up. Grashin ambled over from a workshop—he used a small workbench in one of them upon which he was often writing—talking quietly with several of the older villagers.

Erkan noticed the way Tian was looking at the Grashin and said, "It's been hard enough these past two days. Look around. Everyone is tired, scared. This isn't the time for this... for your egoizing."

Tian snatched her hand away from his, and stood abruptly. She turned her angry eyes on Erkan, now.

"No, Tian, I didn't mean..." he said, reaching for her withdrawn hand.

She got up and left without a word. Erkan didn"t dare follow, and sank to the bench, crestfallen. Tian marched across the Circle, all eyes on her as she went, brushing past Grashin and his companions. The benches were organized in a broad circle, with a large central area for a fire. It had been constructed in this fashion for as long as Tian—and everyone else for that matter—could remember. This was the way it was done, and had always been done.

And, for as long as Tian could remember, there had always been one particular bench almost imperceptibly closer to the fire than the others. For it was upon this bench Grashin had sat, in every village across the forest, in every consensus Circle. Tian had spoken about this to her friends. They had laughed. Then, when realisingrealizing she was serious, they made awkward excuses, changed the topic, or told her it was a trifle.

Right now, it was this bench, that was the focus of Tian"s rage. It was doubtful that any of the other villagers had noticed its position. If they did, it was unlikely that they thought anything of it. But everyone noticed it now. Tian forced herself past him Grashin, throwing herself down on the benchit, staring back ack at him contemptuously, as if daring him to sit on it next to her.

Grashin faltered for a moment as Tian glowered at him. Then, raising his long pipe to his mouth and taking a sip, he smiled and bowed his head. He gave his companions a quick glance and a small shrug. With knowing smiles they sat on an adjacent bench.

Tian was practiced at hiding her true feelings. She was used to the snubs, the condescending nods, the patronizing, smug way Grashin spoke to, and about, her. She had burned with embarrassment and shame the first few times he had deflected her anger with the wave of a hand or a shrug, as if she were a petulant child. She had felt the eyes of the whole tribe on her; they had seen her public dismissal—the dismissal of a rebellious adolescent throwing a tantrum, and nothing more. She had suppressed the blushes, the tears, the feeling of loneliness.

But this time it was different. She felt no shame. She felt contempt—for Grashin and the rest of the tribe. Even Erkan couldn't see what she meant. She remembered the time she had tried to explain to him about Grashin's bench. Like the others, he had laughed it off. When he realized she was serious he became awkward, withdrawn. Erkan hadn't seen it. He was young, sure, but she knew it wasn't just that. No, the only person who ever understood, who could ever understand, was no longer around. That still burned inside of her, more than any shame or embarrassment old Grashin could ever force her to feel.

CHAPTER 2

The Watcher's eyes were bright yellow, almost cat like, a stark contrast to the black, hairless head in which they were set. As it stared down at her, Tian''s hand slipped down to her side, to the knife in the belt she wore. It was the only weapon she had. The Watcher simply smiled.

"I'm afraid your weapon is too blunt to hurt me much, Tian. You should have had it sharpened before you left." The voice was strange, melodic. It was higher than any man's, but too low to be female. It seemed to shift tone after each word, as if the Watcher were singing rather than whispering to her. It was peculiarly calming, and entirely nonhostile. But Tian couldn''t calm herself. The knot in her stomach was awful. She swung wildly with the blade, baring her teeth and attempting a threatening noise. It caught in her throat, and she merely whimpered hoarsely.

The Watcher didn't move, only cocked its head, as if appraising her. Just like Erkan, she thought.

"Am I all that frightening?" it asked. "I thought that someone like you wouldn"t find me threatening. Especially as you spend so much time out here alone. Here," it said, spreading its arms wide, palms facing her. "I mean you no harm, and I apologize for scaring you. I'm sorry to see the problems you've been having with Grashin in the village, Tian. Very sorry." The Watcher shook its head with what seemed to be real feeling.

Tian struggled onto her elbows, the hammock rocking violently back and forth violently as she did so. The panic, the horror, subsided somewhat in the face of the Watcher's urbane manner and sudden change of topic. How in Veyshlur did the Watcher know about Grashin? She sheathed the blade, which seemed like a child's toy in comparison to this huge, lanky creature.

"What— Who are you? How do you know me?" she stammered.

"I'm a Watcher. Don"t you recognize me, from the stories? That isn't my real name, of course, but Watcher is fine. In fact, we sometimes call one another that. Ssme of us are actually rather fond of the name."

"We...?" Tian glanced around her, expecting to see the trees full of glowing yellow eyes.

"Oh, no, you misunderstand. It's just me here. We travel alone most of the time."

"So, what do you want?" she stuttered.

"I told you. We need your help."

"With... with what?"

"The Qah."

Tian took a sharp breath.

"They have killed some of my people. Their bands are ranging fauther and farther south. We need your help to stop them."

* * *

Erkan had not been Tian's first partner. It was common for children in the tribe to lie with others as soon as they desired. Taboos existed, though unspoken. Older adolescents and adults rarely lay with younger members of the tribe, and long partnerships between adolescents of any age were uncommon. Short, casual couplings were the norm.

Tian was sixty seasons old when she first lay with Priash, a girl several seasons older than her. It was later than most of Tian's friends. She had several casual partnerships with friends of her own age after that first time with Priash, but these soon reverted to platonic kinship.

She always returned to Priash.

Tian often thought about Priash in the grove, and late at night in the village. Haydill, a girl who often slept in the cot next to Tian, snored just as Priash used to., and Tian often had to move during the night to an empty bed to get any sleep. Although Tian never remembered them, she knew that she dreamt about Priash from the damp sheets and wet forehead she woke up to almost every morning. If she disturbed the rest of the tribe with her nightmares, though, they never once said anything to her about it.

Tian had never known real loss before Priash. Elders passed away. She saw brothers and sisters die of illness, of accidents, and she mourned them as the community did—publicly, openly. She overcame this kind of sorrow with the help of the tribe. But she was never able to come to terms with losing Priash. It was too personal, the grief too raw. She raged, she cried, she fought. But she could never forget. Priash had been everything to Tian. A sister, a lover, a guide, a friend. She could be intolerable company, but Tian couldn't live without her. Being with Priash was like nothing being with no one else, like the rest of the world dropped into a pale shadow, an insignificant blur next to her.

Priash was taken while Tian was away hunting.

Unlike Tian, Priash was a poor hunter. She worked instead

with some of the elder herbalists in the village. When she went on expeditions with them, she was always one of the first to find what they were seeking. As Priash grew older, her natural ability and burgeoning expertise with the plants of the forest exceeded even Tian's proficiency with the bow. So it didn't surprise Tian when Priash, along with Grashin and several of the other elders went on a long expedition to gather medicinal plants and seeds that didn't grow locally and that were only found high on the wintry mountains slopes, where the community spent the cold winters in a maze of caves.

"Why don't you get these seeds when we go up to the winter caves, Priash?" Tian had asked when Priash first told her of the journey. The mountain range was also where Grashin kept his histories in one of the deeper, more inaccessible caves, and Tian suspected that this was the real reason for their expedition.

"Don't be stupid, sister. If we could do that, do you really think we'd—I'd—be spending twenty days traveling to get them? Twenty days I could be spending with Yuri?"

Tian pinched her hard on the thigh. Priash laughed, a loud, infectious laugh. Yuri was a popular older boy who lay with many of the girls in the village. Priash often teased Tian about him. Priash was one of those Yuri had partnered with regularly before Tian.

"Well, why bother going at all then?" asked Tian.

"Do you really think I'll be going with that stubborn old shit-stool Grashin if it wasn't important? He's going to add at least four days to our journey, whilst he plays around with his books in his cave. No, of course not. The plants are seeding now. By winter they're all gone. Dispersed, buried, eaten. We need them. For one thing, we use the seeds from tulva to make the ointment you hunters put on your blisters. That's why I'm going. And you'll just have to lump it. Unless you like blisters?"

"No," said Tian, sulkily. Tian was no herbalist, and she hated when Priash started talking about the different plants that she worked with. Tian had the distinctly childish feeling of being left out. Reading her perfectly, Priash laughed again, pulling her down to the floor. "Don't worry. I'll be back before you know it. Try not to have too much fun while I'm away."

They kissed. Tian clung to her tightly as they made love that night.

Ten days after Priash left with the others in search of the seeds of the mountain orchid, Tian returned from her hunting trip. Wails greeted her return. She rode up to the Circle, not bothering to dismount from Nimsha'h.

"What happened?" she demanded. She scanned the crowd and saw Grashin, huddled and dusty in the center of the tribe. She asked again, shouting over the weeping. She guided Nimsha'h through the villagers toward Grashin. "What happened? Where is she?" He looked up at her. Looked into her eyes. She was a frightening sight. Astride Nimsha'h, she looked fierce; her long plaited hair swept across her shoulders, her eyes wild, her mouth twisted in rage, her knuckles white on the reigns. "Where is Priash!" she screamed. She saw him cower from her. She saw the fear in his eyes. In that scene of public grief, amongst the entire tribe, in the Circle—the closest the village had to a sacred site—she saw into his soul.

She saw the guilt, and she heard him lie.

"I could do nothing, child. They took her."

"Who took her?"

"The Qah."

Tian left the village. She searched for weeks, roaming roving all over the forest. Eventually she fell in with another tribe. They accepted her without question, without judgment. Unlike her birth tribe, who only moved four or five times an orbit, they were entirely nomadic. They ranged across the vast steppes, where meat and water were scarce and the days were longer. They had no winter caves, no regular settlements, no histories stored away on frail parchments. Life was hard, but Tian grew to enjoy life on the move, never in one place for more than a few nightfalls.

She remembered little of that time now, only the emotional pain and the loneliness, and that the constant travel offered her an escape from her memories. The pain never lessened, but her longing for the forests became greater. Every new face that arrived in her adopted tribe was a disappointment, her hope fading even as the grief remained raw, an open wound. The seasons on the plains were unremarkable. The game never changed, only the color of the grasses and the length of the nights.

There was the threat of violence, there, too. During her time with the nomads, she heard rumors of burnt villages, mounted warriors, and slaver raids. They came across small bands of refugees, brimming with horrific stories of dead brothers and sisters, of enslavement and armies. The tribe welcomed those survivors, just as they had welcomed her. Life was tough, and these people had little, but the principles of mutual aid and the Way were still strong. Some chose to stay. Others feared the threat they had fled and headed onwards.

Away from the Qah.

Tian's return to her birth tribe had been difficult for her, but they welcomed her back warmly. She never talked about Priash, and none of the others mentioned her, at least in Tian''s hearing. She hadn't discussed it even with Erkan. It was too private to talk about, even with him.

* * *

The Circle started soon after Tian had usurped Grashin's bench for herself. The facilitator was Bal, one of Grashin's closest friends. After some short speeches in thanks to the hunting parties—no one looked at Tian—they began discussing the progress of the clean up, and the state of the food stocks.

Sho'een, an elder, stood up and began to talk.

"It seems pointless to begin any rebuilding. I think it's warm enough to sleep out here for a few days, in the open. We''ll be on the move soon, and we should focus on the journey to the new village."

"I agree. Sleeping outside for a few nights won't do any harm. Besides, the smell in the huts is terrible."

"Where will we store our food? If the rains come again..."

"The workshops."

"Good idea."

"Agreed. Consensus?"

"Consensus," echoed all of the voices. Even so, with so many gone, it was much quieter than normal. Eerily so, Tian thought.

"What about these pools of water? The midges are getting pretty bad."

"Mosquitoes, too. I woke up covered in bites."

"There's not much we can do except leave."

Thrake, one of the elders, stood up and took the floor. "There's also the matter of food. Thanks to some of the younger ones, we have some meat, roots, and fresh berries, but we ought to gather more ulgha."

There were a few disgusted grunts.

"I know, I know. Just as a precaution. We can't be too careful. Consensus?"

"Consensus," said the Circle in unison, even Tian mouthing the familiar word, as unenthusiastically as the rest.

Consensus could sometimes be a long process, even on insignificant matters. During meetings of the Circle, many of the tribe occupied themselves with small tasks, especially when consensus wasn't reached at the outset. Marthya'h, Tian's bloodmother, sharpened the knives and smaller spears the hunters used on their expeditions. Erkan whittled or cleaned his nails. Grashin smoked his pipe. Others plaited hair, knitted long socks for the winter caves, or chewed nalga root. Idophes made some of his prettiest necklaces and bracelets at the Circle by the light of the fire.

Tian did nothing at the meetings, except occasionally scowl. As a girl, before Priash, before her time away from the tribe, Tian found Circles long and boring, and a little intimidating. She was always eager to get them over with so she could enjoy the stories and songs before the tribe retired to bed. She used to spend most of the time in the Circle meetings looking at the faces of those speaking, discussing, and arguing by the fire and moons' light. Tian rarely paid attention to the interminable speeches, the constant calls for consensus, the cryptic processes, the intricacies of which she had often heard, but which she never really cared to remember. Instead, she would watch the other children, pulling faces at her friends, or sneaking around and pulling their plaits or tickling their feet, making them cry out, drawing a sharp look from the adults.

But mostly she watched the brown, lined faces. She loved the way the skin around their eyes crinkled when they laughed, the way their dimples showed when they smiled, the way their hands would danced when they explained, the way their eyebrows rose and fell when they agreed and disagreed, the way their noses wrinkled and their lips pursed when they were frustrated or angry. She enjoyed watching and learning the faces and emotions of these people, her people, the brothers and sisters of the tribe.

Tian watched them now in the Circle, all these seasons later, but she felt little of her former love for them. No, she realized suddenly, she didn't belong here any more.

There was a lull in the discussion. Tian knew that most of them were expecting her to speak, and she wasn't going to disappoint. She rose to her feet. The few conversations that had started during the short break ended abruptly.

Before she had slept the night before, she had thought for some time about what she would say. She imagined rallying against Grashin, calling him out for his short-sightedness, his stubbornness, shouting at him, shaking him by his skinny shoulders, to make him understand, to make him listen, making accusations, making the rest of the tribe see him for what he was.

To change things.

She said and did none of this now. Instead, she walked to the center of the consensus Circle. She gazed around at the faces of the tribe.

"I'd like to make a proposal to the Circle. It's one that's been made before, but it's worth making again in light of recent events." She gestured toward the devastated food huts. "I'd like to take the pips of the indus fruit, and the seeds of the ghat grass. I'd like to cut large clearings in the forest, and plant these seeds in the ground in the spring, and cultivate them in the summer, and harvest them in the fall. I'd like to make wine and jam and preserves from the indus, and beer and and bread with the ghat. I'd like to have plenty of food all year round."

As she spoke, she thought of Priash. She spoke Priash's words, Priash's phrases. Gave voice to her dream all these seasons later.

They had had many discussions about this. Priash had strong feelings on the subject. Tian had spent many afternoons with Priash out in the forest, Priash showing her the seeds, roots, grains and fruits that she longed to plant and cultivate. She spoke to Tian of orchards, of fields full of grains, of vast stores of food that would free them from the incessant upheaval, offer them freedom from the hardships of nomadic life. Priash had told her urgently, passionately about the opportunities it would bring the tribe, the opportunity to make a permanent place for themselves in the forest, to build warmer sleeping quarters, make sturdier stables and kennels for the animals, larger and cleaner kitchens and washing areas.

Tian had long known how much Priash hated moving season after season. Before a move, she would be grouchy, snapping at the most harmless comment or remark. Tian tended to avoid her at such times. The horses could only carry so much, and the tribe tended to travel light, carrying only tools, bedding, clothing, and provisions for the trek, as well as a few personal possessions. There was little room for Priash's large collection of herbs, seeds, powders, oils, and extracts that she built up in every village. Priash was forced to leave most of these behind with every move, carrying as much as she could in the horse bags, and in deep pockets she stitched into the her clothing and bedding she used. But it pained her to leave so much behind, to look at the shelves in the herbalist hut and make her choices, and start afresh every move. It was a constant irritant.

It hurt Tian to see Priash so upset, especially about something that was, frankly, alien to Tian. Apart from a few bracelets, she had nothing to take, and nothing to leave behind.

If Tian needed something, she took it, or made it, or asked for it. The hunters shared their gear, and she rarely used the same bow twice; tweaking the tightness of the string to suit her draw took just a moment. If there she couldn't find one she liked, she would cut the wood and bring it to Garuthka, one of the better bowyers in the tribe, or make the bow herself if he was busy. The same went for the knife she used, even the clothes she wore, and the saddle she rode upon. If she needed an axe or a new belt, she took it from the stores and replaced it once she was done with it, or discarded it if it was broken. She remembered a verse from one of the old songs the tribe sang as they were building their a new village, one of Tian's favorites— favorites that she often hummed to herself while she was out alone or hunting.

> Empty and be full;
> Wear out and be new;
> Have little and gain;
> Have much and be confused.

Priash didn't shared these sentiments, but they meant much to her. If she were completely honest with herself, Tian found Priash's dream of settling in one place strange, and not a little boring. She enjoyed moving, and she took great pleasure in the slow treks by horse along narrow animal paths in the forest, exploring areas they'd never been in, that no one had stepped in for seasons. She found it invigorating to clear a virgin area of forest and construct their new home, together, from nothing. This normally took three of four days, and the festivities that followed were always loud and boisterous. Once the final log pole was placed, and the last rope pegged, the whole village would take part in the first hunt. Even those who rarely hunted, the younger children and the elders, would come along. Whatever game they caught, which, with all the noise and commotion, was usually too slow or old to run very fast, was brought back to the village in triumph. The consensus circles on the first night were jovial, full of laughter and dancing. It was in these times that Tian felt most alive, felt the most love for the tribe. It was for these times that Tian had returned from her self-imposed exile with the plains tribe after Priash was taken.

So when Tian spoke that morning in the Circle about the ghat and the indus, she was remembering Priash's dream, not her own. Yet she knew it was the only way to save herself, to save them, from Grashin. The constant rebuilding, along with the circle rituals, was lulling the tribe into a false sense of security. They believed that power, hierarchies, leaders could not exist in their society. But Tian could see that the constant rebuilding was not a source of strength, but weakness. It was one of the sources of Grashin's power, a way of erasing the past, of covering his tracks.

In her heart, she knew that they would shout her down and, perhaps, she longed for it. Besides, Grashin had taught her well; she was setting her own trap.

"I'm tired of moving. I want to settle somewhere and never go hungry, never worry about floods or droughts or the game moving on or the fishing being bad."

The reaction was slow to come, the tribe still tired from the previous day and the sleepless night before. At first there was exasperation. Then anger.

"What you are asking for is *agriculture!*" a voice from the back shouted, spitting the last word.

"Yes," replied Tian. "Exactly."

More shouts rang out; several villagers were on their feet gesturingiculating aggressively. Bal, the facilitator, called for Tian to be removed. The timekeeper, a young woman named Aavyen, shouted an objection, and called on him to ask for consensus. Reluctantly, he called for it. Unsurprisingly, there was none. The ensuing debate was loud, but predictable. The elders used scare words like agriculture, technology, culture, civilization. Some of the tribe called her an egoist, shouted at her for disrupting the meeting. Aavyen called for a break, and walked over to where Tian sat alone, on Grashin's bench.

She had slept with Aavyen a couple of times, but they were not close, and hadn't spent much time with one another for a number of seasons. Now Aavyen appealed directly to her, pleading.

"Why are you doing this, Tian? You know they'll kick you out of the meeting. Stop now, before it turns nastier. Stop being so selfish. Can't you see we're struggling here, that people are afraid, exhausted? The trip to the silo is dangerous, autumn is coming, and we have no provisions. You start talking about indus and ghat at a time like this?"

"This seems like the ideal time to be talking about it," said Tian calmly.

"You're being deliberately provocative. Pursuing your childish agenda, your damned vendetta against Grashin now? You won't withdraw? You want this to continue?"

"I'm afraid so. I won't withdraw."

Aavyen's head dropped. With a sigh, she turned, gesturing to Bal that the Circle could be reconvened.

The reaction was as strong, if not stronger, than Tian had anticipated. The tribe rallied in opposition to her proposal, united by tiredness, worries, and fears. Even her closest friends spoke passionately against her. Never had the tribe turned on a proposal, on an individual, with such a united voice. Aavyen tried to moderate the more extreme speakers, but with little success. The ghat and indus proposal became merely a pretext to denounce Tian and all of her ideas as divisive, dangerous, reactionary. The tribe released all of its fears, all of its frustrations at her recent conduct in the Circle.

Tian sat impassively through it all. She watched Grashin out of the corner of her eye. His face was blank. She wondered what he was thinking, what schemes were fermenting behind those small grey eyes.

Then he surprised her. He stood up, slowly, silencing the shouts. The sun shone brightly in the sky now, and he squinted against it. The tribe was used to hearing his voice. It was gentle and familiar, and he would often read from his histories or recite from memory stories of the old times or the Way, as well as the myths and legends that had scared Tian as a child. He tended to ramble, his stories full of asides and embellishments, but he was a good storyteller. His usual verbosity deserted him today, though. He uttered just one word. The first time Tian, and many of the others sitting in the Circle that day, had heard him say it.

"Block," he said.

Tian smiled.

CHAPTER 3

Tian could see the Watcher's face more clearly now by the light of the fire. She was still wary. Neither of them had spoken since it had mentioned the Qah. It seemed more real, now, sitting across from her its back against a tree. Its face was open, expressive. Its long fingers and big palms were crossed in its lap. It actually looked relaxed, calm. Non-threatening, almost.

After some time she broke the silence.

"I used to have nightmares about you. You were part of our nightfall stories. A myth from the old times. A monster to scare children with."

"Yes, I've heard some of those stories," the Watcher said. "In a tribe far to the east, they call us Zasophan. The night demon. Heard that name?"

Tian shook her head.

"We had a bad reputation there. They said we ate babies. Puppies, too. If someone fell sick, a horse tripped and fell, or a wolf took a fowl, we invariably got the blame. They took to hanging the bones of dead dogs above the doors to their sleeping quarters to ward us off, stop us snatching their children from their cots." An involuntary shiver ran through Tian. She had often woken in the night, convinced a Watcher was creeping around in the shadows. The Watcher noticed it, but continued as if it hadn't. "I'm not entirely sure why they thought dead dogs would work, apart from the smell. Anyway, I wasn't engineered to be particularly friendly looking. But these keep me hidden, safe." It pinched the rough black skin on its arms, ran a big hand over its hairless skull, and gestured at its long legs. Tian watched in silence, drinking in the sight of the monster's weird body, trying to suppress the prickly feeling on the back of her neck. "I'm designed for observing and survival," the Watcher continued. "Not to intimidate, or scare. Or even eat imaginative young children." It smiled again, small blunt teeth a shocking white against its dark face.

"Well, those stories scared me. I still have nightmares about the Watchers," Tian confessed. "About you."

"There are many more dangerous creatures than me in these woods, Tian."

The smile faded. "If I were you, I'd be dreaming about them, not me." The Watcher's voice dropped, as if talking to itself. "*When the people do not fear what they ought to fear, that which is their great dread will come on them.*"

Tian was taken aback by the peculiar phrase; she thought she had heard it somewhere before, but couldn't place it.

"The Qah are coming south, enslaving and killing. Surely you heard the stories while you were on the steppes?"

Tian hid her shock that the creature knew such specific details about her life. "We thought they were rumors, like the Watchers. But what can I do about it? Why do you need my help?"

"The silos, Tian. They are using them as bases, building

sprawling, permanent encampments around them, using them as staging grounds for raids on the surrounding territories. They are sweeping across this continent like a plague, hopping from silo to silo. Now they are here, in the forests, and they are close."

"The silos?" Tian whispered, her heart beating fast. The memory came back to her of the morning after the flood as she'd fled into the forest to avoid seeing Grashin. That last look back at all those loved ones preparing to head out into the forest to the silo rushed back.

"Yes. The Qah have found a way to circumvent our safeguards." Tian noticed the pain in its eyes, its resonant voice expressing the faintest note of anguish. "Once they did so, they've been expanding their little empire exponentially."

"I don't understand. How do you know about the silos?"

"Oh. Simple. We built them, of course. My people live in them."

Tian stared at the Watcher, into its large, strangely friendly eyes, trying to read them.

"I'm sorry, Watcher, but that's hard to believe. It's impossible. Even if you did build them..." she hesitated. The Watcher gave her a little affirmative nod. She continued. "Your people couldn't live there. We'd have seen you."

"It's unlikely. Very little of the silo is above ground. What you see when you go there is just a fraction of what is really there. We live in bunkers underneath, in a cave networklike that of your winter village."

"But, the smell," said Tian, repressing a gag at the memory.

The Watcher laughed loudly in the dark, scaring Tian. Its laugh was melodic, and sounded distinctly, like birdsong. It was strange to see this lanky creature emitting such a beautiful yet frightening noise.

"I'll let you in on a secret Tian. We make the smell, too." Its yellow eyes sparkled, amused.

Tian had been to a silo twice. The first time she had been very young, twenty seasons perhaps, too young to remember the details clearly. She knew it had been a long, dry summer season; she recalled the dust that covered the village, the bedding, and her clothes, in every wrinkle, every crease and fold. She had forgotten the trek to the silo, but she remembered the nauseating smell, the pungent taste, distinctly. Tian had remained behind with the children and their caretakers, three or four days away from the silo, but even there the smell was foul.

The second time the tribe had resorted to a silo she was much older, forty-five seasons. She'd been old enough to remember the hard winter and the long journey to it. The game was slow to recover that spring. Winter had lasted weeks longer than usual, and they had consumed all of the preserved meat and most of the fruits. They even had to eat the gritty ulgha paste.

The smell hit them when they were around fourteen days into the journey. It started as a faint odor, but quickly became overpowering. The others had warned her that the food silos were unpleasant places, and children as young as her rarely made the entire journey. But she had pleaded to go along, unwilling to be left behind.

She later wished that she hadn't been so adamant.

Only a few hours after they left the younger children behind, the smell became overpowering. Her eyes stung, she vomited several times, and she suffered dizzy spells. She stuffed strong smelling herbs up her nose and chewed takka infused with banjali root, as the others did, but it was no good. Tian could *taste* the aroma. It clung to the back of her throat, however much she packed her nostrils. Tears poured down her cheeks. With every step she took closer to the silo it seemed to worsen. She imagined it coating her lungs and insides with a rank, black sludge— feces, dead fish, burnt flesh, and decomposing animal guts.

That night she wrapped long scarves soaked in pungent ointments around her head, as the others did, but she got little sleep. Her stomach turned over unbearably, the stink never abating.

The rest of the journey was a haze, a blur of nausea and the stench of decay.

The silo itself was small, circular, flat, out of place here amongst the ancient trees. Encased in a dazzling hard shell, it was completely alien. It stood silently, the surrounding forest eerily silent. Tian was surprised to see cold fire pits and the remains of small shelters around it. She'd asked an elder what these were.

"Sometimes people live here," he'd said.

"Who?" she gasped.

"It depends. Mostly hermits, freeloaders. Some deviants unwelcome in the tribes. Small groups of bandits sometimes. But they always move on. No one can stand this place for long. Still, this is a very dangerous place, little one. Stay close."

Tian nodded, reaching for his hand. She dreaded staying another night in this place. The thought that people might actually choose to live here, even temporarily, astonished her.

A wide door on the south side of the silo was the only entrance. Above it was a strange circular symbol, with unfamiliar writing around it. She didn't ask what it was, she was too eager to get inside, to get away—she hoped—ffrom the smell. As they approached, the door slid open. Feigning confidence she didn't feel, she followed the others inside.

The silo was cold and very quiet. The smell was horrific, even worse than outside. It was like running into a wall. She nearly fell over. She could see the effect it was having on the others; they too staggered. Someone fainted behind her.

She swallowed dryly, glancing around. The silo was empty. The walls were like those outside, white and shiny, and they seemed to absorb sound. But here they also radiated a soft light. Perturbed, Tian looked at the others, trying to understand. Where was everything? Had the bandits taken all the food? Had they traveled all this way, through the stench, for nothing? Tears welled in her eyes. Disappointment hit her like a punch in the gut.

* * *

Tian hadn't anticipated that Grashin would be the one to block her proposal, let alone that he'd propose to exclude her from the tribe. She'd underestimated him. She thought him too cowardly to act himself, relying on others to do his work for him. But he'd seized his chance to be rid of Tian. He knew that the tribe was exhausted and angry, and open to extreme measures. Yet Grashin had misjudged her, too.

"For proposing the adoption of agriculture, and in doing so undermining the values, customs and traditions of this tribe and the Way, I propose that Tian be expelled from the Circle and from the tribe. Immediately, and indefinitely."

The tribe was shocked. There was a palpable unease the moment he paused. He quickly continued, his voice rising above the murmurs that had broken out.

"Tian has persistently attempted to introduce hierarchical beliefs to our society, has incited the tribe to discard the Way, and has made proposals to the Circle that endanger our way of life. She has pursued a personal vendetta, a feud against me, and in doing so has persistently disrupted the Circle, jeopardizing the safety of our society for the sake of herself. It is for these *crimes*," he said, using a word unfamiliar to many of the villagers, "that I propose she be expelled and excluded."

They had all learned as children that planting seeds or fruits was dangerous, a precursor to exotic, forbidden things such as civilization, hierarchy, law. There were ancient and mostly unspoken taboos in the tribe, ones that ran deep, tangled up with the mysterious and unknown. No one ever elaborated on these things, on why they were so bad, so frightening, and Tian got the sense that her elders didn't grasp the concepts too firmly themselves.

But they often talked about the histories and the Way. Grashin cited these now.

There was still a strong sense of discomfort in the Circle. Tian knew that, despite the things many of them said only mo-

ments before, that most had never contemplated her expulsion.
Grashin sensed this. He changed tack.

"We all know the histories talk about the before time, a time
before consensus, before we understood the Circle and the Way.
The scrolls talk of huge villages living in squalor, tied to one
place for all seasons. Places of misery, where some feasted every
nightfall while others starved, where some toiled all day while
others played, where brothers and sisters killed and enslaved
one another over the dirt, the air, even over the rocks in the
ground. What she," he gestured at Tian, "is suggesting will lead
us back to those times, will introduce to our society all that we
have for generations striven to protect ourselves from. We must
not allow her egoizing to corrupt us any longer, to threaten our
brothers and sisters, to threaten our future. I call for her banish-
ment. I call for consensus."

Tian didn't stick around to hear the result. She walked out of
the Circle, heading towards the workshops. The tribe watched
her in silence as she went. Nobody tried to stop her. Grashin
eyed her closely as she walked by him, trying to figure out her
next move, and whether what he had said was enough to make
her leave. A public humiliation that she would or could not
stand.

Tian had to suppress a smile as she walked through the
flood-wrecked village. All she had intended to do was trick one
of Grashin's allies into condemning the cultivation of seeds. She
expected a mild rebuke, and some choice quotes from one of
his cronies that she might be able to throw back in Grashin's
face in the Circle. She hadn't anticipated that events would play
out like this, so perfectly. When he began speaking, she tried to
calm her excitement, the happiness that was bubbling up inside
of her. She was still half expecting another of Grashin's ploys,
expecting him to have outsmarted and outplayed her yet again.
But as he rambled on portentously, self-righteously about the
Way, she knew he'd stumbled, overestimated. His keen eye for
the right move had failed him this time. Deep down, she even

felt a little sorry for him, this frail old man. Then she thought of Priash.

She peeled back the hide from the door of one of the smaller workshops. This particular one was often used to carve tool handles handles and arrow shafts, and it smelled strongly of wood shavings. The faint smell of ink and yullah pulp, which was used to make the parchments Grashin wrote upon, was also in the air.

She looked at Grashin's bench now. This was invariably his. Nobody else in the tribe used it. Some of the other benches had tools left on them, and one had a dirty plate on it, but generally they were tidy, ready for the next user. In stark contrast to the other desks, Grashin's was piled high with parchments, drying yullah papers, small pots of ink. Several of his pipes and other assorted personal possessions littered the bench. Nobody else had such exclusive use of one particular station. Another of his unquestioned perks, Tian thought to herself. She opened a drawer crammed with miscellaneous junk, empty ink pots, broken nibs, even some moldy havish berries. She opened another, finding stacks of papers covered with small, neat writing filling it to the brim. What she was looking for was at the back. She took it out and placed the bowl on the work surface, gently lifting the lid.

A faint smile came across her face as she peered down at the contents and murmured, "I've got you now you old shitstool."

* * *

Over the seasons, Priash had dropped several hints to Tian about Grashin. They were in the spring camp, where the woodland was less dense, and gave way to wide expanses of plains. Tian had returned that morning from a two-day hunting trip, and she was lounging on the ground, enjoying the sun's warm rays.

"Those damned bloody people! They are so... so primitive!" Tian looked up. Priash came storming over to where Tian lay, caring little who heard her.

Tian had been talking most of the afternoon with Haroon and Reid about one of the brothers, Jaal, who had spoiled yet another hunt. He was young and headstrong and, not for the first time, had tried to spear a bison before the hunting party was ready, while they were still encircling it. It could have been was potentially very dangerous. Fortunately, he was a poor shot and had missed the throw, and the bison had simply charged off harmlessly through an open gap in the hunters' circle. A loud argument ensued, souring everyone's mood.

Seeing the look on Priash's face, Haroon and Reid glanced at Tian and drifted away toward the kitchens.

"What do you mean?" Tian asked.

"It pisses me off that some people around here get away with anything; everyone turns a blind eye. Yet, if I did it, or was even caught dreaming about possibly thinking about doing it, the wrath of the Circle would come down on me so hard my head would spin, and they"d be invoking the fucking demons—Civilization and Hierarchy—denouncing me as a deviant, and condemning me to Veysh'lur for all eternity."

Tian enjoyed listening to Priash when she was angry, and she often had to suppress a smile when Priash began one of her rants.

"Bad day, then?"

Priash glared at her. Tian wondered for a second if she'd pushed it too far. She hadn't. Priash's face softened.

"No. Yes. I'm sorry. Just those fuckers with their Way and their stupid outdated boarshit customs. *But Priash, these are the old ways. But Priash, we tread lightly in the forest. But Priash, these are not our woods, we receive its bounty as gifts. But Priash, we must leave no mark. But Priash, we've always done it like this. But Priash, But Priash.*" Priash did a passable impression of Nealah, one of the herbalists she often worked, and clashed, with. "Fucking barbarians and their stupid Way," she spat.

"You mustn't let them get to you, sister."

"I know, I know. But if one more person says 'harmony' to me today I'm leaving for the mountains and never coming back."

"Can I come?" asked Tian, shifting closer to her.

"Yeah, I guess. I'd need someone to scrub my back and keep my feet warm. Those mountains get pretty cold at night. I missed you last night, by the way," she added, her voice softening. "Did you lie with anyone?"

"No, too busy," Tian said.

When Priash looked at her quizzically, she briefly explained the problems they'd had with Jaal.

They settled down on the ground for. Tian stroked the back of Priash's hand, circling the knuckles and inspecting a few nicks and cuts half-interestedly.

Tian began to drift into sleep. Some time later, Priash rolled over on to her side. Tian could feel her warm breath on her face.

"You remember when I said I couldn't work out what it was that Grashin and some of the other old ones smoke in their pipes, but that it wasn't yusha grass?" Priash asked, her voice hushed.

Tian's eyes opened, alert.

"Yes. It smells like yusha to me."

"Well it's definitely not. But I couldn't tell what it was. I thought maybe they were mixing it with thamba roots or oop leaves. The smoke is too pungent and the ash too white to just be yusha."

"Does it matter?"

"It does to me. Anyway, I think I might know what it is now. You won't believe..." Her voice trailed off; Haroon was walking towards them.

"Forgot the shoes," Haroon said, pointing to them underneath Tian's legs. Haroon sat down to put them on, but lingered for a moment. Neither Priash nor Tian said much; she got the hint and moved to another group after a short while. Priash waited until she was out of earshot before she started talking again.

"I was out yesterday with Nealah and some of the others. We were out hunting for suba saplings."

"Remind me…"

"We mash it up and paste it in on the insides of delicate pots to stop them cracking when we fire them. Anyway, we were down towards the river, around the spot we had the fish festival a few weeks ago. Rremember?"

Tian nodded.

"Well you know how big the rocks down there are, the ones right on the bank?"

Tian nodded again. The river to the south of the spring village was narrow and winding, the banks strewn with boulders, some bigger than their sleeping huts. In places it cut straight through the rocks, leaving cliffs towering over the water on both sides. It also had deep calm pools. It could be a dangerous river to navigate, but great fun for diving and playing in, even though the water, running straight from the mountains, was freezing, heart-stoppingly cold.

"We'd been searching for the suba all day, and we hadn't had much luck. Most of the ones we found had been stripped by animals. We'd stopped on the bank for secondmeal, and I was tired, couldn't keep my eyes open. After eating, I went down to one of the pools to dip in and wake myself up. I told the others I was going for a swim and I'd catch up with them in an hour or two."

"You must have frozen," said Tian, a frown creasing her eyebrows

"Yes," Priash said, grinning. "I didn't stay long, just a few minutes. It was just too cold. But it woke me up. Anyway, I hadn't gone far from the group, and I was climbing up the rocks back towards where we'd eaten. Everyone but Nealah, Bal and Yi'sul had gone already, suba hunting."

"Your favorite people."

Priash ignored the jibe. "They were talking, and there

was something up. Something about their body language, you know?" Tian nodded. "They looked really peculiar, so I stopped. I thought they'd seen me, but they didn't stop talking and none of them looked up at me. I was only thirty meters away, but the sun was behind me and they were too involved in their conversation to notice me. Well, I dropped off the rock I was on, and quietly, like the way I've seen you doing it when you're out hunting, snuck up on them. I got behind this huge boulder about ten meters from them where I could hear them pretty clearly."

"What were they saying?"

"Nealah was doing most of the talking, and I could barely hear her. But whenever Bal or Yi'sul talked their voices carried better, and I heard almost everything they said."

"You should have moved closer," said Tian.

"I couldn't; there wasn't much cover. Besides, I'm terrible at hiding, and I was sure they could hear my teeth chattering even from there. I'm sure you could have sneaked up on them and sat on Bal's lap and heard every word without them ever noticing you, but I'm not that good."

"Well, plants and berries don't tend to run away from you," said Tian, poking her lightly in the ribs. It was true, though. They'd always found Priash first when they'd played hide-and-seek as children. She would shuffle around, hum to herself, pick a terrible, obvious hiding spot—the first place anyone would think of looking. Tian was even a little surprised Priash was able to get close without them noticing her.

"It sounded like they were talking about the winter village. At first I thought I'd made a mistake, that they were just having a regular conversation, even if they were whispering a bit. I was just about to leave and head out after the others. But then I heard Bal mention Grashin, that he was upset, and something about one of the tribes to the east that we shared the cave with. Then they started to talk about ilyup."

"Ilyup? What's that?"

Priash shrugged "No idea. But they were talking about how the last batch hadn"t been dried properly, and I heard Yi'sul saying that it tasted too bitter. Nealah spoke for a while, I think she was saying something about having to get some more. But they kept mentioning it."

"So it's food, or an herb or something?"

"Yeah."

"Well, so what? Is that all?" Tian asked, disappointed. She had hoped for something more exciting, some intrigue or juicy gossip about an elder.

Priash pouted a little. "I've never heard of ilyup. I've read all the stuff Grashin has on herbalism in the histories, or at least everything he's shown me." Tian knew that was true. Priash spent most of her winter seasons holed up with thick tomes with uninspiring titles like *The Uses of the Tanja Genus in the Treatment of Bowel Disorders* and *An Herbalist"s Guide to the Proper Fermentation of Unjia Berries.* Just the memory of those dusty old scrolls made Tian repress a yawn. She resented how much time Priash spent looking through those old papers, but she didn't question that if Priash said it wasn't in the histories, it almost certainly wasn't.

"Perhaps you misheard? Might have been something else, not ilyup," said Tian, feigning interest.

"No, I didn't mishear. I heard them say it clearly several times. You know how deep Bal's voice is. Even when he's trying to be quiet you can hear him in the next hut. And the way they were saying it—why isn't it in the histories? Why haven't I ever heard of it?"

"Did you ask them about it?"

"No, of course not." Tian hid a smile. Priash hated showing her ignorance in front of the other herbalists—one of the reasons she spent so much time alone reading the books in the winter season. "They wouldn't tell me anyway. They're always so... secretive."

"Ursulah would tell you. Poulo too, if you asked nicely. Did you?"

"Nah, they only dabble in it. I like them, but they're pretty casual. They probably wouldn't know anyway. Poulo's memory isn't what it was, and Ursulah only uses what Nealah gives her for her medicines. I doubt she knows what half of it even does. No, only those three would know," she said, meaning Nealah, Bal, and Yi'sul, the three most experienced herbalists in the tribe.

"Maybe Grashin, then. If he was upset, maybe he'd tell you. Plus he'd know if there were something in the histories about it."

"Yes, Grashin." Priash said, her eyes drifting toward the workshops. "That's what I thought. So after we got back to village last night, I asked him."

"And?"

"He lied to me."

Tian's attention had been drifting. She wasn't interested in the herbalist workshop's politics, and she'd started to think about Jaal again. She lifted her head up sharply, her interest quickly returning to the conversation.

"He lied? How do you know?"

"I just do. I was going to ask him straight out, but when I got to the workshop he wasn't around. I waited for him a bit. I had a look through some of the papers on the bench he uses—have you seen the way he keeps it?"

"No," said Tian, shaking her head.

"It's a mess, stuff piled up all over it. Nealah would have a fit if I left a bench like that. Anyway, I was reading one of the papers on the desk that he'd left out. Some story he'd heard in the winter village that he was writing up. Pretty good, actually. Had one of your favorite characters in as a matter of fact. A Watcher."

Tian sorely regretted ever mentioning her childish fear of the Watchers to Priash. She took great delight in poking her about them whenever the opportunity arose.

"So, did you ask him?" Tian said, wanting to change the subject.

"Who? Oh, Grashin. Yes, I'm coming to that. So I was read-

ing this Watcher story, which I'll have to tell you some time."
Tian pulled a face. "Well, after I finished it, I turned to go, but
something caught my eye—one of the pipes Grashin uses. It was
sitting on the desk, already packed. I was just about to pick it up
and smell it when Grashin walked in. Literally the second I was
reaching for it, he was behind me."

"Spooky," said Tian. "He always struck me as creepy."

"Tell me about it. The old shitstool made me jump half out
of my skin. He brushed by me, looking all flustered. He started
dumping the stuff on the workbench into the drawers in big
armfuls. I apologized for disturbing him. He was muttering
something under his breath, the old fool."

Priash had clashed many times with Grashin over access to
the histories in the winter village. She resented not being able
to enter all of the passages that made up the sprawling library.
Grashin always had an excuse for advising against her entry
into the more distant alleys and tunnels, which made them a
no-go area for Priash, unless she were to question his honesty
in public. She made do with sitting on a wooden bench in the
largest cave in the library with Grashin bringing her the parchments and books she requested. Occasionally he would permit
her to take them into the sleeping quarters, if she remembered
to treat them with the respect due to these fragile records of our
tribe's past, as he put it. She resented having to get his permis-
sion, and the patronizing way in which he often spoke to her.

"He asked me what I wanted. I told him I wanted to know
more about ilyup. I could see the question surprised him. He
was still clearing the desk, and his head darted straight up to the
pipe. He looked away really quickly, glancing up at me to see if
I'd caught his slip. Of course I pretended not to have noticed.
But he looked guilty. You know the way children look when
they ask for a second serving of lastmeal? Like that. I saw him
try to hide it, and he attempted this horrible little smile.

"Ilyup, sister?" he said. "Why, I don't believe I've ever come
across that particular herb."

"It's an herb?" I asked. I tried to keep my face blank. He start
ed stammering. He must have realized his mistake.

"Well, since it's you asking me, I assumed that's what it was.
Where did you hear about... what was it called again?" I could
tell he was, trying to deflect me. I could see him desperately trying not to look at the pipe.

"Ilyup." I said. "I thought I overheard someone talking about
it. Thought you might know something about it."

"Me, sister? You'd be better off asking Nealah or Bal."

"I thought it might have been in the histories somewhere."

"Oh, no, not that I can remember. Perhaps you misheard?"

You should have seen his face, Tian, the way he was looking
at me then, trying to figure something about me, trying to read
my mind. It was scary. I started backing away, tried to put his
mind at ease.

"Probably, Grashin. I must have made a mistake. Sorry for
bothering you, brother," I said. I left after that."

"So you think he did know what ilyup was, and was lying?"
asked Tian, incredulously.

"Of course, Tian. It was so obvious. If you had seen the way
he acted, the way he looked at his pipe, the way the others spoke
about it yesterday."

"But a lie? And about something so trivial?"

"He obviously doesn't want people to know what ilyup is. It's
obviously not yusha in his pipe, but ilyup. I've no idea why he
wouldn't tell me about it, though, why the secrecy. Why a lie."

Someone close by had started to beat a drum, slowly picking
up pace as Priash told her tale. Small groups began to sing softly. A few people wandered out from the workshops, and three
boys brought over water flasks and berries from the kitchens.

Tian stood up and said, "Come on. Don't worry about it now.
I'm sure there's a good reason."

Tian extended Priash a hand, to help her to her feet. Priash,
still deep in thought, didn't take it. As Tian stood, hand extended, Lumsha, a small girl of fifteen seasons ran up to them, want-

ing to dance with them, and asking Priash to sing. Her small voice broke Priash's train of thought, and Priash smiled at her, rose to her feet, and began singing with the others.

They danced until nightfall, the ilyup temporarily forgotten in the warm evening.

CHAPTER 4

Tian's head was spinning. She listened to this monster, heard it uttering these bizarre, outlandish things. She got to her feet, her head light.

"I.... I don't believe... Who..."

"I'm sorry, Tian. I don't mean to confuse you. But I've already broken our non-interference policy by speaking to you. Now that I've started, I realize there is so much I've wanted to tell you, so much knowledge I've wanted to share with you and your people. If you're going to help me, I need you to know certain things, things you might not fully understand. But most of all I need you to trust me."

"These things... where are you from?" muttered Tian. She took several large draughts from the water bag, and her head stopped swimming for the moment.

"I was born on a world outside of this star system, a place called Namir, about three hundred standard orbits ago. About a thousand of your seasons."

Tian gasped "You"re that old?."

The Watcher laughed its birdsong laugh again.

"What are you called? Do you even have a name?" asked Tian. She was still trying to gauge it, trying to figure out whether she believed anything she was hearing.

"Well, we normally call one another by our designations. Mine is 578-MORI-AO142."

Tian looked perplexed. "What does that mean?"

"I actually have a much longer designation, but this is what I tend to use to talk infor—"

"I'll call you Mori," interrupted Tian.

The Watcher smiled, nodding. "Mori it is. So, you're willing to help me?"

Tian stood looking across at Mori for some time. It returned her look, waiting patiently. Tian thought about the tribe, about Grashin, about Erkan, about Priash. She remembered the stories of the Qah, the myths about the Watchers, the fragmented tales about the old times, and the journey to the silo. She tried to fit all those pieces together, trying to figure out whether she believed any of this.

"Many of my people are going to the silos. Are they in danger?"

Mori nodded. "Yes, I'm afraid so. Will you help me?"

"A monster from another world who knows my name and details from my past says that half my tribe are in danger from the Qah, and promises to reveal the secrets of the universe to me if I'll help it save them? I don't see how I have much choice."

"You make it sound like I was bargaining with you, Tian. I simply said that I needed your help, but that you'd need to know a few things if you were to come along."

"As you like, Mori. For now, let me sleep. Conversation with you is exhausting."

"We really ought to start out—"

"I'm going to bed, Mori. I'll speak to you at sunrise."

"Very well, Tian," Mori said, almost meekly.

Tian had surprised herself. Only a short while before the creature petrified her, and now she was preparing to go to sleep with it sitting a matter of meters away. She climbed into the hammock, and, with one last glance into those yellow eyes, drifted off immediately.

* * *

Tian disliked the winter village. After the initial excitement wore off of seeing old friends from the tribe they were spending that winter with, she soon became restless and bored. During the cold season, the tribe rarely left the caves. The air outside was bitterly cold, and fog obscured the spectacular view for much of the season.

She found herself with little to do. She would wake up early, eat firstmeal, and spend a few hours chatting. She'd visit the workshops, maybe help fix shoes, wash some clothes or decorate some bowls. Every few days she'd help prepare lastmeal, which, in the winter caves, was a more elaborate affair than usual. Yet, even with all of these small tasks, a lot of the time she simply had nothing to do. As the season wore on, she even began to look forward to her tenth day rotation, where she'd be shovel out the shitstools or sweep the dust from the worn floors.

Her friends spent the winter season occupying themselves with their hobbies. Priash would spent most of her time in the library, reading dusty tracts on herbalism. Haroon and several others would spent days on end fermenting the dried berries and preserves to make strong-smelling, intoxicating drinks for the nightfall festivities. They were convinced that their concoctions tasted better if they kept a vigil over the fermenters. They even set up a rota. Tian's bloodsister, Thayu, spent hours painting intricate murals on the cave walls and patterns on the storage vases and bowls. Yuri tended to sleep with most of the sisters from the tribes they were sharing the caves with. The others spent their time in the biggest of the caves, sharing stories, laughing, joking, singing, smoking, dancing, meditating. Winter was a period of relaxation, a chance for her tribal brothers and sisters to enjoy themselves and indulge their passions. Even the Circle went unused for weeks at a time with there being so little to discuss or plan for.

Tian often ended up in the nursery or one of the education rooms. She enjoyed teaching the young ones about hunting and fletching, about the different seasons, about the stars, about how to read the clouds and how to preserve meat. She took pleasure in listening to the others explaining how to mix herbs, how to fire a kiln, or how to jury rig a broken shelter in heavy rain. She especially liked playing games with the children, many of which she remembered from her own childhood, her cries mingling with their excited shrieks echoing through the cave tunnels.

Yet Tian missed the woods. Missed the sun, the rain, the mud, the trees. Missed the adrenaline rush of a hunt, the soft forest floor under her feet. Missed galloping through the undergrowth astride Nimsha'h, swimming in the cool rivers, lying on her back looking at the stars, making love with Priash under the moons' light. She would get pangs in her stomach, like hunger or thirst, when she thought about that. The others enjoyed the winter village. They were comfortable, safe, warm; they had more leisure time and fewer worries. But Tian felt cut off from her passions and her freedom by the snow, and the long winter days were hard on her.

It was the winter after the conversation with Priash about ilyup. Priash had only mentioned it two or three times since the previous spring. Tian had urged her to ask Nealah about it, but Priash refused. Priash had bided her time. She now spent most of it going through the histories, often looking for a mention of the mysterious herb, her curiosity piqued. She had contemplated taking some from Grashin's pipe, but she was too ashamed to do it. Instead, she'd waited until winter, when she could go through the histories again.

Tian was preparing lastmeal when Priash approached her. They'd seen less of one another since coming to the winter village, and Tian had lain with several others since she had last been with Priash. Tian felt the smallest twinge of guilt when she saw Priash coming toward her now.

She asked, "How have you been?"

"Busy. I've missed you."

Tian stopped mashing the legumes she was preparing. "Yeah, me too. What have you been up to?"

"Well, that's why I'm here. I need your help with something... I want to look at the archives myself, while you watch for Grashin."

Tian gasped, thought for a moment, and agreed, pleased that she could make up for her recent distance, and secretly happy to have something scary and exciting to do.

They passed the cavern with the long-term food stores—far too many large earthenware vessels to count, filled with dried fruit and berries, wild grains, jerky, honey, all sealed with beeswax—and found themselves in the library. Neither Tian nor Priash had realized quite how labyrinthine the library itself was. It was part of an apparently endless network of narrow passages replete with blind alleys and sudden, potentially lethal drops. They quickly abandoned the plan for Tian to remain behind in the main room and keep watch for Grashin.

Crude bookshelves lined most of the tunnels, the order cryptic to Tian but apparently clear to Priash. Their candles cast long shadows as they stumbled on the uneven ground.

"Not much farther, I think, sister," Priash said, her hand squeezing Tian's. "Here we are. Look, *Ilyup!*"

Several well worn scrolls perched precariously on the end of one of the shelves. "Ilyup" was clearly inscribed on two of them.

"Just take them, we don't have time to read them now," said Tian.

"What if he notices them missing?"

"Well, you can't read them by this light," said Tian, indicating their small candles.

"I don't want to take them; let's go a bit farther. Perhaps we can find more candles," said Priash.

Priash took the scrolls off the shelf, and they pushed on into the maze.

"Are you sure you can find the way out again?" whispered Tian.

Priahs sighed. "Yes. I can tell by the books..."

Her voice trailed off. The narrow passage opened into a cavern. On the floor in front of them was a plot of muddy soil on the cave floor, divided by thin wooden planks into small squares the size of a hand. On the mud sat hundreds—no, thousand—of seeds, small white shoots sprouting from some of them.

Tian looked at Priash, her mouth wide open in disbelief. Priash looked down at the parchments in her hand. She lit one of the big candles perched on a nearby wall. She read aloud to Tian, their astonishment growing at every word.

* * *

Tian looked down at the bowl she'd found in the back of Grashin's drawer. The sweet smell of ilyup rose to her nostrils. She'd thought many times of doing this, of revealing what Priash and she had found in the labyrinth all those seasons ago. Their discovery was a precious memory. They had both begun to question things they had always taken for granted after that day in the caves. Her respect and love for Priash also grew after that, their shared secret brought them even closer together, binding them inexorably.

It was also the last winter Tian spent with Priash before she was taken.

She could heard someone approaching. She replaced the wooden lid, turning. It was Erkan.

"Tian, are you all right? What are you doing? What is that?" he said, pointing toward the bowl on the bench behind her.

"You'll see," said Tian. She picked ithe bowl up and walked by him back to the Circle.

Bal was speaking, but he stopped and turned when he saw them approach. Tian walked up to Ursulah who was applying ointments to mosquito bites. She was very old, an experienced herbalist, and once a friend of Priash's. The old woman looked uncomfortable at the unwanted attention. Tian handed her the bowl.

"Do you know what this is?" she asked. Ursulah looked down at the bowl in her hands, then around at the faces of the tribe.

"Open it," said Tian.

Ursulah's frail, wrinkled hands removed the lid. She looked over to Grashin, who was standing motionless next to Bal in the center of the Circle.

"Well?"

"I don't know, sister."

"Is it yusha?"

Ursulah pinched a little between her fingers, bringing it up to her nose.

"No, it's not yusha. I don't know what it is. I've never seen it before."

Tian turned about to face Grashin, and spoke.

"I'm not surprised, sister. This is *ilyup*. It doesn't grow anywhere around here. It isn't native to this area, and it can only be grown under special conditions. The seeds have to germinate in warm, dark, dry places, like some of our winter caves. They then have to be planted in special soil, fed and watered with peculiar mixtures, and protected from the sun and the wind. In other words, ilyup has to be planted, cultivated, nurtured, and harvested. When the leaves are harvested, they have to be hang in a warm, dark place for a couple of weeks to cure. There's a guide on how to do it in the histories."

The Circle was silent. Tian walked up to Grashin.

"If you check the pipe Grashin uses, you'll find some more ilyup in there. The histories say it smells the same but tastes sweeter than the yusha everyone else smokes, and is much stronger, with no bite. But he only has a couple of bowls of it, so you might have to ask him nicely if you want to—"

Grashin hit her open-handed across the mouth. Tian fell to the floor as much from shock as from the force of the blow. The violence was so unexpected. It was the first time she'd ever been struck on purpose, or ever seen a brother raise a hand to another in anger. Tears sprang to her eyes. She stayed on the damp ground, sobbing.

The tribe was quick to act. Bal and the other elders led Grashin away. Erkan and to help Tian up, but she resisted. There was no more talk of expulsions or ilyup. Many of the tribe remained dumbstruck on the benches.

After she regained her composure, her cheek now a deep, stinging crimson, Tian got up and headed straight for the stables. Erkan and a few others begged her not to leave, but she had to escape. She jumped on Nimsha'h and galloped into the woods, the cries of her people swallowed by the forest.

Part II

Chapter 1

Tian woke two hours before sunrise. Mori was already awake, and had rekindled the previous night's fire from the embers. They sat cross-legged on the ground. Even in the flickering firelight, Tian could make out very little of its features.

"Good morning, Tian. Did you sleep well?"

"Yes, thanks, sist— I mean . . ."

Mori smiled. "Your confusion is understandable. You have no androgynous gender here. I am genderless, so you canmay take your pick."

"Should I call you brother or sister, then?" asked Tian. It was far too early in the morning to get her head around this.

"Well, we normally call one another by our designa—" It stopped, catching her look.

"Never mind. Mori, what's for firstmeal?"

Mori reached out to the small pack of supplies Tian had hooked over a nearby branch.

"Well, you seem to have some food left," Mori said, rummaging through the canvas bag. "Some dried rabbit and berries."

"Aren"t you having any?" asked Tan. If Mori wasn"t going to eat the rabbit, what would it eat? Such a large predator would need a lot of meat to sustain itself, she thought to herself, more than a measly rabbit and a handful of berries.

"Oh, no, thanks. I ate a couple of days ago," said Mori, casually. "Besides, I"m an herbivore."

"A what?" Her imagination was running wild, the stories of the Zasophan coming back to her suddenly. "Never mind. So you don't eat... much?"

"No, my metabolism is designed to be variable. I can go without food for months, and water for weeks, if I need to."

"What do you mean, 'designed'? You said it last night when we were talking about the smell. I don't understand."

The first hint of sunrise crept across the star-filled sky as Mori replied.

"Do you remember Hashna'h?"

Tian's eyebrows shot up in surprise. Hashna'h had been one of the tribe's swiftest horses. She remembered him from her childhood. He had died many seasons before. She hesitated and then answered, "Yes."

"He was a fine horse. Strong, powerful."

Tian nodded, remembering. It was true, Hashna'h was an excellent horse, but he had a poor temperament. He often bit those who came near him, and would only let the most experienced of the tribe ride him, and even then only after much coaxing.

"I don't think you realized it, but his eyesight was poor; that's why he could be aggressive. But you studded him for his qualities, to pass down his traits to his offspring, despite this flaw. I think Nimsha'h is related," said Mori, nodding to the where the horse stood grazing. Tian hadn't noticed it before, but Nimsha'h was completely comfortable around Mori. The night before she hadn"t made a sound when it had approached the camp.

"Yes, she is. She runs like him, too."

"Well, my people have the means to pick and choose the qualities we want in a newborn, and discard the less desirable ones. So if we wanted a fast horse, we'd choose all of Hashna'h's good qualities, like his speed and stamina, and we'd drop the bad qualities, like his poor eyesight."

"So, when it came to me, they did the same thing. They chose the most desirable qualities. Only, an anthropologist doesn't need the strong legs of a horse. I need thick black skin for camouflage and protection from the sun. Long, agile limbs for climbing. Big eyes that can see in the dark, and a slow metabolism so I can survive in a hostile environment for a long time. I need advanced neural implants to record the massive quantities of data that I observe. Essentially I was designed, created, for my environment, my role here, in just the same way you studded Hashna'h for his qualities."

"Did you pick it?" asked Tian, interested.

Mori frowned. "Pick what?"

"Your 'role'? You said you were born like this. What if you didn't want to be a Watcher? What if you wanted to cook or grow herbs?"

Mori was silent for what seemed like a long time.

"No, I didn't pick this. But I could do those things equally if I wanted."

"Yes, but—"

"You're ignoring your food."

Tian ate in silence in the long shadows of the rising sun.

They set out a little after dawn. Tian often lost sight of Mori in the canopy above. Tian had plenty of time to think, to mull over some of the things Mori had told her. She was brimming with questions. She wished she'd been more interested in the histories, asked Priash more questions, been more curious.

It wasn't until the sun was high in the sky that she realized they were heading away from the village. She'd been too wrapped up in thought, going over the conversations with Mori and the events in the village, to notice. She felt a growing sense of unease. Had the Watcher been lying to her? Was she being led to some monstrous underground lair, Mori's friendly appearance just a show? All of the stories she'd heard about Watchers came flooding back.

She slowed Nimsha'h to a trot, calling up to Mori.

"We're going the wrong way," she cried, trying to keep the

panic from her voice. She couldn't see Mori. She squinted, trying to catch a glimpse.

A voice right above her made her jump. "No, sister. The silo is this way." Mori pointed in the direction they had been heading all morning.

"I thought we were going to the village, to warn them. To get their help."

"There isn't time."

"But we can"t take on the Qah alone. We need them."

"The people in your village would be a hindrance, not a help. Besides, there are only a handful of you, and most of the horses are with the others. No, we must carry on, and hope we get to the silo before your tribe does."

Mori turned to go. Tian called, "Mori, what will happen? What if we're too late?"

"We won't be, but we need to hurry. Do you need to stop for food, or can you continue?"

"I can eat and ride, but Nimsha'h will need to rest soon. She's tired."

"Wait here," said Mori. The Watcher leapt to the ground and ran into the undergrowth. It returned a moment later.

"Here. Let her chew this. It contains ubutu, a stimulant. It'll also appease her thirst for a while." Mori handed Tian some broad leaves. "Don"t eat any yourself, though."

Tian gave the horse the leaves. Nimsha'h ate them greedily.

When the leaves were gone, Mori said, "Come, let"s press on. We have much distance to cover." With that, it clambered up a nearby tree and was flying across branches within seconds. Tian looked up, marveling at the acrobatics. She dug her bare heels into Nimsha'h's flanks, spurring her forward after the shadowy figure.

They stopped at nightfall. Tian was exhausted, and Nimsha'h was weary. It didn't seem like Mori had broken a sweat.

"I'm so tired. I'm not sure I can keep this pace up. I'm worried about Nimsha'h."

"We have traveled a great distance, Tian. This country is tough. On the steppes, we would have travelled twice as far."

"What do you know about the steppes?" asked Tian, rubbing her aching thighs and butt.

"I spent many seasons there observing the nomadic tribes. They are a tough people."

"You've traveled that far, Mori?"

"Oh yes. We rotate around the tribes every generation or two, so I have ranged far across Dodona. It's a beautiful place."

"More beautiful than Namir?"

"Oh, yes. Much. My world is a hot, unforgiving place. We are the only life there, and we have to live under big domes. Like your caves, but for all the seasons. This place? It is a wonder. So much life, so much unspoiled beauty." Mori breathed the air in, deeply, before letting out a sigh. "A real paradise."

"Aren't there more worlds like this out there?" asked Tian, pointing to the sky.

"Some, yes. But Dodona is unique. Most of the inhabitable planets in our sphere are settled. Even some of the uninhabitable ones, too, like Namir. Here it is so empty, so wild."

"But we"re here," said Tian. "My people."

"That's different, sister."

"How?"

Mori looked at her. Tian could see that it was trying to decide how much to tell her.

"It's difficult to explain. We are so cut off here. I'm not sure you'll understand many of my references."

"Try me. I enjoy hearing you speak, even if I don't understand all of the words." She had once said this to Priash when she had been explaining to Tian some obscure recipe, a long list of exotic herbs and roots and fruits, a mesmerizing display of knowledge. She blushed at the memory, and especially that she had spoken these words to Mori now.

Mori looked reluctant, but relented when it saw her earnestness. "This world is different. Maybe I'll explain exactly what

I mean some other time. But I can tell you now some of the history of this world. I don"t think anyone would begrudge you that. I suspect something like it is in your histories, anyway."

Tian frowned. "We never see the histories."

Mori shook its head.

"That is a real shame. It might have prevented all this trouble, not only with the Qah, but with Grashin too. Anyway," it said, waving Tian's curious expression aside with a hand, "this world was discovered by our civilization about two-and-a-half thousand seasons ago. We'd travelled to many, many worlds before we found this one. This place was a miracle. It was teeming with life, with sentient life. With vast oceans and plains and forests and all of it full of life! You must understand how how special that makes this place. We had traveled for a long time and never before found such abundance, let alone intelligent life that we could understand and communicate with Our people, by which I mean both of our peoples—"

"Wait!" Tian interrupted. "We share the same *ancestors*?"

"Yes. Like I said, I was designed for this environment, but the people on our worlds look quite similar to you. We're the same on the inside."

Tian wasn't sure what to say. *Does that make me a Watcher?* she thought as she looked into Mori's strange yellow eyes.

* * *

In the weeks before Priash was taken, she and Tian had been especially close. They spent almost all of their time with one another in the village, and took long trips together out in the woods. They'd become inseparable. The tribe began to notice. Priash and Tian stopped receiving invitations to lie with others. Even Yuri recognised that their relationship was becoming exclusive, and had ceased his advances towards them. Or at least most of his advances.

Keeping the secret of the winter village had changed both of them, Tian especially. They talked about their dreams and their frustrations. Priash told Tian about her imagined pharmacopoeia, and vented her anger about the way the tribe was organized. Tian became more interested in the histories, in the way things were before, the way they could be if the Circle and the Way and Grashin weren't around.

Priash also talked often about their ancestors, the other tribes, and the way the Circle worked. She sometimes used words that Tian didn't understand, had never heard before, words even the elders didn't use. When Tian asked her what they meant and where she'd learned them, Priash admitted going back into the library tunnels without her. She said she didn't think it was important, and Tian, wanting to preserve their closeness, accepted the explanation.

Yet they both still enjoyed communal life, and took great pleasure in the festivals and shared the work. They laughed at the jokes, told stories around the fire, cooked lastmeal with smiles. Their secrets and thoughts, however, they kept to themselves, sharing them only when they were alone in the woods or under the furs in bed.

Priash often talked about leaving the tribe. Tian always refused.

Travelers often visited the tribe, and it would sometimes come across small groups that had chosen to live separately from the tribes and villages. The tribe sometimes came across deviants, too, outcasts who were unwelcome in any of the tribes because they had abandoned the Way. The glimpses of such a life, cut off from people, frightened Tian. The bond of community, the belonging and sharing, was too strong for her to abandon, even for Priash's sake. So they dreamed. They spoke of traveling across the oceans to the west, across the sky to the moons. They imagined living high in the trees in wooden huts, or following the winding rivers on canoes big enough to live on.

"We could live with the Watchers in their underground nests," Priash had joked. "You could lie with them, grow round with their ferocious babies with sharp teeth and claws that would tear their way out when they were ready to be born. Meanwhile, they would teach me all the secrets of the forest." Priash laughed hysterically at the panic-stricken look on Tian's face.

"I think they'd pick you to lie with first," replied Tian. "Your tits are bigger. And screw the secrets of the forest. I'd get them to teach me the secrets of the *universe*. You think too small, Priash."

* * *

The foraging party verified Grashin's story. They had camped early for the night near a small lake. The weather had been terrible, and they had been traveling into a strong gale all day that had whipped up fallen leaves, making their journey treacherous, slow, and suffocating. The lake was in a small valley that had offered them some protection. It also gave the horses a chance to recover; they were weary, and the relentless wind made them nervous.

They said Priash had been restless in the camp and had said they shouldn't be intimidated by a bit of wind. She told them she had seen some ubutu on the trail a couple of kilometers behind them, and that she was going back to get some. They had protested, but she was adamant. Whether she wanted the ubutu or just wanted to be alone, they couldn't tell.

"I'll be back at sunrise," she said, hefting a pack with her sleeping gear.

With that, she was gone. They never saw her again.

Tian was numb when they finally told her the story, after being so long away with the plains tribes. A small voice inside her cried out: Why did you let her go alone into the night? Yet she knew in her heart that when Priash said she was going to do something she could not be swayed.

In time, she forgave them.

But she could never forgive Grashin.

CHAPTER 2

"When we arrived, we found that we weren't alone on Dodona. Our explorers discovered a space station and two abandoned ships in orbit belonging to an ancient, space-faring race, the name and origins of which are lost to us. They were apparently long gone from here. Their station was hundreds of thousands of orbits old, perhaps older. It was a bitter disappointment, despite our joy at discovering this world."

"Dodona?" asked Tian. "That's what you call this place?"

"Yes. It's a very old word. Anyway, our scientists painstakingly translated the old libraries aboard those alien vessels, and found fragments to suggest that they too had appreciated this world as the miracle it is. Even though we couldn't speak to them directly, we could read some parts of their histories, and understand a bit about their civilization. We learned that they had introduced species to this world. Massive, intelligent monsters, as tall as the trees and faster than Nimsha'h. They used to hunt them here. The same way you hunt, now. This place was a vacation planet."

"Vacation?" said Tian.

"Yes. You know how everyone in winter village does whatever they like, pretty much all of the time?" Tian nodded. "That is a bit like a vacation. A long festival without any cooking or washing up or tenth day rotation. Well these aliens enjoyed hunting big game, so they came here to hunt. For them, this world was a hunting festival."

Tian could appreciate that. She often wished for a festival when she was cooped up in the winter village, and a land full of huge creatures to hunt all day sounded appealing.

"Why did they have to travel across the sky to hunt? Couldn't they hunt on the world they came from?"

Mori laughed. "Oh, no. By what we could tell, their empire was militaristic—they had lots of weapons, and spent much of their time fighting other species, and even themselves. That takes a lot of resources. From the little we know about them, they seem to have cut down all of the forests, dammed all of the rivers, settled all the plains, poisoned the skies, and killed almost all of the life, except themselves." Mori laughed again, seeing Tian's reaction.

"How horrible."

"The same probably would have happened here if it had any strategic value. Fortunately for you and me and this forest, it didn't."

"They would destroy their home world so they could destroy others? But . . . why?"

"I'm afraid that would take too long to explain, Tian. But I can tell you that when they abandoned this world, they left it in almost the same condition as they found it in, which is a credit to their civilization, despite all of its flaws."

They sat in silence for a few moments, Tian digesting all that Mori was telling her.

"Where are all the monsters you said they left here?"

"Most of them died out. The native ecosystems couldn't support them and they ran out of food and starved. The largest thing that survived on land was the bison-analogue you call a mollkah. But Dodona is over eighty percent water, and that's why you and I are here."

"What do you mean?" asked Tian, rubbing her eyes. She desperately needed to sleep, but was too engrossed in Mori's tale to say so. Even if only half of what Mori was saying was true...

"Unlike the land, the oceans can sustain some of the large intelligent life that they introduced to hunt, even without artificial support. Actually, they thrived. They were the first non-extinct sentient alien life we ever made contact with."

Tian didn't reply. The flurry of unfamiliar words and concepts made her tired head hurt. They had been talking for a long while, the forest filled with Mori's remarkable, hypnotic voice. The silence that ensued was deafening.

Finally Mori said, "It is late, and we should retire. I have been telling you things you are probably not ready to hear yet. We should sleep. We still have a long way to travel."

Tian looked at Mori. "I don't know what to say. All these things you speak of are beyond my wildest dreams. They're like a crazy dream, like you've been smoking too much yusha."

Mori smiled. "I know, Tian. But I promise you they are true."

They rode out at dawn. The morning was fresh, the first taste of autumn in the air. The season was turning quickly, and the trees would soon shed their leaves and the rains and snow would come. For today, though, the sun shone brightly, bathing the forest in its red glow.

Tian ate firstmeal on the move, thinking about the tale Mori had told her the night before. She didn't understand most of it, and she longed to ask Mori what a ship looked like, and what the ocean animals had said to them when they spoke. But another question tugged at her: how would they fight the Qah alone?

The tribes never fought. They had no reason to. They settled small disagreements in a joint Circle, and where personalities clashed irreparably, the tribes would go their separate ways, just as two people within a tribe would if they could not live with one another. There was plenty of space for everyone on this world. Even the deviants and hermits and could be left in peace.

The Way also had a stringent ethical mandate that the tribes help each other out, and many youths spent several adolescent seasons traveling among other tribes, so there were always familiar faces and relationships whenever a tribe came across another in the forest. The tribes also prided themselves on their hospitality to outsiders, often attempting to outdo one another even in times of relative scarcity.

Occasionally, there would be problems in the winter caves. Despite the relaxed attitude that prevailed, differences in prac-

tices and the mixing of people that were not kin in such a re-
stricted space sometimes led to misunderstandings. But that
was what the Circle was for: to resolve problems and to deper-
sonalize arguments, "to find the Way in the Circle," as the old
saying went.

So, the tribes abhorred violence. It was unthinkable. To raise
a hand against another was an act of moral cowardice, a personal failure, shameful. It was treated with revulsion across the
tribes, from the northern nomads to the southern coastal tribes.

Yet it had happened. There had been murders and rapes.
Despite the tribes' permissive attitudes, there were some who
could not fit into social life, who were quick to anger, who lust-
ed after those not old or interested enough. They were rare, so
word would spread. Some were accepted into other tribes, to
be cared for, if their birth tribe could no longer tolerate them.

There were some, though, who were irredeemable. They deliberately chose a path of violence, a life that endangered others
wherever they went, or they deliberately abandoned the Way.
They were cast out as deviants, shunned by the tribes. They
lived alone, or in small groups of bandits, eking out a life in the
woods without the protection of a tribe. They led a parasitic
life, out of step with the Way, stealing from the tribes or living
off the silos.

The Qah were different. Traveling elders told terrible tales
about them. Like the deviants, they led a life out of balance with
nature. They had abandoned the Circle and cared little for the
Way, for mutual aid, or for the old ways. They used violence to
settle personal disputes, had leaders who told others what to
do, and attacked neighboring tribes as a group, with weapons
normally used to hunt. This was unheard of. For one person
to raise a hand against another was an act of cowardice. For a
group to do so was a disgrace, a breach so gross as to threaten
the very basis of tribal society.

Yet to Tian and her tribe, the Qah were still a distant threat,
even after what had happened to Priash. Most of the tribe still

thought of them as a bedtime story. The Qah were a lesson, a parable, a warning against the horrors of civilization and leaders and violence. They underlined the importance of following the Way and all of its customs and traditions.

Tian remembered one of the stories vividly. An old one from another village had been staying with the tribe for a fish festival. He was a source of great entertainment. Most of the tribe were too young to have heard any of his stories, and the old ones appreciated the novelty of his voice, his dialect peculiar but fascinating. The sound of him clearing his throat on a warm spring night was a pleasure, a prelude to another exciting story.

On one night, though, the story he told terrified them.

There were once two bloodbrothers named Jaka and Hosan from a distant tribe, the elder began. They were closer than any bloodbrothers before or since. They were strong and brave, and they spent all of their time with one another, hunting, dancing, singing, cooking, sleeping. They were inseparable; they lived the same life.

But one day, when they were out in the woods, they came across a hunting party from another tribe. They saw the most beautiful girl they had ever seen. She had long, raven hair and eyes so big you might fall into them. They had to have her.

They asked her name, but she was shy, and wouldn't tell them. They asked again, and again. They asked to lie with her, there, in the forest, with both of them.

Unfortunately for Jaka and Hosan, Yultra, for that was the girl's name, was too young to lie with anyone. The others from her tribe told the bloodbrothers this. "She has not yet bled," they said. "She lies with no one. Come and see us next season, brothers."

But Jaka and Hosan didn't believe them. "Look at her," they cried. "She is too beautiful. We must lie with her," they pleaded. Yultra's tribe refused. "Come, brothers, eat with us and share our kill, but be on your way after that, for she is too young."

"Let her tell us that herself," they said.

Yultra couldn't. The men were big, and she was frightened of the way they looked at her. They looked like wolves at a kill.

"See," the brothers cried. "She doesn't deny it. She will lie with us now."

"No, brothers," her tribe said. "It is not the Way. You are thinking with your cocks, not your brains. She is afraid of you. That is why she does not speak."

But Jaka and Hosan wouldn't listen. They took Yultra there before her tribe, both at once. One of her tribe tried to stop them. Hosan struck him in the head with a rock, and he was dead. Once that one was dead, the others began to scream and strike at them; and the bloodbrothers hit them all with rocks . The forest was red with blood that night.

They were too greedy in their frenzy for the beautiful girl, though. They took turns lying with her all through the night, the bodies of her brothers and sisters all around them. Yultra died at dawn, of sorrow.

After this, all of the tribes shunned the bloodbrothers. They tribes drove them off whenever they came near a village. They fought between themselves and blamed one another for Yultra's death.

One day, they met up with some bandits near a silo. Three women were with the bandits. They hadn't lain with anyone for many seasons, since they had lain with Yultra. They killed the men in the night, took the women, and lay with them until they were dead, too.

The brothers stalked other villages at night, when everyone was asleep, looking for a woman as beautiful as Yultra. They told themselves that this time they would take care of her, and and that she would live forever. Although they visited many tribes, they never found a woman as beautiful as her, and they killed many in their search.

After a while, women were not the only thing the brother-sy took from the villages. They also took food, drink, horses, clothes, bedding. They met other bandits, but didn't kill the men, only beat them until they were almost dead. They made these men find food for them, and bring them women from the villages.

But they had grown weary of their search, and they hated each other's company. They lived in separate huts that they forced the bandits to build for them, made them plant seeds and fruits, and dig holes for water so they could stay in one place for all seasons.

The bandit village grew large. They seized other bandits and took boys from the villages to turn into bandits. They stole horses so they could steal more and kill more. When a bandit tried to run away, they would hunt him down, then lie with him in the center of the village, like they had lain with Yultra many seasons before, until he was dead or they were tired and they got others to lie with him instead, or used spears.

Even though they tried to avoid one another, one day Jaka and Hosan got into an argument in the middle of the bandit village. They were saying that whoever had lain last with Yultra was responsible for her death. Jaka said it was Hosan, Hosan said it was Jaka. Jaka took a knife and ran it across his blood-brother's belly, and Hosan's guts spilled out onto the ground.

But Jaka missed Hosan. He smoked yusha and drank fermented juices, and told the bandits what they could and couldn't do. He dreamt about Yultra and Hosan every night, dreaming he was lying with both of them in that forest amongst the bodies all those seasons before.

One night, one of the bandits decided he'd had enough of Jaka telling him what to do, so he crept into his hut and struck Jaka's head from his body. Then he smoked Jaka's head over a fire for several days. He strapped it to the saddle of the finest horse and rode it through the forests in front of the other bandits looking for more heads to put on his saddle.

They say that the bandit who killed Jaka was Yultra's blood-brother. His name was *Qah*.

CHAPTER 3

For the next three days, they traveled from before dawn until long after sunset. Nimsha'h was close to collapse, despite the concoctions Mori fed her. It was clear that they would have to rest her for at least half a day.

Tian marveled at Mori's stamina. Its legs were thin and sinewy, and it had no excess fat anywhere on its body. She had only ever seen Mori drink water and eat a handful of berries. Yet, despite the Watcher's modest appetite and skinny appearance, it was as fresh as the day she had met it.

"I can carry you, Tian, if you wish, to give Nimsha'h a rest. We really can't delay any longer."

Tian's fear when she looked at Mori had all but disappeared, but the idea of it carrying her like a baby monkey was out of the question.

"No, Mori. I'll go on foot."

"This terrain is difficult, Tian, and you would delay us."

The way Mori said it, so neutrally, impassively, as if talking about the weather or the color of the sky, took most of the sting out of the insult. That was not to say it didn't hurt, though.

"I can manage fine," she said, huffing. "Lead the way."

Mori had told her more of the story about Dodona while they traveled, mostly during short breaks and while they cooked first and last meals. Mori occasionally walked next to Tian, relating a snippet of the story as they made their way through the trees.

"Even with all the great moments in our history, the adoption of global consensus, the implementation of universal mutual aid, the construction of our first deep space vessel, the discovery of food synthesis from basic elements, even the infosphere itself that makes our civilization possible, we were shaken by what we found in orbit around Dodona. Those ships undermined everything we ever believed about the universe and our society. We believed that organized violence, like leaders, states, and exploitation," Mori paused to explain the words, "came about through poor socialization and ignorance that could be cured with care and education. A an early, infantile stage in a civilization's progress, that would be overcome through the bonds of community, mutual aid, and solidarity.

"Very early in our history on our origin world, we faced these sorts of cultures, but we evolved and overcame them, mostly without violence. They were self-destructive and stunted. They were also notoriously fragile, and constantly in turmoil, consuming themselves with wars. Our society outgrew them, and our technological and industrial prowess surpassed theirs. Where they competed and fought each other to acquire material wealth, we cooperated, created wealth together, and acquired scientific insight. They withered while we prospered. Our people were free, our society was egalitarian, our development was unimpeded by tithes or wars or masters or superstitions. They were no match for us."

Tian had caught a whiff of something unpleasant in Mori's tone, a childish air of boasting that went beyond justified pride. It disturbed her to see it in Mori, whom she was coming to admire more and more the longer that she spent in its company. She didn't say anything about it now, though, and listened in silence to Mori's strange story.

"We hadn't seen a civilization like the barbarians of our ancient past for millennia. We didn't think it was even possible. We never anticipated that they could survive for longer than a few generations. So to find a civilization that had lasted long enough to acquire the technology to venture into space and create an empire that replicated their indigenous societies was horrifying. The ships we found up around Dodona were transports, yet they were brimming with advanced weapons technologies that were vastly beyond anything we had ever dreamed of. I dread to think of what the arsenals of their warships were capable of. The universe suddenly seemed a much darker place. The discovery transformed our perceptions of science and technology. They were no longer neutral, not after what we found."

"What do you mean? Neutral?"

"Okay. Let's take an example. That knife you carry," Mori said, pointing at Tian's belt. "You use it for all kinds of things. Cutting, skinning game, marking trees to show paths. I'm sure there are a thousand other uses for it. But without you, itt would just be a bit of sharp rock. You give it purpose, meaning, you see?"

Tian nodded.

"And while most of the time it is used for those things, it could be used for other things, too. Things that are against the Way, that are wrong. A Qah might use it to kill a man or threaten someone. So depending on how it is used, on who is using it, this blade stops being neutral. You could use it as a tool, but another might use it as a weapon. You see what I mean?"

"I think so," said Tian.

"Well, the technologies and science we have are far more advanced, but it's the same idea. Only in our case, in the wrong hands, things that we've used to help make our lives easier could be used to decimate entire populations or destroy planets, not just kill one person."

"You have things that could destroy all of this?" Tian said, gesturing at the trees around them.

"No, but we could. We use our knowledge to make the world a better place. But if someone like the Qah or a bandit could understand these things, they could use that knowledge to make the world a much darker, more dangerous place. Destroy these forests, for example, or design machines that would enslave and control. Technologies could be turned around and used to hurt, even where they had been used for thousands of years to help. Like the knife."

"You shouldn't have such things, if they can be used that way."

"Would you give up your knife because it could be used to kill someone?"

Tian thought about that for a moment. "I suppose not," she said finally.

"Exactly. Even though the technologies and knowledge we have could be used to hurt people, we have used them for as long as we can remember without using them that way. We could not live without them, just as you couldn't live without your knife. They have improved our lives vastly, to the point where, without them, our civilization would collapse. Besides, as I said, we never anticipated that any advanced species would be hierarchical, let alone militaristic and hostile. The idea that science and advanced technologies could be used in this way was—well, we just never thought it could happen."

They paused for a break. Nimsha'h needed a rest, and began chewing at a patch of long grass, happy for the moment. Mori continued, "We live on densely populated worlds. We learned early on the perils of over-consumption. Much of what you call the Way is an embodiment of some of our ancient ideas.

"There was little dispute over the use of technology to create better lives for our people. We found ways to mass produce all the food and energy we could ever need by harnessing the sun and oceans. That fueled a scientific golden age, a post-scarcity society in which every person's needs could be met many times over and no one ever goes without.

"The things we found on those ships caused a rupture in our society. Many began to question the value of leaving our star systems, proposing that deep space exploration and the founding of further colonies stop. Others, a very vocal minority, argued that if we were to continue our expansion, then we needed to be prepared to meet hostile species and defend ourselves. They called for the development of weapons technologies, for our scientists and engineers to take what we found on the vessels around Dodona and develop it. We were naive to venture into space without expecting to encounter hostility, they argued.

"Some even began to question whether technology, the way we lived, and even civilization and the infosphere, were natural or morally right. A few began to drop out of the infosphere, setting up communes in the wilderness. They, even refused to eat mass produced food and drink, and instead revived ancient agricultural practices to grow food. They called themselves "Ferals," and they had many sympathizers. It was a trying time. It looked at one point that the Confederation would break apart. It took over forty standard orbits to find a solution, and no one was entirely happy with it."

"What did you decide?" asked Tian. She was still trying to piece together the way Mori"s society was organized, so different, so much much more complicated than hers. It helped that they had something like the Circles and consensus, something she could relate to.

"We adapted some weapons to equip a small self-defense fleet; and we used the shielding and other defensive technologies in our cities and colonies. We also sent many more unmanned probes deep into the neighboring star systems to ensure we wouldn't be caught unaware by a militaristic advanced civilization, and in the hope of finding friendly alien species.

"And, after much negotiation, we sent settlers to Dodona."

"Settlers?"

"Yes. The Ferals. Your ancestors."

* * *

Standing in the empty silo all those seasons earlier as a child, looking around at the faces of her tribe, Tian had been scared. Her belly was empty, and their only hope for food had apparently failed them in their time of need.

Had the other tribes taken all of the food? Why hadn't they shared it with them?

Yet the adults didn't seem concerned. Though they were clearly suffering from the stench, they were readying their bags and baskets. She held her breath, willing a miracle to happen.

And it did. The door behind them closed, an eerie light, almost as strong as sunlight, bathed them, and a cool breeze tickled Tian's feet. Fresh air! The stench was swept away, leaving only a faint trace on her skin and clothes. The relief was sublime.

There was movement in the center of the room. Part of the floor began to rise up in front of their eyes, transforming into a peculiar, circular table. Tian could see strange figures inscribed on it. The tribe backed away in awe.

An elder spoke an ancient word, the word for their tribe. Before her eyes, the figures on the table changed. She could now read some of the writing. The old one who had spoken approached it, and touched the writing. She uttered the name of the tribe again, pressed the table, and said, "We require food for one hundred and ten adults, and thirty-eight children. We require fifty days supply. The reason for our request is," she paused as she scanned the table, "flooding."

At this final word, the table lurched downwards, swallowed up by the floor. A portion of the floor lit up against one side of the silo. A hand guided Tian away from it as everyone stepped back.

Then something extraordinary happened. The glowing part of the floor dropped away entirely, leaving a gaping hole. Then, as quickly as it had disappeared, it returned. But it wasn't empty. Food covered the floor. There were stacks and stacks of canvas bags, all packed full of grains, fruits, dried meats, honey, roots, preserves and seeds. There was even raw meat and fresh fish.

The smells were wonderful to Tian. After the long travel through the stink around the silo, the smell of the food brought tears to her eyes.

Tian watched as the tribe began filling its bags and baskets, realizing that it was real—the silo had saved them from famine.

"Why can't we live here?" she asked herself.

She didn't have a chance to ask any of the adults before the stench began to creep back into the silo. Tian could smell it over the food, now, and she groaned as smell grew worse and worse.

The doors slid open. Outside, two figures awaited them. The elders pushed the youngsters behind them, but the smell inside drove everyone out, those in the rear pushing those at the front nearer to the two waiting men. When the last of the tribe left the silo, the doors closed behind them.

"We want no trouble. Just give us a couple of bags of seed and we'll let you by," one of the men said, the words obscured by the towels wrapped around his head.

"You"ll get nothing from us bandit. A few of the larger brothers and sisters edged to the front of the group. Between the legs and bodies in front of her, Tian saw that one of the bandits had a long, double-edged axe. Tian was old enough to know he didn't intend to chop wood with it.

"We will take it, then."

Another voice rang out. "We have no quarrel with you, bandit. Let us be. We'll give you a sack." There were whispers of discontent at the capitulation.

"How are we to live on a sack? Come now, think of your precious mutual aid. We are in need. Surely you can spare more than a sack?" The one with the axe grinned maliciously.

"We will not be threatened or lectured to about the Way by a freeloader. You'll get nothing, now."

The man with the axe was quick. He lunged for the nearest villager, covering the distance in a heartbeat. Tian jumped at the sudden flurry, legs and torsos blocking her view. She heard shouts, and a blood-curdling cry that abruptly cut off.

She worked her way forward and saw the two bandits. The man with the axe had an arrow through his neck, and another protruding from one of his cheeks; he lay sprawled on the ground, dead. The other man was struggling for breath, a spear through his body, jutting out his back. Bubbles of blood emerged from his lips, his lungs pierced, and his life ebbing painfully away. Tian saw one of the villagers approach him and, without hesitation, cut his throat from ear to ear. Blood gushed down his bare torso.

Tian watched as the man, Yehla, wiped the blade on the bandit's shirt and sheathed it before turning back toward the group.

The journey back was silent, mournful, despite their full packs and the gradual easing of the stench.

* * *

Tian had been pestering Mori with questions for hours, her thirst for knowledge insatiable.

"Don't you get lonely out here, away from the other Watchers?" she asked.

"No. I have the infosphere, so I can always talk to someone."

"Talk to them?"

"Well, almost. It's like talking, but not the way you and I talk. When I want to talk to someone, they hear it in their heads. It's silent, and a lot quicker."

"You can read one another's minds?"

"It's a little like that, but it's a lot more compli—"

"That sounds scary, Mori. Can you read my mind?"

"No. You need the implants before you can broadcast and receive data, or talk to... read each other's minds." Mori smiled. "So your thoughts are safe."

Tian went quiet for a few minutes, trying to imagine what it would be like to have someone else inside her head.

"What are you thinking, Tian?"

"Oh, nothing. The infosphere. Explain that to me more."

"Well—"

"Without all the fancy words," said Tian. "Sometimes you sound just like Priash used to."

"Okay. It's a bit like... like an invisible cloud that is always around us, storing information—recording the histories, if you like—about us."

"So everything that you think about and do is being watched by the cloud?"

"Not everything. There is separation between what we think

or feel and what we choose to broadcast to the cloud. Although perhaps not as much as you'd expect."

Tian stopped to think about this. She didn't like the idea of other people being in her head or watching what she was doing—she could just imagine what Grashin would do if he had the infosphere. She'd constantly have to check her emotions if the tribe talked like this. She wasn't sure she could separate her thoughts and emotions from whatever she said to the cloud, as Mori said it could.

Mori continued, "It isn't just a communication device. It stores information—memories—and so on."

"Memories?"

"Yes. We're Watchers, so we're good at recording every event in great detail. But we can't keep all of those memories in our heads. It'd be too much, even for us. So we store our memories in the cloud, and just keep a much smaller memory, an outline, like a memory of a dream, in our heads. Then, if we need to remember something from a few orbits before, we access it from the cloud and fill in the gaps."

"So all of your memories are like dreams?"

"I use that word loosely. To me they are hazy, a bit like your dreams, but to you they would probably be clearer and more vivid than most of your own memories. You have to remember that I'm recording—remembering—everything about every moment: the sound of that bird in the tree, the ambient temperature, your heart rate, as well as what we"re saying and doing."

Tian fidgeted, feeling rather self-conscious all of a sudden.

"Can I see them, too?"

"No. Not without the implants."

"Can't you send them to me? Just think them into my head?"

"No. Sorry Tian." Mori paused. "What did you want to remember?"

"Priash . . . I'm beginning to... I can remember what she looked like, but her voice, Mori . . . I'm beginning to forget her voice. Is there a way?"

"No, not without having the implants."

Tian's eyes swelled with tears, and she let her hair fall across her face to hide them.

"Do you remember her?" Tian asked Mori, her head still turned away.

Mori replied immediately, "Of course."

"Do you know what happened to her? Was it the Qah, or..." her voice trailed off.

"No, I wasn't there." There was something strange about Mori's voice. It had lost the its singsong quality.

"But you remember her, remember what she looked like, her scent, her voice?" asked Tian quietly.

"Yes."

"Do you think she's still alive? Do you think the Qah have her?"

Mori breathed in deeply.

"Listen, Tian. You need to let her go. She's gone."

"You say that, but I bet you've never felt—" she cut herself off before saying something she'd regret. "You've never forgotten anything, anyone, that you love. You don't know what it's like to clutch at a memory, to struggle to remember. Is there... is there a way I could get the implants?"

Mori looked at her in surprise. It had no wish to lie to her, but telling the truth might put it in a very awkward position.

"It is possible," Mori finally admitted.

"It is? I'd be able to remember her?"

"Well, they'd be my memories, but yes, you could. But you wouldn't be able to change anything, Tian. What happened—you can't change that."

"I know that Mori. I just need to see her again, hear her voice again. Just to say goodbye. If I can do that with the implants, then maybe I need them. I should get them. Does it hurt?"

"Yes, but don't get ahead of yourself."

Tian could never see those memories. That memory. Mori would always keep that one to itself.

CHAPTER 4

The smell was the first sign they were getting close to their destination. Tian had hoped they would find the tribe before they got this close, but Mori had told her they were still a day or two behind them. The pace at which they'd traveled had been hard on her. Her legs and butt were raw from riding, and her sleep was troubled, too, full of strange, barely comprehensible dreams of alien worlds. The smell was what she found hardest to bear, though.

"I'm sorry, Tian, I know the smell is hard to bear, but we have to keep going. I'm still hopeful we can find your tribe before they get to the silo. If not..."

Tian had begun to make camp, unrolling the bedding. Mori had started a small fire, following the familiar routine established early in their journey.

"Are you sure the Qah are there?"

"Fairly. The Qah have been following a predictable pattern. I've seen their scouts as far south as here, which indicates that they'll be moving through the area."

"What makes you think they'll be at the silos, though? They could be anywhere. It's a big forest."

"Since they figured out a way to subvert our defense mechanisms in the silos, they use them as resupply areas. Their scouts find a silo, then send a messenger back to their main village, or to another silo where they've built a new village. When the war party gets word from the scouts, they ride in, build a village around the new silo, and then start raiding the surrounding area."

"So will it just be a scouting party at the silo? Not the slavers?" asked Tian.

"I really don't know what we'll find."

"You said your people lived in the silos. Can't they help my tribe, or fight off the Qah?"

"No, there are too few of us, and we're unarmed."

"But why didn't you get together, make weapons, fight them off when they first appeared in the forests?"

"My people were… unwilling to get involved. We are bound by an agreement, a pact of non-interference, that we made with your people's ancestors many centuries ago. The Qah hadn't even appeared then. And when they did, we thought them a passing aberration that would disappear within a generation."

"But they didn't, did they?" said Tian.

"No, they didn't. You must understand, we'd seen something like this before. A coastal tribe followed a similar path; they forgot the histories and abandoned the Way. Their society became cruel. The women killed most of the men, and used the rest for hard labor. We tolerated it, even though their society breached the settlement agreement. We concluded that it would not last long. Such societies never do. This proved to correct. The men rebelled and escaped, scattering across the continent, and the remains of their tribe crumbled."

"So, you thought the Qah would be like that? That they'd just disappear?" Tian was sitting across from Mori, chewing some roots. "From what you've told me, tribes like the Qah can survive, and prosper, as long as they have enough supplies, enough slaves, and a ruthless leader who makes all the decisions." Tian paused, nudging the fire with a stick. "They have access to the food in the silos, don't they?"

Mori looked away from her. "Yes," it said. "They do."

"So they"ll never go hungry, if they can stand the smell. So all they need is slaves. The forest is full of them, full of *us*. If what I've heard about the Qah himself is true, then they have a leader brutal enough to enslave the entire continent. And you," Tian said, pointing a finger at Mori, "just let them do it."

"No, Tian. We didn't. When we saw them for what they were, we immediately took precautions. We tolerated them for as long as possible, but we realized that we'd have to do something sooner or later, otherwise we'd breach the agreement through inaction. You must understand though, this world was ... an experiment."

"You're talking about my life, my home, here!" Tian nearly shouted.

Mori waved her objection aside. "The Qah seemed to prove that the universe could and would be full of advanced, hostile civilizations. Even here, in a world of plenty, beauty, and simplicity, where everyone lived in harmony with nature and the Way and rejected almost all technology, even here an aggressive culture arose. But what you see as our cowardice and complicity was really inertia. We *expected* them to die out, so we waited. Probably too long."

"You said yourself that they forgot their histories, that they abandoned the Way, and that they use your technology," said Tian. "The Qah don't represent us. Without your technology they could never had done these things."

"Who knows, Tian? Perhaps they would have collapsed without the silos. Perhaps they wouldn't have."

"They would have," said Tian firmly. "Our culture is better than that, stronger than that. They are not like us. We'd never do what they did to us, even if we had all of the food we could ever want, whenever we wanted it. If half the stories are true... they are disgusting, violent, egoist. We are not like them."

Talking about the Qah had upset Tian more than she realized. The distant smell of the silo lingered in her nostrils, and the memory of Priash tugged at her.

Mori sat quietly, looking at her. "Perhaps you are right," the Watcher said. "But then again, perhaps not. Your people have forgotten almost all of the histories, holding on to only a loose understanding of what the original settlers believed in. You have superstitions and employ rituals, and you have chosen a path of ignorance over enlightenment, locking away your past in deep caves. You use consensus Circles as forum for political games and tedious routines rather than innovation and a places for sharing ideas and ideals. You have *de facto* leaders, who breach the Way that they themselves interpret as they wish, who engage in activities they publicly condemn, and who encourage intolerance of difference. You are even violent to one another. You expel those who don't conform to your particular way of life, from which there can be no divergence or evolution, and even invent or forget parts of your ethical code when it suits you. Consensus can only function where there is a free exchange of information and ideas, informed debate and complete equality of position, resources and knowledge.

"There was an ancient saying of the Way, no doubt preserved on some dusty scroll in one of Grashin's caves that you'll never see. 'When the Way is disregarded in the world, the war-horses breed in the border lands.' Our society, the Confederation, might be responsible for helping to make possible the Qah's actions with the silo technology, but your tribes are responsible for creating the conditions in which they could flourish to begin with. You even made—" Mori stopped mid-sentence.

Tian sat in stunned silence. Her face was flushed with indignation. She longed to run to Nimsha'h, to ride away from this evil creature, this twister of words. How dare it judge her, her people? However, just as she had been paralyzed with fright when she first saw Mori, now she was now paralyzed with rage.

Mori continued, as if the damning judgment it had just made on the tribes tribe was nothing more than an informative aside, as if it had been explaining the meaning of an unknown word to Tian. Mori hadn't even raised its voice.

"We"ve known about the Qah for many seasons, but something changed about a season ago. Before, we'd only seen their slaves around the silos, forced to endure the smell while the Qah themselves waited. Because of our precautions, they could only get enough provisions to last them a few days. Yet recently we began to see Qah warriors in the zones, in the silos. They seemed unaffected by the smell, but all of the slaves still exhibited symptoms. Then they started leaving their villages, and headed south. And then they killed one of my people."

There was a pause. Mori swallowed. Tian held her breath, waiting for Mori to speak.

"Somehow, they found an open service entrance to the tunnels beneath a silo, and one of my people, AO17, was inside it repairing the entrance mechanism. The others locked down the tunnel, but not before the Qah had captured 17. They tortured 17—hurt 17 for a long time but didn't kill it—and forced it to reveal some of the basic security systems in place around the silo. 17 refused to tell them how to stop the gas, or how to enter the tunnels below, for which they tied 17's legs to a tree and arms tied to a horse, and ripped 17 in half." Mori paused, looking away. "Then they cooked and ate 17."

Tian's mouth opened in horror, her thoughts immediately returning to Priash.

Mori continued, "When you tell me then that we are responsible for the Qah, you see why I disagree with you. The Qah were a violent culture long before they started abusing our silos. Our silos do nothing but help those in need. We did not teach the Qah such callous disregard for life. We didn"t teach them how to tear apart 17, or remove 17's fingers and toes and eyelids and ears, or pierce their anus or burn their feet or peel off their skin to make them talk so they could do the same to 17's friends, who were forced to watch every moment. They learned that long ago on the steppes."

Mori paused for a moment to regain its composure. Its melodic voice had become heavy with grief, and the story had riled Mori up to the point where its words were becoming almost incomprehensible. After a few moments and some deep breaths, Mori continued.

"Even then, with the remains of 17 digesting in the stomachs of Qah warriors, my people did not call for help. But the Qah spread quickly once they knew how to force the silos to give them what they wanted. They could range farther afield and force their slaves to carry weeks' worth of provisions. They captured four silos in the north during the first season, and killed two more of my people who were attempting to deactivate a silo before the Qah arrived. That was three seasons ago. Our reports are sketchy, but they seem to have stepped up their raids on villages, too, taking more slaves in one moon than they did in a dozen before it. Now they have at least thirteen silos, ranging from the far northeasten desert in an almost straight line across the steppes and the plains to here, the southern forests. And believe me, Tian, we are taking them very seriously."

"Here," said Mori, abruptly ending its long, terrifying story. "Take this before you sleep tonight. It will block the smell."

Mori handed Tian a small white pill. She studied it in the palm of her hand. She was still furious at Mori for what it had said about her people, but the story about the Qah frightened her even more. She hadn't realized how much danger they were all in. The Qah had seemed faintly unreal to her, a myth, a bedtime story. No longer.

"It will make everything taste bland, but you'll be spared the stench," said Mori, taking Tian's hesitation as reluctance.

With just a brief glance at Mori, Tian swallowed the pill, turned her back, and silently retired to bed.

* * *

The next day they came to a broad river deep in the forest. It was swollen with the mountain rains, and was a murky brown. Tian had smiled when she first heard the churning of the river in the distance, looking forward to eating fish. When she saw how swollen the river was, though, she knew bowfishing was out of the question. The water was too fast and muddy to catch anything.

Mori noticed her downcast mood.

"You wanted to fish here?"

"Yes. I'm tired of rabbit and berries, and that seed you gave me... I couldn't taste firstmeal at all this morning."

"A small inconvenience to be free of the smell, I thought. Wait here. I'll fetch you a fish."

To Tian's surprise, Mori walked straight into the raging river. It must have been at least four meters deep, and the current was strong. Tian watched as Mori walked far out from the bank, only its head and shoulders showing. Despite being almost entirely submerged, Mori didn't seem at all bothered by the massive amount of water that must have been pummeling its body. It walked as if it were crossing a stream. Mori stopped and reached down. Its head disappeared for a second beneath the water. Then there was a sudden splash, a glint of silver, and long black arms bursting from the water's surface. A large flapping-silver fish came to rest on the bank near Tian. She watched the fish with amazement, before realizing it was struggling its way back into the river. With a hard stamp, she bought her bare foot down on the fish's head, stopping its wriggling. In the time it had taken her to kill the fish, another had come sailing through the air, landing on a rock a little farther from Tian. She killed that one, too.

"That enough?" called Mori, over the roar of the river.

"Yes!" She stood holding the two dead fish in her hands, watching Mori walk through the river, its naked, hairless body emerging from the torrent, showing no sign of exertion.

"That was unexpected," said Tian.

"I hope they make up in some small way for my behavior last night."

Tian looked up at Mori, unsure of what to say.

"I have no right to judge you or your people. This is a difficult time, but that is no excuse for my self-righteous lecturing, and I apologize for what I said. I was angry, and I'm scared. I am not used to conversing with people, especially those who aren't other Watchers. I honestly meant no offense. I hope that you can forgive me, and that you can still trust me. I will need your help when we come to the silo, and I need you to trust everything I say. I hope that you will." Mori placed a wet hand on

Tian's shoulder. The hand was warm, comforting.

"I trust you, Mori. I just hope... I hope I'm not like them. I hate them. They took my sister Priash away from me. To hear you say that I was like them, it hurt so much."

Mori's face was blank. "Yes, I know. I'm sorry I said those things, Tian. I know you are not like the Qah, and it isn't your fault. Come, I'll cook you these fish. Let's see if you can taste them."

Tian watched with something close to tenderness as Mori gutted and prepared the fish. She remembered the words Mori had said the previous night, and how much they had stung, but the more she thought about it, the more she realized how right Mori had been about her people. Mori had said, although with less tact, what Priash had often said to her, and what Tian had thought to herself after her many frustrating encounters with Grashin and his cronies in the Circle. Deep down, Tian knew that Mori was right, and she couldn't stay angry at it for saying what she herself had so often thought.

Mori handed her the fish, having warmed them over the fire for only a moment or two. She thought she could taste a hint of raw fish as she chewed, but it might have been her imagination. They set out not long after, leaving the river behind.

They were walking side by side, Nimsha'h trotting slowly, taking a break from the fast pace she'd maintained all morning, Mori's long legs easily keeping up with the horse. Their conversations were now merely excuses for giving the horse and Tian a break from the hard ride, but Tian welcomed the conversations as much as the breaks.

"Tell me about Grashin," Mori said after a while.

"You told me that you remember everything you see. You probably know more than I do about Grashin."

Mori nodded its head, smiling its smile.

"Yes, probably. But just because I watched you and Grashin doesn't mean I know what was going on inside there"—Mori tapped the back of Tian's head—"or inside Grashin's head, either. Tell me about it." The tap sent a small shiver up and down Taian's neck and spine, for reasons she couldn't quite explain. She wasn't afraid of Mori any more, but there was something about Mori that made her skin shiver whenever she looked at it or heard its hypnotic voice, about the way Mori explained things she didn't understand so slowly and patiently, without ever patronizing her. Just like Priash used to. Then, remembering what Mori had said about being able to hear her heartbeat, she quickly began talking to disguise the unusual effect the touch had had on her.

"Well, he's an old shitstool."

"You don't need to joke with me, Tian."

"Well, what do you want me to say? You've seen the way he acts. I hate the way he is, the way he talks to me. The way he talks to everyone else, like he knows more than them, like he knows best."

"Why do you hate that?"

"*Why?* I don't know why. He just... he just has no right to act like that. Does he? He abuses his position and hides parts of himself from others. And he uses people, I've seen him do it. He treats people like objects. He's just a horrible man."

"Give me an example," said Mori.

After a few moments, she said, "You know the Arphan festival?"

Mori nodded. The festival was one of the most elaborate in the forest tribes' calendar, marking the spring equinox. It was especially important for Tian's own tribe, and they always spent weeks preparing for it.

"Yes," Mori said. "I know it."

"Well, you know that we pride ourselves on hosting the best Arphan festival among the forest tribes, maybe even all the tribes. Everyone knows that we host the best Arphan festival. People travel days, even weeks to attend. Some of them come every year."

Mori nodded again.

"I don't know why I'm telling you this. You probably already know the story I'm about to tell you."

"Maybe not. There are hundreds of people at the festivals, and we have to keep our distance to avoid being seen, especially when everyone is in such a... rambunctious mood," Mori said, smiling. "If something happened between Grashin and you at one of the Arphan festivals, I don't recall witnessing it."

"You were too busy watching everyone fuck?" Tian laughed. The celebrations at Arphan lasted several days, and there were always a lot of new faces. The tribe prided itself on showcasing the very best of its beer, too, at the festival.

"No, I— Oh never mind, get on with your story," Mori said, nudging her playfully on the shoulder.

"You don't fool me Watcher," she said, laughing. "Anyway, I was with Priash and we were hanging around in the Circle, chatting about who knows what. It was the Arphan before she went missing..." Tian's smile faded. "Do you remember?"

"No, I don't recall anything special about that festival."

"Well, I remember that it was just getting dark. I think we were joking about one of the stories someone had told the night before. She was teasing me about it, because it was about a Watcher."

"Why?"

Tian hoped her cheeks weren"t turning too pink.

"I told you. Those stories used to scare me. When I was little," she added hastily.

"And she knew that?" Mori asked, who of course knew the answer.

"Yes. She always used to poke fun at me about them." She flicked her hand as if pushing aside the memory. "So we were in the Circle, and suddenly Grashin and a few of the elders came over and sat down on the benches. None of them looked particularly happy. I don't think they'd been dancing or drinking. If anything, they looked pretty serious. At first we ignored them.

But they made it pretty obvious that we weren't welcome."

"How did they do that?"

Tian smiled. "It's clear you live on your own out here, Mori. When you live in the tribe, you get to learn when people want privacy, when you're intruding, even just from the way someone is sitting or holding themselves. Even how they're breathing. They were all talking quietly too, and throwing us long glances. It wasn't very subtle, even by Grashin's standards."

"I see. What were they doing there?"

"I'm getting to that. So Priash and I—we'd had a bit to drink, and we were having a good time. We were enjoying ourselves. Maybe we felt a bit put out that they'd marched over and were trying to get us to shove off, when we'd been there most of the afternoon."

"But isn't the Circle used for important discussions?"

"Well, yes, but it's not like we were being that disruptive." She threw Mori a cheeky grin. "Okay, maybe we were. But who cares? It was Arphan. We were having fun, and then they came along with their long faces and their whispering to ruin it. Maybe we were playing up a bit to get a reaction from them, but we had every bit as much right to be there as they did."

"So what did they do?"

"I saw Grashin whisper something into Bal's ear. You know Bal?" Mori nodded. "Well, he's one of Grashin's cronies. When Grashin wants something done without getting his hands dirty, he gets Bal to do it. So Bal listens to Grashin, then stands up, puffing out his chest and starts swaggering over to us."

"Did he make you leave?"

"No. When we saw him walking over like a pompous old fool we both burst out laughing, which just made him push out his chest even more. He's an idiot, but you probably know that already."

Mori smiled. "He does come across as being a little self-important, yes."

"Well when he did that we just dug our heels in. He gave us a long speech about distinguished guests and appropriate behavior, then started in about the Way. We just sat there, not budging. This was back before Grashin really knew how to get under our—my—skin. He's come a long way since then."

"So did they leave?"

"No. I could see that there was someone else from another tribe with them, and she was getting uncomfortable watching Bal giving us this stupid long lecture, and she tried to intervene. I think her name was Sesh, or maybe Salesh. She tried to get us to join in."

"Join in with what?"

"They were having a Wayfinder."

"A what?" said Mori, frowning.

"You've never heard of the Wayfinders?"

"I don't think so, no."

"Well, sometimes something happens in the tribes that the Circle can't agree on, but they can't just leave it, either. They need a decision; they can't just put it off like most things. No matter how much they might try, sometimes they can't resolve their differences and reach consensus, and the Way isn't clear. So when they've exhausted all possibilities at finding the Way in their own Ciircle, they hold a Wayfinder. They travel to one of the other tribes to seek guidance, to help them reach consensus."

"I see," said Mori. "I knew this kind of thing happened, I just didn't know that's what you called it. I've heard it called other things elsewhere. It's like a mediation process."

"Yes. People sometimes come from very far away to have Wayfinders. Even though I hate to admit it, Grashin and the other elders probably know more about the Way than any of the other tribes, and anything they don't know Grashin can check in the library. So our tribe holds a lot of Wayfinders."

Mori gave Tian a peculiar look.

"What is it? Why are you looking at me like that?"

"Oh, nothing. I've already passed judgment enough."

"You don't approve?"

"Well, do you, Tian?"

"I'm not sure. Like I said, they know almost everything about the Way, and they did seem to help the people who came to them. Sometimes the people were in real trouble."

"But?" asked Mori, catching Tian's hesitatance.

"But sometimes it seems unnecessary. They come to our tribe for a Wayfinder, even about the smallest things. It seems, to me at least, that they could reach consensus a lot of the time if they just worked harder to find their own solution, instead of relying on a few elders, strangers, from another tribe to make the decision for them." Tian was half-joking, but Mori responded with a stony silence. She continued, "And when they go back, their tribes almost always accept the decision, because they'd found the Way, the right path...." her voice trailed off.

"Why doesn't anyone besides elders participate in the Wayfinders?"

"That's another thing. They say it's because they're neutral, and because they know the Way the best. Which I guess is true, but it's all so informal, like a secret. They never let us even watch, let alone join in. Most of the time we only found out that there'd been a Wayfinder after it had already happened. Plus they say discussing it in the Circle might lead to more problems. We might not be able to come to a decision either, which would just make everything worse than it already is."

Mori pushed aside a branch and asked, "What if the elders can't reach a decision?"

"Well, they almost always do, as far as I know."

"And if they don't?"

"Then they consult the scrolls Grashin carries with him, check what the Way says."

"But what if the Way doesn't say anything about it? What do they do then?"

Tian paused. "Well, that's never happened."

"It always says something?"

"Yes. Sometimes it's a bit cryptic, and needs interpretation —some of the language it uses is a bit strange. But yes, the Way always produces a decision. It is the Way, after all."

They walked in silence for a moment, both deep in thought.

"Anyway, like I was saying, they were trying to have a Wayfinder then, during that Arphan. Sesh or Salesh tried to get us to join the Wayfinder. From the way she spoke, I could tell she was from a long way off, one of the coastal tribes. It was clear she didn't really know how Wayfinders work, but once she'd suggested we joing the other elders couldn't stop it."

"Why not?"

"It's a bit complicated. But since she'd invited us, and it was supposed to be her Wayfinder, they had no choice."

"I bet that annoyed them."

"Like you wouldn't believe. They were fuming. Priash and I could barely contain ourselves. To be honest, I was more than a bit curious to see how it worked—like I said, they were normally very secretive about it."

"I can't say I've ever seen one up close, either."

"Exactly. . . Anyway, it all started pretty much like a normal Circle. It was boring, but it sobered us up. It turned out Sesh's tribe actually had two problems. She'd already been to a neighboring village but they hadn't been any help and she'd left without a decision. They suggested that she come to our tribe."

"So what did she need help with?"

"The first problem was straightforward enough, although I could see why it had caused such problems for her tribe. She explained to us that a bloodbrother and bloodsister had lain together, and that the girl was now on the path."

"Pregnant?" asked Mori.

Tian gave Mori a sardonic glance. "Yes. There was no question that the fatherchild would be the bloodbrother's, and they had no idea what to do."

"Do? What did the Wayfinder suggest?"

"I've heard about this happening before, and they didn't need to discuss it, or even consult the Way. If the child lived and was free from the blight, they should care for the child and raise it as usual. Leave it for the forest—or in their case, the tides—if not. Common sense, really."

Mori didn't say anything, but looked up at the sky.

"The second problem was much more difficult."

"Really? Why?"

"A few of their tribe wanted to build huts made of wood that would float, they said, out on the ocean."

"They wanted to build boats?" asked Mori incredulously.

"I'm not sure. It sounded a bit crazy to me. What's a boat?"

"Pretty much what you said. A floating hut. Like a big canoe. Why did they want to do that?"

"They said that they couldn't go far enough out on their canoes, that the waves were too strong. They'd lost two men who'd been dragged far out into the ocean.

"They said that if they built big enough canoes, and according to Sesh what they had in mind was as big as our sleeping huts, they could be safe. They'd be able to go farther out where the fish were, away from the rocks and the undersea pull. She said a few of them were convinced that these things would float better than the canoes. It sounded like nonsense to me. As if a hut could float!"

"What did the elders say?"

"They laughed at her. Grashin said, "It sounds like some of you have been drinking too much beer" or something equally dismissive. I could see that upset Sesh, and it got my back up straight away. I don't think she really thought they could get the floating huts to work either, but I could see she didn't like the way Grashin and a few of the others spoke about her tribe."

"What did you do?"

"I didn't have to do anything. I was with Priash, remember. You know what she was like. I'm a mouse compared to her. Or at least, I was then." Tian smiled sheepishly. "She started on about how it couldn't hurt to experiment, how they had nothing to lose, that they might actually be able to catch even more fish or stop others from being dragged out to sea. When they saw that she was serious, well, that's when it all started getting nasty. They said she was ignorant, that she didn't know anything, as if an herbalist knew anything about the ocean or fishing. When Sesh started to explain that some of her tribe had actually started testing it out, apparently they'd felled a few large trees and tied the trunks together and they floated just as well as a canoe, they turned on her, too. Saying it was a waste of resources and time, that it was dangerous, people could drown. I admit, I sort of agreed with them, but they were being so mean about it. It was obvious that they'd made up their minds already. By this point everyone was getting pretty heated, so Sesh asked for guidance from the Way."

"I thought that's what you were doing already."

"No, that was just like a normal Circle. Everyone was just giving their opinions, but it was clear that there wouldn't be consensus. So Sesh was asking what the Way said about it."

"So what did the Way say about boats?" Mori asked, with a little grin.

"Well, that's where the problems really started. Once Sesh mentioned the Way everyone got all serious."

"They weren't serious before?"

"No, I mean, they started . . . I'm not sure I can explain it. They were joking, laughing at her and the idea. But as soon as she mentioned the Way, it was like they all put on a mask, like they were about to start a performance. But a grave one, like the funeral rites. It was strange. They were talking about the Way, but not like I'd ever heard them talk about it."

"How so?"

"Oh, I don't know. I can't describe it. But it was weird. Grashin began to recite parts of the Way."

"But he does that all the time. Almost every night."

"Yes, but as he was doing it, the others would repeat what he'd just said, like an echo. He and the others normally tell it like a story, and they don't use the old language when they do. This time he wasn't even stopping to explain the old words. He just said them, in this deep, rumbling voice, which the others would chant afterwards."

"How odd. I've never heard or seen them do anything like that," Mori said.

"Exactly. Well, I was too distracted by this weird performance to listen to what Grashin was actually saying, and I could see it was having the same effect on Sesh, too. But of course, Priash was listening, and she wasn't distracted by the performance. She was always a lot smarter than me. Well, after they said about ten or eleven lines like this, they stopped, and they all looked at Sesh. I could see she was overwhelmed. She didn"t say anything, just waited for what was going to happen next."

They'd stopped dead in the forest now, Nimsha'h eating some juicy looking leaves from a low branch.

"And?" Mori asked, breaking the silence. Tian smiled; it was nice to be the one finally telling the stories.

"And Grashin said, 'The Way forbids it,' of course."

"Of course?"

"Well, you didn't really expect anything else, did you?"

"Well, no, but the whole pretense of 'seeking the Way'—what was the point? They all know the Way by heart, so why the charade?"

"Charade?"

"Yes, performance. A fake ritual. Why did they bother with that?"

"I guess that's just how the Wayfinder works. But that's not the point. After Grashin had said that it was forbidden, Sesh just nodded and accepted it. She'd gotten what she'd come for. She looked intimidated. I don"t blame her. To be honest, so was I. But then Priash piped up. She said that the lines they'd recited said nothing about floating huts, canoes, fishing or the oceans. Or anything to do with the situation at all."

"Was she right?"

"I have no idea. Priash knows the old language much better than I do—she can read almost everything in the library. Besides, like I said, I was too shocked by the way they'd said it to follow what it was they were actually saying, and the Way can be pretty confusing even when it's spoken normally. But if she said that the lines they'd recited didn't mention fishing or the oceans, I believed her."

"So what did the elders say when Priash challenged them?"

"What do you think they said? They said she couldn't possibly understand it, that it required years of training, contemplation, and the 'wisdom of age,' to understand the true meaning of the words, which weren't all they seemed. Some nonsense like that. Anyway, I could see that Sesh was looking confused. She thought she'd gotten an answer. Bear in mind she'd been traveling most of the season for it. And now, when she'd finally found the Way, there was this half-drunk girl disputing it. I could see her fidgeting when the others turned on Priash. Then she asked whether what Priash was saying was right, asked for an explanation of what the Way said. If Priash hadn't been there she'd have just gone away without questioning it, but now the elders had to explain it to her."

"Did they explain?"

"No. They said the same things they'd said to Priash. That she couldn't understand it, that it was too complex, needed long meditation and seasons of readings before anyone could hope to interpret it. Said some horrible things about the coastal tribes too, implying that they were backward or that they'd strayed from the Way. It was awful. Then they began saying that Priash was being disrespectful to the Way. They even called her some words that I won't say, but basically said she was an egoist."

"But all she was trying to do was to get them to clarify the Way. Why did they react so badly? Was she being disrespectful?" asked Mori.

"To the elders, maybe a bit. Though I think she had every right to be that way. But no, she wasn't disrespectful to the Way.

She never said it was wrong or anything like that. She was just questioning whether the part they chanted had anything to do with Sesh's question, whether the elders' interpretation was right. If anyone was disrespectful, it was Grashin and the other elders to Sesh and her tribe. For all of their rules about how to treat guests, they treated her like a piece of boarshit."

"So that's when you and Grashin started to—"

"That was one time of many, but that's one of the earliest memories I have of him and the other elders being so openly mean to get their way. Hiding behind things, manipulating people for their own ends."

"How did it end? Did Sesh's tribe ever build boats?" As it spoke, Mori scanned its memories for records of any coastal tribes developing seafaring vessels, but came up empty.

"No, of course not. Grashin and the others faced Priash and Sesh down. Gave them this long harangue about Way ethics and so on. Browbeat them into submission. Grashin isn't as forthright these days. He uses other tricks now to get what he wants, but that day when there were just us three outsiders, Sesh, Priash and me, I saw him for what he really is."

"Which is?"

"A leader," she spat. "A coward too, hiding behind his Way. But without doubt, a leader."

* * *

Three weeks before Priash was taken, she spoke in the Circle. It was the first time she'd done so for a long time.

The meeting had been a long one. She had proposed that the library be opened to all the tribes, and had offered to help construct better shelving and assist in organizing the books and parchments so that more people could use them. Most of the tribe didn't see the need. The tribes already have access to the library, they said, and the narrower, more dangerous tunnels only contain damaged or useless books. There was no need to start pulling out all the dusty old scrolls only to have to put them back again, or waste time building new shelves or widening caves for books that nobody reads. Everything that is important is in the main library cave, they said, and Grashin can get you anything else you need.

The discussion was still going on when it was time to call for consensus. Many stood up to show their objection to Priash's proposal. The whole process was tedious and tiring. It dragged on and on, with its customs, etiquette, and procedures. Tian saw Priash's shoulders slumping as the evening wore on. Eventually, the facilitator called a break.

Grashin ambled over to Priash, his beady eyes bearing down on his prey. Tian couldn't hear what he was saying, but she could see Priash's face clearly across the Circle. She saw Priash's eyes widen in surprise, looking up eagerly at the old man. Whatever he was saying to her, she seemed to be happy about it. Her dejection fell from her shoulders in an instant.

With a final nod, and a quick tap on the shoulder, Grashin walked away. Priash was smiling.

When the Circle resumed, she withdrew her proposal.

Three weeks later, Priash was gone.

CHAPTER 5

The day was overcast, and the sunlight barely reached the forest floor. The ground was uneven, and Tian's back was stiff, the pain enough to take her mind off the Qah and the approaching danger.

The woods were different here. They were almost empty. The only sounds were faintly buzzing insects and the rustle of leaves under Nimsha'h's feet.

They didn't talk as much now as they had earlier in the journey. Tian was often deep in thought Nimsha'h's sure footedness allowing her mind to wander.

"Where are all the birds, Mori?" she asked.

"An unintended side effect of the gas. We thought it would only affect the settlers, but for some reason it seems to disturb most of the animals, too. I see even Nimsha'h is a little nervous."

"Will she be okay?" asked Tian, anxiously.

"Yes, as long as you stay with her. The gas won't harm her. Still, let me know if she becomes distressed." Mori stroked Nimsha'h's neck, murmuring something under its breath to her.

"You put the gas here to stop people from living near the silos?" asked Tian. The sight of Mori talking to Nimsha'h, the way its big hand was rubbing her neck with such compassion, caused a small flutter in her chest. She already knew the answer to her question. She just wanted to subdue the peculiar feeling she was having.

"Yes. It was part of the settlement agreement. It was actually a compromise. When the first settlers came here, we felt very uncomfortable about leaving them to fend for themselves. The tribes on this continent agreed to our request that we build the silos in case of emergencies. But your ancestors were worried that the silos might eventually lead to permanent settlements and agriculture, and with it everything they were trying to escape. So we put countermeasures in place. The gas is the most obvious."

"Who were the settlers?" asked Tian. They had resumed walking now, Tian's strange feeling fading away.

"I never finished that story, did I?"

Tian shook her head, glad that she'd enticed Mori into relating another story.

"Well, I told you about those that dropped out from the infosphere, and who tried to create a new community based on harmony with nature and so on."

Tian nodded, remembering. "The Ferals," she said.

"Yes. Some of them were very critical of the Confederation. They said that the infosphere was alienating, depersonalizing. That consensus could only truly be reached face to face, in circles like the ones you have here. They spoke a lot about our decision to acquire weapons technologies, and our use of technology in general, saying that it would lead to the kind of society we said we were trying to protect ourselves against."

"Did it?" Tian asked abruptly.

"No. But their critique definitely moderated some of the more extreme ideas about the new weaponry. We didn't go all out to build weapons and armed forces. We modified the gas here from a formula we found in the records on the ships. We use it as a nonviolent dispersal method, where we suspect they used gas to wipe out whole peoples and species.

"Anyway, while all this was going on, and we were having this long, existential debate, Dodona was sitting here untouched. We'd sent exploration teams, and their reports caused a sensation. It seemed perfect for settlement. Only, we didn't settle it. Despite all of the fuss about the station and abandoned ships, what was more important was that we had found intelligent life in the oceans.

"Our civilization is very developed. We have settled thousands of worlds and moons. Most of us live in vast, sprawling communities. Beautiful, too, but still.... Even the smallest of them would have a major impact on the ecosystem here. In time, the population of Dodona would expand; we'd start encroaching on the oceans for tidal power and maybe even living space. We'd have to clear large tracts of forest or steppes for homes and infrastructure, disrupting natural habitats irrevocably. In a few millennia, given Dodona's perfect conditions for settlement, we predicted it would be covered in vast cities with a population of billions. We deemed the threat of settlement to the sentient marine life unacceptable, so the Confederation decided to keep this world as it was. It was given Protected status, and we only established a few monitoring stations to study the oceanic culture and creatures."

"Why did you let the Ferals come, then?" asked Tian.

"There are only a few worlds we'd visited that can support

life without technology or terraforming. Almost none of the planets or moons we settled had a breathable atmosphere or developed ecosystem. Our origin world was heavily populated. There are the sprawling cities, space lifts, the infosphere hubs, transport systems, energy plants, manufacturing plants, and so on. There are areas of wilderness, too, but most of them are close to populated areas.

The Ferals who dropped out to reconnect with nature struggled. It was too artificial for them, even in the remotest areas. So they reconnected to the infosphere, and proposed that they resettle here. They planned to live as our very early ancestors had, as nomads living off the bounty of the land, without even the most basic agriculture, technology, or medicines, let alone the infosphere. They pushed hard for it, claiming their right to a self-determination. In the end, we allowed it, though with some provisions."

Tian tried to imagine those first settlers, their lives so unhappy, so desperate that they left their homes and even their planets to travel across the stars to an alien world. "What were the provisions?" she asked.

"Only two of the continents would be settled, and the Confederation would monitor them to ensure that a destructive civilization would not threaten the oceanic life specifically, and the wider ecosystem more generally. The rest you know. We built silos on this continent as a precaution against disaster, as well as to allow anyone who wanted it access to the infosphere. You see, at the time... well, some thought that the settlers would get bored or discontent living outside of the Confederation. They wanted to ensure that anyone who changed their mind about this place, about this life, could be reintegrated if they wanted it. We put the silos here for the same reason; we worried that settlers from cornucopia worlds would have a much harder time living this "pure" life the Ferals imagined."

They stopped for a break, the night drawing in. Tian had picked some cherries and was eating them as she listened to

Mori talk. Nimsha'h had strayed a few meters away, leaving Mori and Tian alone in the darkness. Tian considered lighting a fire but it was a warm night and she thought better of it; instead they simply sat on the forest floor, talking. She could barely see Mori's body, just the hint of a silhouette across from her, but its voice sounded as if it were sitting next to her.

"Nobody had lived this life, the way you do now, for many tens of thousands of seasons. But here scarcity was a possibility. Indeed, that possibility was a fundamental part of the culture. That was worrying to us. We weren't sure the settlers could cope with it, and Dodona is a long way from assistance if they got into trouble."

"But they did cope," said Tian.

"Clearly, we underestimated them. They are still admired throughout the Confederation."

"You mean the whole Confederation is watching us? I'm not sure I like that, Mori."

"Oh, no, Tian. The anthropological teams send reports, but we're not being watched. We're not linked to the Confederation's infosphere."

"Did more people try to come here, after the first ones?"

"No one else came," Mori said.

"Why not? Did you stop them?"

"No, we didn't need to stop them, as you put it. People do as they please, as long as they don't harm or intrude on others."

"But why didn't they come, then, if they wanted to?"

"The vast majority in the Confederationn admire you, but your tribal society is very narrow. For one thing, the ecosystem strictly limits your population, as long as you remain hunter-gatherers. Only agriculture would allow the population of this continent to grow to even a fraction of the size of one of our smallest cities. Once the first settlers came, there could be no others. Most people in the Confederation know the impact studies we did. That is the reason Dodona is officially 'Protected.' And as much as they admire it, and as much as your culture has had an influence on the us in many ways, there is no real desire to adopt this lifestyle. People understand that any further immigration would unsettle the fine balance here, push the tribes in a direction that their founders and members wouldn't want them to go in. That knowledge, and Dodona's Protected status, prevent anyone else from coming here, as much as that might appeal to some personally. Just because you can do something, doesn't mean you will do it.

"Most of my people are content to do their lifestyle experimentation within the protections of the Confederation, with access to the infosphere. I've tried to explain to you what the infosphere is, but it is difficult to put it in a way you could understand. For most people, living without the infosphere is a frightening prospect. It isn't just a cloud of memories for them. To be cut off from it would be like losing part of their personality, part of their mind. Like living in the dark, almost."

Tian popped another cherry into her mouth. It was strange talking, or rather, listening, in the night without the fire. She hadn't realized how much she relied on it. As much as she hated collecting firewood, she couldn't remember a time with the tribe when they wouldn't light a fire, even on the rainiest or windiest days, even when they had no meat to cook or stew to warm. Even on their hunting trips they would always have a small fire before going to bed, to sing songs around or tell stories over. It gave a sense of safety, of hominess.

"Without the infosphere, we couldn't have the Confederation or consensus," continued Mori, breaking the train of Tian's thoughts. "Consensus means more to us than just a decision-making forum, as it does here. To us, Consensus means harmony, it means intellectual freedom and cooperation, sharing everything using the infosphere. With that comes reasoned, humane ethics. Consensus forms the basis of our culture, the concept behind our entire civilization, the Confederation. Everyone has a voice and a chance to shape any and every decision. Consensus allows every single one us to have a say in the future of our civilization, and to shape the beliefs, values and culture of that civilization."

If they'd had a fire, Tian might have seen Mori's eyes sparkle as it talked, its hands gesticulating excitedly. Instead, she just heard Mori's voice, but even that was enough to convey its excitement. Even though she understood few of the words, she understood the basic principle behind Mori's peculiar culture. People had taken the tribe and scaled it up to the point where it spanned many worlds. The huge distances and the vast numbers of people in it left Tian's mind reeling as she tried to imagine it.

"You see then, sister, why this world is a novelty, not something most of our people would like to—or even could—emulate."

"Then why are you here?"

"Me, personally?"

"No, I mean the Watchers. Are you here to protect us?"

"No, not at all." Tian thought she heard a faint uneasiness in Mori's voice. "As I've said, we're curious about how this society will develop, but we're ethically forbidden from getting involved, unless something really terrible threatens you. We're just here to observe, to expand our knowledge."

"But you don't watch anybody else on all those other planets, do you?" asked Tian. She continued without giving Mori a chance to reply. "Why didn't you just leave us alone? Just let the people here lead their own lives? It sounds like they just wanted to get away from this Confederation, and the way you lived. And you followed them here."

"It's true, we did. But, the silos and you and I aside, we've always stayed clear. It was part of the agreement. We're here to ensure that the settlers don't jeopardize—no, let me put it another way...The only reason *any* of us are here, permitted to live in this unspoiled wilderness, is on the condition that we don't threaten it."

"But what if someone did? If the tribes decided to build cities or make canoes that travel through the sky? What would you do?"

Mori thought about that.

"I'm not sure. We permitted the Ferals to live here on the condition that their societies were in harmony with the natural world and didn't destroy or threaten the biodiversity here, and we, the Watchers, were permitted to study the settlers on the condition that we kept out of sight and acted only in case of dire emergency. Both sides were happy with that arrangement. We reached consensus, if you like. We always assumed that any disaster would be environmental, rather than something like the Qah."

"But what if the Qah are just another natural progression, like the dead civilization who left the things in space? Who are we to say they're wrong?" She was being deliberately argumentative now, and she knew it. A trait picked up from seasons of confrontations with Grashin.

"I'm not sure you really believe that," said Mori. "Anyway, I don't think that most of them do actually have a choice in the matter. The threat of violence can never be the basis for a fair or free society."

"No. But who said the way we live has to be free, or even fair? The forest isn't fair. The Way teaches us that. And you could just swoop in and stop us if we did anything you don't like."

"That would only be in extreme emergencies, and we would always limit the extent to which we did interfere. It's true that your Way teaches that the forest isn't fair, but it's for that very reason that cooperation and consensuall societies are necessary. I don't think that anyone could survive here without a tribe, without mutual aid, and some measure of equality. It's regression back to infantile, self-destructive behaviors that can't last."

Mori paused. "Besides, as you've probably guessed, there are plenty of things that the tribes do that we find upsetting, even morally wrong. We never interfere in those, though, and we never would. And trust me, there have been plenty of times I would have liked to. But this is your life and your mistakes, and we cannot and will not be the judge of that."

Nimsha'h came trotting back to them. Tian stood and stroked the horse, appreciating its familiar warmth. The forest was eerily quiet. Even the insects were silent.

"Don't you miss the Confederation though?" Tian asked after a while.

"Yes," Mori said without hesitation. "I do, even after all these seasons. We have a limited community here, of course, but nothing like the Confederation. That culture is so... it just buzzes with life, with ideas, with energy. It feels deep. Alive. The feeling of connectivity, of belonging and contributing to this massive society, this huge organism that you are a small, but vital part of..." Mori's voice had become distant. "You're never alone in the Confederation, Tian."

She looked at where she thought Mori was, trying hard to imagine. "I sometimes prefer to be alone, Mori."

Mori's voice was more direct now, its reverie broken. "Yes, of course. We all enjoy some privacy. I'm sorry, I haven't explained it very well. I've bored you long enough. Good night."

With that, Mori climbed up a tree trunk, the conversation abruptly over, leaving Tian's head filled with thoughts of alien worlds, clouds of memories, and Qah slavers.

* * *

The weather had calmed during the night, and the foraging party awoke to a clear morning. They went out to search for Priash after firstmeal.

Nealah said that she thought she'd seen the ubutu bushes that Priash had gone to forage from. Leaving three of their party at the camp in case she returned, Nealah, Grashin and another girl of Priash's age, Valun, set out in the direction Priash had gone.

They had only traveled a short while when they saw that many horses' hooves had churned up the wet ground of the path they were following. They were certain that no tribes were in the vicinity, and it was unlikely that a hunting party would be this far out. There was only one other explanation.

"The Qah," said Grashin.

"And Priash?" asked Valun anxiously.

Grashin and Nealah looked at one another. Grashin shrugged and said, "We have to get off this path. Nealah, go back to the camp and inform the others. Valun and I will wait in that copse until the sun has moved a handspan and then go search for Priash, if the Qah do not return. If we haven"t returned to camp by midday, leave without us."

Nealah told them where she had seen the ubutu bushes, about a kilometer farther along the track near a large, fallen yuja tree.Grashin and Valun found the ubutu exactly where Nealah said it would be. Priash had made a small fire under the shelter of the fallen yuja tree's roots, and had hung her hammock between two of the smaller roots inside the natural shelter. A small leather bag had some food and ubutu leaves neatly packed inside. She wasn't there. The fire was cold, the ground around them churned to mud, horse tracks everywhere.

The Qah had found her.

They walked into the surrounding woods and called her name repeatedly in case she had heard the Qah coming and had hidden, though it seemed unlikely she had heard them coming over the noise of the wind. They found no trace of her.

Grashin rode ahead of the others back to the village; he was the lightest of the party, and he took the fastest horse. There had been no talk about trying to rescue Priash. They knew it was futile. They only hoped that her death had been swift. They all secretly doubted it.

Even though the Qah had never been seen in the southern forests, the tribe decided to move villages early, heading away from the place Priash was taken. It sent messengers to the other forest tribes telling them of the tragedy; word spread quickly. The prospect of Qah slavers in their woods was horrifying.

For a while, no one left the new village alone, and the tribe posted sentries with dogs on its outskirts at night. They did this for two seasons, but there were no signs of the Qah: no tracks, no more people abducted. The Qah had vanished without a trace. The village began to suspect it wasn't even the Qah who had taken Priash, but a group of bandits. The tribe's memories faded. They stopped posting sentries and ventured out alone into the woods at night again. Priash had just been unlucky; in the wrong place at the wrong time, they said.

Tian knew better.

CHAPTER 6

They were traveling at a much faster pace now. Tian forgot for the moment the reason for the journey, and simply enjoyed riding Nimsha'h through the beautiful, autumnal forest.

There was a rustling in the undergrowth ahead of them. At first she thought it was Mori, but Mori was never so clumsy. Instinctively, Tian reached for her bow. As she did so the bushes rustled again. Then, suddenly, a dark shape emerged, bursting from its hiding place and away from Tian and Nimsha'h. Without hesitation Tian squeezed Nimsha'h with her knees, but the horse needed little prompting, knowing what to do instantly, hurtling after the fleeing animal.

Then Mori screamed, louder than Tian thought possible: "Tian! Stop!!"

Shocked, Tian pulled back on the reins, stopping Nimsha'h short as Mori burst from the trees, still yelling: "What are you doing!? We can"t waste time and we can't risk you or Nimsha'h getting hurt!"

Seeing the shocked expression on Tian's face, Mori relented.

"I'm sorry Tian, but we can't waste time."

Tian sat still for a moment and then turned to Mori, her face flushed, and said. "No, I'm sorry. I'm just tired, and scared. I wasn't thinking...I'm exhausted. Can we sit down for a few minutes?"

"Of course. . . Look, Tian, I'm scared too," Moris said.

"About the other Watchers?"

"Yes, and your tribe. But I'm also worried about what will happen afterwards, even if we reach them in time. I'm not supposed to make contact with the tribes, ever."

"The others will understand, I'm sure."

"I don't know. It will make things difficult, now that you know about ..."

"Starcanoes and other worlds?"

Mori's look of worry faded, its yellow eyes crinkling into a smile.

"Yes. Precisely."

"Well, I won't tell if you won't."

They sat together for a while on the grass. Tian's leg muscles were twitching, and the hard ground hurt her sore butt. She began to think again about what they'd do when they got to the tribe and warned them. Would she tell them about the Watcher? What could she tell them that they would believe?

She also realized she'd have to go back to the tribe, back to Grashin and the Circle and the Way. But she wasn't sure she could go back to that life.

And the thought of not seeing Mori again made her stomach turn. Whatever their differences, this was the closest she had felt to anybody since she'd been with Priash all those seasons before.

"Try not to worry about them," Mori said, misinterpreting her anxious look.

"Will I see you again?" she blurted. "I mean, once we save the tribe. Will I see you again, or . . .?"

"I'm not sure. We're not supposed to."

"I thought you had no taboos in your Confederation."

"We don't. But that isn't to say we don't have ethics and self-imposed restrictions. As much as I'd like to see you, it probably isn't right. It would contaminate your lives here too much. It would interfere."

"So? Let's not tell them. Maybe we can see each other at

night?" Tian blushed, the insinuation for some reason embarrassing her.

"I don't like keeping secrets, Tian."

This made her blush even more.

"No, not a secret. More like . . . Oh, I don't know."

"Let's worry about the tribe for now."

"Okay. But promise me that when we find the tribe and we're safe from the Qah you won't just run off into the woods. At least come and speak to me before you go. Okay?"

Mori hesitated, then rose to its feet, brushing leaves from its backside.

"Okay, Tian. I promise. Now, are you ready to go?"

* * *

Tian began to see the tracks of her tribe now, too. Before, Mori had gestured to a snapped twig or patch of ground when Tian asked if they were on their trail, as if nothing else need be said. Tian didn't like to ask, and had just nodded, pretending to understand.

She did know that the more time she spent with Mori, the more she came to like her, him, it, whatever. Its big yellow eyes were passionate, kind, intelligent. Its voice was hypnotizing. When it spoke to her about its world, the life it led here in the forest, or about the other Watchers, it was a pleasure to watch, its animated speech and desire to explain and share with Tian apparent. It was like being with Priash again. When Mori had talked with her, it was as if she was the only person in the world that mattered, that everyone and everything else dropped away. Physically, too, Mori was mesmerizing to watch. As agile as Erkan, but graceful, too, giving ita feline quality that was matched by its placid, self-confident expression.

She realized that she was becoming attracted to Mori, despite its bizarre looks, but she had no idea whether it was appropriate to share a blanket with it, or whether she even could. Besides, there wasn't time, as Mori kept reminding her. She began to ask Mori questions just so she could be near it, to hear its voice, see its weird body. And more than anything else enjoy its intelligence and mysterious personality.

To Tian's disappointment, Mori kept their conversation to a bare minimum now. They no longer lit camp fires, no longer cooked. Mori said they were close, only half a day behind the tribe. Tian asked whether Mori had seen any trace of the Qah. It hadn't.

Tian seized her chance that morning. Mori hadn't told her that they needed to be quiet.

"What's it like? Living alone, watching all the time, away from your people? Having to hide, not talking to anyone, not lying with anyone..." Her voice trailed off.

"I love this life. I am free."

"But you must miss the warmth of being around others," Tian asked, trying to sound as innocent as possible. She didn't succeed.

"As far as intercourse goes, I'm genderless, so I don't have any sexual cravings. I'm asexual. That doesn't mean I don't feel love and affection. It's just … it's more intellectual for us, if you understand that word. We lie with others, but for comfort and pleasure, rather than sexual gratification. Do you understand?"

Tian blushed..

"Did you want to lie with me, Tian?" Mori asked, quietly.

She couldn't bring herself to say it. She nodded, like a child admitting to uttering a taboo word.

Mori smiled. "I don't scare you any more, then? That's a relief. I'm very fond of you Tian. There was a reason I asked you specifically to help me. You're strong willed and question much more about your society than many others. I'm not sure it would be a good idea for us to lie together now, with the threat of the Qah so near."

"But afterwards?" Tian said, trying to keep the hope out of her voice, and failing miserably.

"Once this is over perhaps we could spend more time together, learning about one another. At least I hope so. I think I've probably already breached the non-interference agreement beyond repair, so perhaps no one would object too much," Mori said, laughing. It stopped when it saw her expression. "I'm sorry, Tian, I hope I didn't upset you. I am serious about my feelings towards you."

"No, Mori, it's not that. I just don't understand you. One minute you seem so familiar, the next so different, so alien."

They walked on in silence.

"What is your favorite food?" asked Mori.

Tian laughed. "What?"

"I asked what your favorite food is."

"But . . . why?"

"This whole journey the most I've heard you say is a couple of sentences, while I've been talking endlessly."

Tian laughed. "I told you about Grashin, didn't I? And you have so much to tell, so many stories. Besides, you know everything about the woods, about my tribe, about me."

"That's not true, Tian. Yes, I've watched your people, but only from afar. I've watched you for many seasons. I even witnessed your birth; your bloodmother was so happy, she actually shed tears when she saw you."

"That's what I mean," said Tian. "You know everything about me. I don't know anything about you."

"You don't understand. I've seen all these events in your life. But I've no idea what you've been thinking all these seasons. I've never been able to ask whether you enjoy cooking or see it as a chore. I don't know what you dream about, I don't know what you're thinking when you watch the stars at night. Sure, I know most of your habits. But I don't know *you*." Mori placed a hand on her chest, holding it there there slightly longer than needed to emphasize the point. "After Priash, you changed. Your face used to be so expressive. Since you came back, I can"t tell what you're feeling."

Her throat constricted, tight with grief. She swallowed, turned away, fiddling with a strand of hair, suppressing the urge to cry. Mori reached out and held her. Tian didn't say anything, just hugged Mori tightly as she wept silently, her shoulders quivering.

Later, without a word, she let Mori go, and remounted Nimsha'h.

"Let's go, sister," said Tian.

Mori smiled at the pronoun, nodding. They walked side by side for a while. They glanced at one another occasionally, but kept their thoughts to themselves.

***

They took short break after traveling hard for a couple of hours. Nimsha'h was becoming increasingly weary, and their breaks more and more frequent.

"What are we going to do if they aren't there?"

"They will be, Tian."

"But if they're not? What if we need more help."

"I'll talk to my people. We"ll contact the Confederation.".

"Wait. You can talk to the Confederation? I thought they were half-way across the galaxy?"

"Sort of. It isn't like here, where we can talk to one another whenever we like. Connecting this world to the Confederation-infosphere wasn't an option. We're pretty remote out here; there aren't any other settlements or colonies nearby. We're very isolated. The distances are unimaginable. I find it almost as hard to think about as you probably do."

"Really?"

"It's true. Back in the Confederation they have something called ansibles. They send vast quantities of information—lifetimes of memories, for example—across space, almost like that," Mori said, clicking its long fingers together. "The infosphere is available everywhere in Confederation space."

"But not here?"

"No, like I said, we're too far away."

"If it's not like that here, how does it work then? How can you talk to the other Watchers? How can you talk to the Confederationsensus worlds?"

"We do have a planetary infosphere here based in the silos. And we can talk to each other directly if we're close together. If we're farther apart, the silos relay our messages to each other. But if we want to send a report, or call for help, to the Confederation, we have to send our reports or requests via the silos in short, massive bursts, like a really loud shout across a valley"

"So they just shout back when they hear you?"

"Basically yes. It does, however, take a while for help to arrive once we call for it."

"How long?"

"Two seasons."

"Two *seasons*?"

"Two seasons is better than never. "

"Why didn't you use an ansible in a silo, before you came to find me?"

"The nearby silos aren't working. And . . . well, that's another one of our shortcomings. A failure of imagination, a failure to anticipate the worst. The designers who made the ansibles and infosphere here on Dodona didn't consider physical attack or intrusion into the living quarters when they created them. They couldn't conceive that the silos might be attacked. Because of its nature, the ansibles and infosphere require the AI to be functional in order to work. But there were enough silos that they didn't worry about that. If one malfunctioned, the others could always contact the Confederation."

"So, any help from Consensus will take seasons to get here and now you can't even reach the other Watchers?"

"Yes. That's correct."

"And the Qah must have broken into the nearest silo, so it's not working."

"Again, correct. I'm the only one anywhere near here, the only one who could help your tribe, which is why I contacted you. Let's hope we reach your tribe before they reach the Qah."

The sun was low in the sky before Mori spoke again.

"We're close to the tribe now, but we're almost at the silo. It's only twenty kilometers ahead. I'm not sure we're going to be able to reach them before they get there. I was hoping we'd have caught up to them by now... I'd like to keep traveling all night, to see if I can reach them alone."

Tian breathed in sharply. They'd come so far together, the thought of Mori leaving her now made her stomach lurch. "No, Mori. They'll go crazy with fear. They won't listen to you. They'll try to kill you."

"That's the reason I asked you to come with me. But it's too late to worry about that now. If the Qah are there at the silo, even if it's just a scouting party, many of your people will be killed. I'm not going to let that happen again."

"What if the Qah are there? What are you going to do on your own?"

"I'll warn your tribe, then try to get to my people under the silo. This can't go on any longer. I'm going to call for help from the Confederation with the emergency beacon."

"Can't you use the infosphere?"

"No. I told you, the planetary infosphere is broken."

"Carry me," said Tian, as Mori turned to go. "Take me. I don't want you to leave me here. You can carry me, right?"

"Yes, I suppose. Are you sure?"

"Yes, let's go."

"What about Nimsha'h?"

"She's so tired she won't go far. We can find her after we warn the tribe."

Tian dismounted Nimsha'h, walking to Mori. "Oh, wait." She turned back, unslinging her bow from where it was tied along the horse's flank, strapping it across her back.

Mori grasped her by the waist, swinging her on to its back with a graceful motion, seemingly without exertion. She felt tiny gripping to that big back. Mori was far larger than even Nimsha'h. Feeling somewhat embarrassed, even though the forest around them was empty, Tian smiled as she squeezed her legs around Mori"s broad chest. Mori leapt forward at a remarkable pace.

The journey was exhilarating, terrifying. She could see nothing but Mori's back and branches flashing by. It was even worse as night fell. Plunged into darkness, she gripped on to Mori for all she was worth, feeling its chest rising and falling, its powerful muscles relaxing and tightening as they raced through the trees, sprinted across clearings, leaping across obstacles, on a cloudy, pitch-black night. Tian felt as if she were riding a panther. Her heart raced, and she panted with the excitement, the wind rushing past them as they raced toward the silo, to save her people, *their* people.

* * *

Priash had been very quiet in the days before the Circle where she had proposed that the library be opened to all. She and Tian had left the village to spend time on the river, where the tribe kept fishing canoes canoes, and to escape the tribe.

"It's all boarshit anyway, Tian. Their stupid Circle, even the bloody Way, they don"t tell us the whole story. I bet if you asked most of the others about the taboo words, they wouldn't have a clue about what they mean. The Way says nothing about planting seeds. It says nothing about half the shit the elders say it does."

"What do you mean?"

"I've seen the Way, a lot more of it than on the scrolls Grashin carries with him. It's in different scrolls in one of Grashin"s back corridors. I've seen other stuff, too. About how we came to be here, about who we used to be."

"You went back to the library?"

"Of course I did. If they were germinating ilyup seeds back there, I figured they must be other secrets too. So I poked around after everyone moved to the spring camp."

"You should have told me. I'd have come with you."

"I didn't want to get you into trouble." Seeing that Tian was hurt, Priash touched her cheek with the back of her fingers. She sighed, and then went on.

"That library is so disorganized, though, that it's hard to find anything specific. It was pure luck that we found the ilyup scrolls.....That old shitstool Grashin could be a big help if he wanted."

Tian snorted.

Once they arrived at the cave at the riverside where the tribe stored the canoes, they pulled one out and dragged it across the sandy bank to the river below. They let the current take them downstream for a while.

"What did it say, Priash? The Way?"

"Not much. I could barely read it. Nothing in there about Circles, at least that I could find. I can tell you though, our ancestors never wrote it. Nobody from the tribes could have written it. The stuff it talks about in there, the people who wrote it, they didn't come from here. Some of i's completely irrelevant, bizarre. It sounds as if... as if it was written a long time ago, and a very long way from here."

"Grishin, like the elders of all of the other tribes, says there was a time before the Way. A time of agriculture and massive villages. Structures were kilometers high were, people lived in caves their entire lives and didn't live in harmony with nature. Nobody talked to each other, people were always unhappy, and they ate food they didn't find or hunt themselves.

"Then the tribes discovered the Way and started living in accordance with nature. They left the big settlements and started smaller ones, and created the consensus circles, rejected agriculture and civilization."

Priash looked away and added, "I also found books that describe the before times in a completely different way. I'm not even sure we're living in the same place. I think we must have traveled a long way from there, across the oceans perhaps."

Tian noticed Priash's wandering gaze and wondered if Priash was holding something back.

"Maybe you read the scrolls wrong," said Tian. "Maybe they were written down by one of our tribe, but everyone just forgot about it."

"No. I've read some of the other, older scrolls he has back there. What they describe, it seems unreal, like a dream."

They had started paddling lazily, the current doing most of the work. The branches of the trees on the banks hung down low, almost touching the water, ripples sparkling in the sun, and insects buzzing around the canoe.

"I can't explain. it all Next winter, I'll show you what I mean. But the Way was definitely different back then from the Way we have now, and the other books use words in a different way than we do. Even taboo words like technology. You need to read it, the style of it, to understand it, I think."

"I'm not sure, Priash. Perhaps they're just dreams, fantasies like we have?"

Priash turned to look at Tian directly.

"No, sister. They aren't fantasies. I'll show you next winter. I might ask in the Circle to see the scrolls and books. I bet there are more. I only found a few before I had to return to the village."

They drifted for a while.

"They even had herb gardens in the before times, Tian, just like I always wanted. Why we ever gave up the life some of those books describe... I wish I could go back. I wish *we* could go back."

Tian didn't say anything. She watched a skein of geese fly overhead honking noisily, as she thought back, trying to remember the things she'd heard about the Way, about the Circles. A creeping feeling of doubt began to come over her. She looked at Priash's naked brown back, her plait running down her spine. She seemed so sure. So, happy. Priash seemed so excited about what she had found in the library, as if it justified all of her dreams. She hummed to herself, dreaming about the before times, probably about the layout of her herb garden. Yet Tian couldn"t share her happiness. All she felt was fear.

* * *

They came to a stop at the edge of a clearing. Tian could make out very little in the dark, though she thought she could see a faint light in the trees ahead.

"Is it the tribe?" she asked. Mori shrugged. It bent down so that she could climb off its back, her front wet with perspiration. "Are we near the silo?" she whispered.

"Yes, it's just ahead," said Mori. "Near where the light is. I smell smoke, but I can't hear anything. Perhaps you should wait here."

"No, I'm coming."

They walked into the undergrowth, the bracken parting before Mori. It had started to rain, again, and large drops pattered the forest floor from the canopy above. It made the forest seem eerily alive.

Tian could see lights ahead now, through the trees. She sniffed hard to try to catch a whiff of the smoke Mori said it had smelled, but Mori's odor-blocking seed was still working. She trod lightly, bow in hand, trying to follow Mori closely, wet leaves squelching under her feet. Mori, as ever, was almost completely silent.

Mori whispered for her to stop. There was clearly something ahead, but Tian still couldn't see anything. Tian felt the Watcher's hand on her shoulder, then heard it whisper, "Stay. I'll try to get a better look from up there."

Tian nodded and nocked an arrow. Mori looked at it and

shook its head, but didn't say anything. Instead, it climbed up a nearby tree.

Tian knelt, feeling a cool breeze wafting around her wet. She checked the quiver; she had seven arrows. Her bloodsister, Thayu, had made them. The memory of her now made Tian take a sharp, anxious breath. Thayu was one of those who had traveled to the silo. The thought of her sister made her remember all the others who had gone with Thayu. She thought about their faces, her heart pounding at the recollection.

All of the things she had thought about them, her curses about their ignorance and inability to see through Grashin''s manipulation, all of the horrible things she had imagined saying to them, came back in a wave of guilt. She desperately wanted to speak to them all, to apologize, to be together again. Whatever was in the forest ahead, all those people—her people—thought she was a petulant egoizer. She wanted to tell them what Priash had found, all that Mori had told her, why she had challenged Grashin and the old ways. It was all for them. So they could all lead better lives. She knew now she'd done it all wrong, gone about it as a child would. She should have spoken to them, reasoned with them, not gotten angry or frustrated and forced them to defend themselves. Only now, when half of her village was in immediate peril, and the forest close to being overrun by Qah slavers, did she realize how much she loved them, why she had come back to the tribe even after losing Priash.

But, just like with Priash, she had failed to protect them, and now the Qah were closing in.

She was taut as a string with pent-up anger, frustration, despair, and loneliness. She gritted her teeth and gripped the bow hard, her knuckles turning white. She thought she heard a familiar voice in the distance: Thayu's. She leapt to her feet, running through the forest toward her tribe, her people.

The lights were close, now, and she could make out the silhouette of the silo ahead. She ran through the clearing, dim shapes and shadows on the ground around her. There were several small fires around the silo, but the long shadows they cast revealed little. The grass was wet, and she nearly lost her footing, running blindly towards the silo. She saw movement ahead near what she assumed was the silo entrance, a painted face, caught by the firelight, the whites of eyes looking at her. She didn't recognize it. *A Qah.*

She stopped short and loosed an arrow, catching him in the throat. She saw two more faces look up towards her. They dropped what they were carrying, reached for their weapons, and began running toward her. She loosed another arrow. It plunged through one of the warriors' shoulders, and he went down, screaming.

Then, before she knew it, the other one was on her. He swung at her, catching her hard in the chest. She fell awkwardly. She felt a crushing blow on her knee. She shrieked in agony. Looking up, the man was bringing a huge club down on her hip. She rolled to the side, the pain in her knee causing her to bite her tongue. The man missed. She spit blood and rolled away.

Behind her, the man screamed. He was a meter off the ground, his legs thrashing beneath him. Mori had the man's head between its hands. Tian saw Mori's expression. It was shocking in its intensity, its hatred. The man squealed like a stuck boar, trying desperately to strike and claw at Mori. Mori squeezed harder. The man's eyes bulged from their sockets as Mori crushed his head like an overripe fruit. There was a wet crunch as his skull caved, and then a soft thud as Mori dropped the corpse.

Tian lost consciousness. When she came to, she saw Mori above her, a look of worry on its face in the dim light.

"Tian, are you hurt?"

Her eyes widened in terror. "What about the Qah?"

"They were just stragglers."

She tasted blood, her jaw and tongue hurt, and her knee was badly twisted and bruised, and had begun to swell. Mori touched it carefully. She recoiled in agony.

"Tian, I must go check... I need you to wait here."

She nodded, lying back down. She felt faint, but didn"t lose consciousness again. She remembered Mori's face as it held the man's head in its hands; the expression had been so close to what she had dreamed the Watchers looked like as a child it was terrifying. The same Mori she had hugged the day before... She tried not to think about it, and lay back, gasping from the pain.

Mori returned after a few minutes later, sobbing. She felt the Watcher pinch her on the thigh, murmuring something about pain relief. She quickly numbed out. But this wasn"t like the numbness from the narcotic plant the tribe used when setting broken bones; she was awake, alert. She glanced at Mori, who was still crying, nearly hysterical. The sight of Mori in the grip of such emotional pain was hard to bear She hugged Mori tightly.

After what seemed like ages, Tian managed to sit up.

"Mori, you had to kill him. It was him or me."

"I know," Mori said, its voice breaking. "It's not just that, Tian. The silo..."

Mori couldn't continue, and started weeping inconsolably. Tian looked at Mori, then at the silo.

"Where are they, Mori? Where is the tribe?"

Mori continued weeping, head down..

Tian looked around her and saw her attacker's club a few feet away. She crawled over to it, grasped it, and using it as a crutch hobbled to her feet. She limped her way toward the silo.

She grasped a burning branch from a fire near the entrance. The doors were ajar, and smoke was billowing through them. She wondered about Mori's people underneath, about whether they had got out.

She could feel the heat, now, from inside. She took a deep gulp of air before stepping into the silo.

Inside, Tian found her tribe.

PART III

CHAPTER 1

The alarm for firstmeal sounded, filling the rooms with a deafening klaxon. The children stumbled from their beds and out of their rooms, hastily dressing and wiping sleep from their eyes. They stood to attention just as an adult appeared at the doorway at the end of the corridor. Each of them stood as straight as possible. The adult began walking down the collinear line, hovering in front of each child for a cursory inspection, the children's right arms outstretched for scanning. Even at such a young age, most of the children towered over him, and he had to get several of the older children to bend down so that he could inspect their near-identical faces.

Once he reached the end of the line of tall black children, he barked a command. They raced toward the cafeteria; those that reached the cafeteria last would be left with just the scraps, and, as usual, there was a lot of pushing and shoving as they raced through the corridors.

Mori, although that was not yet its name, reached the line in time to get a full plate. Mori ate greedily, knowing that it would need the energy for the day ahead. Although violence was strictly forbidden, the older children often stole from the younger ones, but usually the threat of violence was enough to convince them to hand over their food without any punches being thrown. Mori wasn't bothered by anyone now though, and finished its meal without incident.

Today was an induction day. Mori wasn't looking forward to it. Usually Mori and the other children would have the morning to themselves; classes and games wouldn't start until later in the day. Mori had hoped to spend the morning accessing a favorite holovid, but had been informed the night before that it was assigned one of the new children for the next few days. Mori could probably get out of it by tomorrow, but this morning Mori would have to attend the introductory seminars and sit holding some kid's hand.

So, Mori didn't rush when the klaxon sounded for the end of firstmeal, and hung back with a few others who probably had the same assignment. When the cleaning bots began shooing them out, they all shuffled down the corridor towards the lecture hall.

"Come on, come on!" called a voice ahead of them, from one of the scientists, Amezla. She was a bit of a pushover, so they didn't heed her admonishments. "They're all waiting for you. You remember how it was when you arrived here. Let's not keep them waiting. And try to be nice."

The children smiled at one another. It was rare being told to be nice by one of the scientists, who usually scolded them for being so. In her hurry though, Amezla had dropped the act and let slip her real self. When this happened, the children would always exchange knowing, mocking glances with one another. It happened fairly often with Amezla, who was new to the project.

She finally managed to herd them into the nearly empty lecture room. It was weird, creepy being here so early in the day. It was like being in the cafeteria on your own, or walking down the corridors at night when everyone else was asleep, Mori thought.

There were five kids sitting inn the first row. They were tiny, shorter even than Amezla. Their legs dangled over the edges of the seats, not even reaching the floor. They looked at Mori and the other older children anxiously, chattering amongst themselves and sending out a burst of nervous energy into the facility's infosphere. Mori scowled and filtered their uninhibited jabbering out. They couldn't even control themselves. Their verbalizations and laughter mingled with their infosphere transmissions, and now Mori had to look after one of them, probably for most of the day.

One of the scientists at the front of the lecture room began to speak. "Okay, settle down. Your mentors are here now, so we can start." Mori heard it as both a vocalization and as a proxisphere broadcast. Although the children were discouraged from doing this, the scientists themselves often used both for direct communication, apparently unable to break the habit. Mori preferred the infosphere for communication. Vocalization was simply too slow, not to mention too public.

Amezla ushered Mori and the other older children into the second row as the man at the front continued to speak. Mori looked down at the child in the seat in front and, lowering its filter for a few seconds, heard the uncontrolled buzz of thoughts and feelings from the child over the proxisphere. Mori could feel everything the kid was thinking, and it gave Mori an unexpected thrill to hear it, this young mind so open, so naked and vulnerable. The kid couldn't have had its neural implants and other bioware for more than a few weeks. The scientists would soon train it to control itself. That, or it would learn the hard way from being around the older children.

"I'd like to welcome you on behalf of the DSE staff," the man began.

"What's DSE?" Mori heard one of the children whisper on the proxisphere to its neighbor.

"Dunno."

"Dodona Scientific Expedition," Mori tightbeamed to them. Five little round heads turned to look at Mori. Mori frowned back.

"We're about two hundred kilometers from the nursery you've been in for the last five orbits, and we're a much larger facility than you're used to," said the man at the front of the room.

"We still on Namir?" blabbered one of the kids.

"Dunno."

The heads turned again to look at Mori, who frowned before nodding.

"... and as such we have a lot more rules than you're used to. If you'll please access the list I'm sending you, we'll go through them individually. If you have any questions, do speak up."

Mori switched off as the man read the long list of rules, ones the older children had heard a thousand times. Mori saw five sets of shoulders begin to sag as the man droned on, and the older children fidgeted incessantly.

Finally the man finished. None of the kids had asked any questions. "So now we're going to talk a little bit about why you're here. Actually, before we start, perhaps you'd like to tell me what you know first?" This was a classic trick that the scientists employed during lectures—they tried to engage the children by asking them questions. Most of the older children met these direct questions with silence, but these younger ones were eager for the chance to speak up.

"To look after Dodona!"

"To protect the oceans!"

"Yeah, and to keep the forests clean!"

"No you idiot, we"ve got to look after the little people in the forests, to make sure they don't bash each other over the head!"

All of them tittered with excitement. The scientist held up a hand, appealing for silence. Mori could hear the kids' proxisphere whispers continuing even after they'd stopped vocalizing. The scientist did too. He sent out a sharp reprimand that cut their whispering dead.

"Quiet! You're all wrong." He swelled out his chest; Mori knew that to be a prelude to another interminable lecture. "The DSE has a long history of anthropological research on the world known as Dodona. Before this facility was created, the requirements for prospective candidates were extremely high. Given the nature of the posting, we could only send the very best, most capable observers. Unfortunately, candidates with the right skills were hard to come by. Every single one of our anthropologists failed in their task. The urge to assist was so compelling, so inherent in every single one of them, and the first settlers so prone to mishap, that the settlement agreement was breached on many occasions, even by seasoned scientists who, at the sight of suffering or pain, forgot all of their training. Obviously, this was not what we wanted.

"The absence of pain, of disease, of starvation, or any of the many ailments that afflicted the early inhabitants of Confederationsensus worlds makes its presence on Dodona upsetting, shocking. But we must never approach the settlers on Dodona *for any reason*. Our continued presence on the planet is predicated on our abiding with the settlement agreement, which forbids contact. So we began to recruit those with abnormal, asocial personality traits. Even then, that wasn't enough to prevent a spate of interventions.

There was serious talk about removing all Confederation personnel from Dodona, and replacing them with AI and satellite observation only, in order to maintain the integrity of the settlement agreement. Yet that clearly has its own drawbacks, not least being the prospect of technological contamination, which we want to avoid at all costs.

"This is where you come in. We decided to create and train the brightest, most capable anthropologists from scratch." The man stopped and cleared his throat. "Our experts began to experiment." Mori saw Amezla swallow, looking distinctly uncomfortable.

Mori knew the rest. The DSE genetically engineered an entire cohort of asexual, highly intelligent subjects in an isolated desert settlement on Namir, that was cut off from the infosphere, and beyond all Confederation oversight.

Most of the Confederation's citizens had undergone some form of gene therapy, primarily for medical purposes, such as the prevention of hereditary diseases, altering the rate of cellular senescence, and strengthening of the immune system. But

Confederation bioethics did not condone genetic alteration of fetuses beyond these basic purposes, except for the still-controversial purpose of intellectual or physical enhancement. The absence of consent made that practice problematic, and one that many parents avoided. If adults need significant alterations, if to become marine specialists, spend time in non-standard gravity environments, or outside of the domes in harsh atmospheres, Confederation medical science could provide them with the necessary augments and alterations long after they were born. But even that was uncommon. Jobs that required profound physiological alterations and adaptations were now almost universally automated.

But the DSE scientists were obsessed, and disregarded all ethical boundaries in their desire to maintain their observational presence on Dodona. They made drastic alterations to intellectual and emotional capacities, as well as significant alterations to physiology. Mori had been horrified to discover the extent to which it and the other children had been altered. DSE had made them freaks, then hidden them away from the rest of the Confederation.

Mori's disgust had quickly turned to outright rebellion, which was met with considerable force. Mori spent a number of months in solitary confinement, followed by being forced to take copious amounts of mood-enhancing drugs, which it had only recently been allowed to stop taking. The overt rebellion was gone, but Mori still fumed underneath its placid, compliant surface. That seemed to fool the staff at the facility.

The scientist at the front of the room said nothing about all this now, of course. He told them the lie he'd told a thousand times, and probably half-believed himself. The children would soon find out though. When they were a bit older, they'd hack the facility firewall or, more likely, hear about it from one of the older children. For now, the scientist talked of creating "perfect" anthropologists, better and more brilliant observers who would carry on the noble DSE project for centuries to come.

And the kids lapped it up. Mori remembered when it had first heard this speech. How special and proud it had made Mori feel at the time. Mori looked at the children in the row in front of it, feeling their excitement. Mori thought about puncturing this bubble with a few choice tightbeamed images or words, but thought better of it.

Despite all of the scientists' valiant efforts to limit Mori's emotional capacity in preparation for a lifetime of detached observation, Mori felt a great deal of pity for the five small freaks in front of it.

CHAPTER 2

Tian awoke with the sun beaming down on her face. Mori lay next to her on the clearing floor. Her knee ached, and her tongue felt too big for her mouth. She looked down at her feet. They were covered in blood.

She jumped at the words, "I'm so sorry Tian." She hadn't realized that Mori was awake. "I should never have let you see that. It was just... I'm sorry."

Tian said nothing. She examined her knee, it had swollen up and had turned a dull blue. She tried to open her mouth, but she couldn't. Her jaw had stiffened during the night.

"Your people?" she mumbled. Mori shook its head.

"They got to them. I don't know how. I think they had deactivated the Cornucopia, and the Qah took revenge." Mori's voice trailed off.

"We were too late," she said.

"Yes. I think the Qah killed them all yesterday. We couldn't have done anything, sister. Not without the help of my people. You see what they're capable of."

Tian nodded, laying a hand on Mori's leg.

"Not your fault," she managed to mumble.

They lay in the sun for a long time, neither willing to stir, neither knowing what to do next.

"Let me fix your knee," Mori said, rousing Tian from her thoughts. "We must go underneath the silo, to the living quarters. Hopefully it's not completely destroyed. I might still be able to use the beacon."

Mori helped her up. There were still bodies in piles dotted around the clearing. Mori offered to carry her. Tian refused.

About two hundred meters away from the clearing, Mori stopped and pushed aside a stand of thick ferns, revealing a small hatchway. Mori touched the door in several places, and it opened silently. Mori went in first, climbing down into the darkness.

They went down a ramp for about thirty meters before touching level ground again. The light was the same generalized glow as in the silo, and the tunnel was large, clearly designed for someone of Mori's height. The walk had made Tian's knee more painful, and she leaned on Mori more and more as they made their way down the tunnel. Eventually they reached the Watchers' living area.

All around them were signs that the Qah had been here: Tables and chairs overturned, the walls smashed, plants ripped up, and debris strewn around about the room. Tian tried to make sense of it all, but it was so strange, so alien, that she could barely understand anything she was seeing.

A big central table dominated the room. A dead Watcher was strapped to it, its torso shredded and minus its limbs. Mori went into one of the side rooms and returned with a large, white sheet; Mori covered the body, patches of blood seeping through and staining the sheet the moment it touched the corpse.

Mori, seeing that Tian was shaken, tried to reassure her.

"I checked for Qah last night after I found the bodies in the silo. There isn't anyone here. When they couldn't get the Cornucopia to work, they smashed up everything and killed my friend . . ."

Mori set a small table upright and motioned toward it. "Come, sit up here. I'll go find some medical supplies, if they haven't taken them."

Mori left again. The big room made Tian nervous. It was full of technology. She wondered if all their rooms looked like this, so big and white and formidable.

Mori returned with a small, clear bag.

"We're in luck. Lay your leg out flat, if you can."

She did, wincing.

"Hold this for me."

Mori passed her a short white stick, smooth to the touch. She held it in her hand, turning it over, an uncomprehending look on her face.

"See this button here? Press that, and hold it over your knee, but don't let it touch the skin. It will feel strange; it will tug. Just keep it there. I'll be back in a moment. Keep holding the Panacea above your knee until the light stops blinking."

Tian watched as Mori walked over to one of the control tables, and began touching its surface; lights flashed as it did so.

"Looks like the AI, communications, and sensors are all damaged, probably beyond repair. The beacon, too." Mori continued to touch the table, its fingers racing across the surface, then looked at her and said, "I'll be back," and left.

Tian desperately tried not to think about what she'd seen in the silo. The sight of all those burned bodies, faces, clothes, hair smoldering ... She looked around the room at the destruction here, trying to figure out what Mori's people used the different items for—anything to keep that awful memory at bay.

A few moments later, Mori returned. "I have something to relieve your pain." She felt a pinch on her arm. "How is the knee? Let me look." Mori took the white stick from her, touching her knee hesitantly with its fingers. Tian looked down; the swelling had disappeared.

"You won't be able to put any weight on it for a few minutes. Here, let me do your jaw." Tian felt the same tugging sensation in her cheek. It didn't occur to her to ask what the Panacea was; she was too preoccupied by what had happened the previous night. She avoided looking up at Mori's face.

Mori reached down and touched her cheek. "Listen carefully, Tian. Once you're fixed up, I need to leave here. I need to find a working silo. I can't even warn the other silos from here. I have to go before the Qah reach the next one."

She felt Mori shift closer to her. As it held the Panacea over her swollen face, it looked intently into her eyes, trying to make sure that what it was saying was getting through to her. Tian felt Mori's smooth hands touching her chin tenderly.

"There is something I haven't told you. Something has changed—I think I know what itat is now. It's more important than ever that I alert the Confederation. The three men we killed last night had masks that protected them from the smell; that's why the Qah are able to enter the gas zones uninhibited. One of them also had this. It's a Kaiinish weapon. We were fortunate they didn't use it on us."

Tian mouthed an unspoken question.

"They are an alien civilization. They complicate things. The Kaiins are everything we dreaded finding since we discovered the Dodona orbital, exactly the kind of society Grashin and the elders warned you about. They are a hostile empire, as bad as the Qah, but on a much bigger scale. They are hierarchical, they are xenophobic. They attacked us without provocation when we first made contact, around forty standard orbits ago."

Tian tried to speak. Mori shook its head and didn't release its hand from her chin.

"Stay still. Fortunately, our fleet was able to defend us due to the Dodonan technology. We won that battle decisively. Since then, though, there has been a stalemate, and they are slowly winning the war, even though they can't face us in open battle. Our technology is far superior to theirs. However, when they began to realize the nature of our society, they initiated a different kind of war. They took advantage of our openness, the autonomy of our worlds and regions. They tried to foment revolt on our outer worlds; they armed small groups to fight us from within, which we were completely unprepared for. They began disrupting the infosphere. They sent agents into our cities and our habitats, destroyed Cornucopia machines, destroyed assemblers, assassinated prominent artists, all in order to demoralize us, to split us. For the first time in the history of the infosphere we had to close certain parts of it off from general access, so thoroughly had the Kaiin infiltrated us. They forced us to undermine the values our entire civilization is based upon by restricting the flow of information.

"Now it looks like Dodona is in their sights. A soft target. Tian, we—I—had no idea they knew or cared about this place. Their civilization is many lightorbits away, on the other side of Confederation space. I desperately need to warn the Confederation fleet. If the Qah have acquired Kaiinish technology, then this is bigger than you and I thought. It explains why the Qah have left their homes, why they are sweeping over the continent. It could be the prelude to an invasion. This is much worse than we imagined. What they did to your tribe could happen to this whole planet."

Mori moved the Panacea away from her jaw. Tian flexed it. It felt normal. The pain was gone, and the swelling had disappeared.

"I need you to go and warn the rest of your tribe about the Qah. Tell them what happened here. Take them to the winter village. I'm going to try to contact my people here on Dodona, although I suspect the Kaiins are jamming the planetary infosphere. That would explain why we've been having so many communication issues. I'm going to head towards the nearest silo and try to call for help there.

"Make contact with the other tribes and get them to join you in the winter caves as soon as they can. Try to make the caves as safe as possible, don't call attention to yourselves, and be prepared to stay there for a while. I"m sorry to place all this on you, especially after what we went through last night. But I really have to go. Here. Take this." Mori gave her the small Kaiinish weapon. "Point this end and pull here to activate it. It will kill instantly, so use it only if you absolutely have to. Go out via the tunnel we came in by. Try to find the trail if you can. Goodbye, Tian."

With that, Mori touched her face, briefly, and left.

Tian didn't say a word.

Dazed, bewildered, still suffering from grief and the shock of the previous night, Tian slid down from the table. Her knee was fine, her tongue and jaw back to normal. She looked warily at the Panacea that Mori had left on the table. She placed it in the belt she wore, alongside the black Kaiinish weapon, not wanting to think too hard about either. She only barely understood what Mori had said to her. It had been talking so quickly she'd only caught the basic concepts. Another species had armed the Qah, the Qah had killed her tribe, and she needed to get everyone to go to the winter caves.

She cried out when she realized that she would have to be the one to tell the tribe what she had seen.

Her shout of grief echoed in the weird, alien room.

Tian didn't go back into the above-ground part of the silo. She was tempted, and she hated the thought of not saying goodbye to her brothers and sisters, but she couldn't face it alone.

She arrived near dusk at the place where she left Nimsha'h, and whistled. Nimsha'h came ambling back within a few minutes. Tears rolled down her face as they rode away from the silo, away from Mori, away from the Qah. Away from the dead.

On the way home, she wished many times that Mori was with her. She longed for its company, to see its black figure emerge from the trees. She ran Nimsha'h ran hard, giving the horse breaks by alternating walking, trotting, and running, from before dawn until after the sun set.

Tian, totally exhausted, met Erkan and the others in his hunting party two days from the village. When she rode up, they were glad to see her, but surprised. She broke down when she saw their faces, despite telling herself the whole ride that she would be strong. She collapsed as she got off the horse and fell limply to the ground. Erkan caught her as she fell, and laid her on a mat near near the fire.

* * *

Mori was worried about Tian. It wasn"t sure it had done the right thing. It missed her.

Mori sat now, five days from the silo where they had last seen each other, perched high in a tree, wet from the rain. Mori hadn't been able to use the planetary infosphere at all since a few days before meeting Tian, and the loneliness was becoming oppressive. Even here, in the forest, in its home, Mori felt alone.

Mori hadn't realized how close it had become to Tian until the evening that they reached the silo. When Tian made her stumbling proposition, Mori had understood how special Tian was, and how much it enjoyed her company. Although Mori had watched the tribe, and Tian, for many seasons, it was only then that Mori realized how much it had longed to talk to the tribes, to help them, to tell them about their world and the galaxy they knew nothing about.

It was hard being a Watcher. Mori and the other anthropologists often used the tribe's term, after after hearing it over and over again. The time since they'd left Confederation space had changed all of them, but Mori especially. Mori was now unquestionably a Watcher, in every sense of the word. That meant that most of the time Mori felt totally helpless, frustratingly distant from the tribes, unable to assist, even when it wanted to.

* * *

The event came when Mori was fifteen orbits old.

Things had been coming to a boiling point for a long time. Many of the original DSE scientists had burned out and been replaced by outsiders, who didn't have the fervor of their predecessors. The children knew too much, too, and the façade was beginning to break down; their lives and the routine had become untenable.

The genetic enhancements had only been the beginning of the DSE program. The facility was designed to condition the enhanced children out of their natural, social instincts. It was a training facility as much as a nursery, created to inculcate scientific detachment, to sculpt a new generation of impartial observers—watchers, not actors. Anthropologists who could stand by as the tribes hurt themselves or got sick. Anthropologists who could resist the urge to assist those in need or peril, even when they could easily do so.

Things reached a critical point one memorable day. Too many of the children knew what life outside the facility was like. The small trickles their supervisors allowed them from the Confederation infosphere were enough to show them that their rigid, competitive lives were abnormal, abhorrent. It was clear to them that life outside the facility had none of the rules and boundaries that deformed their lives. They had been taught to compete, to isolate themselves from one another, and the more competitive and isolated they became, the more they were rewarded with bigger rooms. But recently, the more the scientists attempted to divide them, the more they attempted to break down their natural social instincts, the more the children had rebelled, seeking solace in one another's company. They began to stand together, to resist together.

The revolt started with small acts of defiance: refusing to participate in the more physically competitive games, ignoring some of the stricter rules on conversation and interaction among themselves. These minor acts of rebellion began to snowball. To the horror of the scientists, the children began imitating the behavior they saw on the Confederation infosphere. The competition and secrecy that had been the norm for decades melted away.

This was intolerable to the DSE staff. They cut infosphere access and food rations, and even started drugging en masse in an attempt to maintain order and the illusions necessary to a detached, competitive ethic. But nothing worked.

Mori vividly remembered the morning of the fateful day. They'd been up most of the night chattering on the infosphere. The odd behavior of some of the newer DSE scientists the day before had indicated that something was up. There were too many anxious glances and worried frowns.

The klaxon sounded for firstmeal. One of the more recent rebellions against the strict rules had been slowness to respond to the klaxon. Today was no exception. But when the first of the children finally deigned to go out into the corridor, it radiated surprise and fear; it was too frightened for words. Soon, all of the children came out of their rooms to investigate.

Nearly all of the facility staff were in the corridor, but nearly unrecognizable in heavy looking, waterproof suits, their faces obscured by helmets with blackened visors.

Then they turned on the hoses.

The kids in front were thrown down by the blast, skidding across the floor. Mori and many of the others tried to get back into their rooms, but the doors had sealed behind them the moment they stepped out. Then Mori felt a searing surge of cold strike its leg, and down Mori went.

Shouts filled the corridor. A mixture of, both verbal, proxisphere and infosphere in one jumbled, frightened cacophony. It was complete pandemonium. But it only took seconds for Mori to realize why the DSE scientists were doing this: it was an exercise in domination. Others realized it, too. The children's confusion turned to anger, which surged when one child's arm snapped. The pain rippled out amongst the children as if it were their own.

The children snapped. One of them ripped down a vid screen and heaved it at the line of scientists. Another screen hit one of the men with the hoses in the chest. Then a few of the suited figures were tried to stop the men with the hoses, who emitted a surge of panic. Then a child threw another screen. It landed squarely on one of the suited men, who crumpled to the ground.

That pushed them over the edge. Four of the suited men charged the soaked children, batons raised. They all felt the jaw of the first child break, then the ribs of another. One of the children lashed out, striking blindly at its suited attacker, but only managed to break its fingers on the hardened suit.

Mori saw the man who did it. The one who ended it all. Mori saw his expression even through his plated visor: pure hatred. Mori could feel his rage pulsing out into the proxisphere like a supernova. Mori experienced the blow as both the victim and the attacker. Mori felt the pain, then the sudden, terrifying abyss of blackness. Mori felt the thrill and the surge of lust surging through the man as he split smashed the child's skull with his baton.

The hoses stopped. The shouts ceased. Everyone in that corridor felt the terror of that child in that moment.

***

"What will you do now?" Amezla tightbeamed to Mori. She was sitting just opposite, but the noise of the shuttle's engines made voice communication impossible.

"Go to Dodona, of course."

"But won't you stay in the Confederation for a while? Enjoy your freedom?"

Mori looked across at her tear-stained face. It had only been a few hours since the child had died in the corridor, ending the DSE and its experiments in a stroke. There was already a Confederation-wide scandal. Mori was bombarded with requests and communications from thousands of individuals, which Mori filtered out.

"You might not have succeeded in brainwashing us, but you did one thing pretty well."

"What?" she asked, uncomfortably.

"You sold me, us, on Dodona."

Her eyebrows shot up in surprise. "We did?"

"I was a captive on dusty, boring Namir, with all of its rules and fear, all the time dreaming of escape. Where do you think I'd want to go? The one place where life could be perfect for someone like me? A world free of all these rules and restrictions. Why would I stay in the Confederation as a freak when there's a paradise waiting for me?"

Fresh tears rolled down Amezla's face, but the child that was not Mori, not yet a Watcher, turned its face away from her.

CHAPTER 3

The village was quiet when Tian awoke. At first, disoriented in the dark, she didn't realize where she was. Then she nudged against Erkan, who was still asleep. She rose, taking care not to disturb him.

The grey dawn was cold. She shivered. There was no one in the Circle, though she could see activity in the kitchen. She headed toward it; her long sleep and longer journey had left her hungry. The kitchen crew didn't say anything when she walked up. They looked frightened, grieving. She wasn't sure whether they knew. Whether she'd told them before passing out. Either way, they were visibly shaken.

She sat in the kitchen chewing takka root. The villagers started to rise, much later than usual. People came in and out of the kitchen and nodded in greeting. Tian sat chewing the takka until her jaw began to ache, staring into the distance.

She saw Erkan approaching out of the corner of her eye. He seemed to want to avoid talking to her, like the other villagers had, but when Tian looked up at him he walked over to her.

"Hello," he said simply. The others in the kitchen drifted away. "You've been out for three days. I... we were worried you were really sick."

Tian hid her surprise at how long she'd been asleep. She couldn't remember traveling from the hunters' camp to the village. She looked into his eyes with an unspoken question. She watched them moisten, tears forming.

"We know. Tullan rode in late last night. On the last day, he'd fallen ill and decided to rest while the others went on to the silo. The Qah were already attacking when he rode up. They were so busy they didn"t see him. He told us everything this morning."

Erkan moved toward her. Tian stiffened involuntarily. He stopped, his arms dangling at his side.

"Tian, are you okay? Do you want to talk?"

Tian sighed. How could she even begin to tell him about all the things she had learned, about Mori, about the Confederation? She had no idea where to begin. Instead, she simply said, "Not yet. But we have to leave the village. Right now. Why aren"t we preparing to leave? The Qah are coming. They're going to attack all of the villages. We need to leave now, go to the winter caves, defend ourselves."

Tian's throat ached and her head throbbed. She spat out the takka, and took a long drink of water. She wasn't sure what she really meant by "defend ourselves," especially after what she'd seen what the Qah had done at the silo, but she"d worry about that later.

Erkan said, "We can't leave here yet, Tian. Not now. We're in mourning. When we do go, we need to travel to the silo, and say goodbye to the others."

Tian stood up. "No! It"s too dangerous! The Qah have alien technology. One of the Watchers has gone to another silo to get help, but we have to leave now."

Erkan looked at her strangely. "Alien technology? Watchers? Listen, Tian, go back to bed. We can talk later." He turned to go, a bemused expression on his face.

Tian reached out, put her hand on his shoulder, and glared at him. "Call a Circle now. I need to talk to the whole tribe."

She squeezed his shoulder gently and softened her gaze. "Please, Erkan."

He sighed, "Okay. If you're sure."

She released his shoulder. "Thanks. I'll be back in a moment. I want to go check Nimsha'h. She squeezed his hand and hurried off toward the horses.

There were so few of them. Nimsha'h was grazing a little way from the stable. The structure was simple, a few vertical logs supporting a long hide roof that Tian had helped tan the previous winter. Tian felt a flutter of relief at the sight of the tawny horse. She walked over to her, clicking her tongue gently. Nimsha'h looked up when she heard the noise. Tian spoke to her about what she was going to say to the tribe, her worries about Mori, the Qah, and the Kaiinish.

She stepped away from Nimsha'h, withdrew the Kaiinish weapon from the belt she wore, and examined it in detail for the first time since Mori gave it to her. She noticed how small and light it was, and how peculiar the jet black, cold material was. Almost the color of Mori's skin. She considered testing it, but decided against it. She would trust Mori's word that it would kill any Qah. Until then, she wanted as little to do with it as possible. She placed it back into her belt, and began to groom Nimsha'h.

She'd finished and was leaving when Nimsha'h walked over to her, hobbling. Tian walked her back towards the stables. She hadn't imagined it. Nimsha'h was lame. Tian frowned, the thought that the long ride might have crippled Nimsha'h gnawing at her. Tian felt Nimshah's' leg, but couldn't find anything obviously wrong. But it was clear that Nimsha'h was uncomfortable on the leg, and, after another inspection, Tian saw that the the problem was the lowest joint.

The Panacea. The Confederation tool had healed her injuries almost instantly. She had no idea if it would work on a horse, but she knew that Nimsha'h's injury was potentially life threatening—there was no way the tribe could take a lame horse with them when they left this village in a day or two. She pulled the Panacea out, speaking to the horse gently as she held the white stick over the place she thought the tendon was torn. Nimsha'h didn't react, and lowered her head to graze..

A shout startled Tian: "What are you doing!?" It was Bal, who was walking, no, swaggering, toward her. The sight of him brought all the events of her last night in the village flooding back. She looked around to see if she could spot Grashin.

"Nimsha'h's leg is injured."

"What is *that*?" he said, pointing at the Panacea.

"It's called a Panacea." The word sounded strange in her mouth. "It's mending the wound."

"Where did you get it?" He was looming over her now. Tian continued to hold the Panacea over Nimsha'h's leg. She wasn't sure what would happen if she removed it before the flashing light on the tip stopped, and she wasn't willing to find out.

"Give that to me now, child," he said, reaching down for it. Nimsha'h flinched at his tone, and Tian looked up at him, her upper lip curled in anger.

"Don't fuck with me, Bal. I'll tell you what it is in the Circle, but for now let me do this." He didn't move, and Nimsha'h was becoming nervous, trying to turn around to face whoever was standing so close to her back legs, her tail flicking around violently.

"Also," Tian said, "talk to me like that again and you'll regret it." Even after the clumsy warning left her mouth—a violation of the taboo against making threats—and she saw Bal's surprised reaction, she didn't regret it. Keeping the Panacea in place, Tian moved her left hand almost imperceptibly toward the knife sheathed on her belt. Bal saw the movement. He turned and walked hurriedly away from the stable. Nimsha'h calmed down as Tian stared at Bal's retreating back, dark thoughts in her mind. She shook her head to clear her momentary anger, looked down at the Panacea, and noticed it had stopped flashing. With a final, wondering glance at the stick, she tucked it back into her belt, and after a few more words led Nimsha'h across the pasture—the leg was completely healed.

Tian headed toward the Circle, where some of the villagers had already begun to gather. while others wandered over from the kitchen area, where they had been eating firstmeal. She could see that some of them were uncomfortable. She hadn't yet seen Grashin, and wondered where he was, what had happened to him after she left. Erkan and a few of her old friends approached her. She smiled at them, and they moved closer and hugged her. She almost cried when Erkan kissed her behind the ear. His familiar warmth was reassuring.

Erkan and the others sat down, and waited for her to speak.

"Brothers and sisters, I'd like to thank everyone for looking after me, even though I brought such terrible news. I know you want me to explain what happened at the silo, and I will, but for now it's too painful for me to go into any detail. All I'll say is that they're all gone. The Qah massacred them."

Yahna, a young man who had stayed behind, interrupted her. "Why were you there, sister?"

"One of the Watchers warned me that the Qah were close. We were trying to stop the tribe before they arrived."

The mention of the Watchers made the tribe uneasy. Some of them clearly wanted to say something, question her, but they were reluctant.

Erkan stood up. "Tian, I'm sure everyone wants to know.... What do you mean by a Watcher? Not a Watcher from the stories?"

"Yes, exactly. I know it's difficult to believe, Erkan, but they exist. . . . And thank brothers and sisters for not shouting me down when I mentioned them just now. "

"How do you know it was a Watcher?" asked Erkan.

"It looks like a Watcher, tall and as black as charcoal. Plus it told me so," she smiled thinly. The expressions on the faces around her remained doubtful. "It came to me a few days after I left here, and said that the Qah were moving toward the silos. It asked for my help."

Circle etiquette broke down at Tian's revelation.

"It spoke?"

"What did it sound like?"

"How can we trust it?"

"How did it know about the Qah?" Erkan asked, his question tumbling out over the others.

"It was obvious that it wasn't a Qah, or anyone from this world. I took it at its word, and it was right."

Yahna stood up again. There was no facilitator, but Tian and Erkan yielded the floor to him.

"Tian, you've seen terrible things. Perhaps you... imagined it?"

"No, Yahna. I know you find it hard to believe, but it told me things about itself, about us, about our histories. I spent many days traveling with it, and it told me about worlds out in the stars.

It was helping me to find the tribe, and it needed me to warn them, but it also wanted to help its own people. They live in under the silos."

Murmurs bubbled over audibly. It was clear that most didn't believe anything she'd said. Julam stood to speak now, and voiced the sentiments of the tribe. "You're asking us to believe that a Watcher, a creature from a fairytale, that lives with its kind at the silos, talks our tongue, and comes from the sky, told you stories about its past and helped you find the tribe? Tian, sister, I don't know how you can expect us to believe any of this. Is this about Grashin?"

Tian felt Erkan tense next to her as she stood up.

"I wasn't going to come back here. I was so angry with all of you. I see how childish I was, now; perhaps we all were. I don't care about Grashin any more. I don't care about any of our petty squabbles. I know you don't entirely trust me after my behavior before the flood. So perhaps this," she said, passing Erkan the

Panacea, "will help convince you. Everyone have a look at it. It's a Watcher healing tool."

With that, she sat down. People had already begun huddling around Erkan as she spoke; now others walked over to him, to look in wonder and fear at the technology.

CHAPTER 4

The Panacea passed through most of the tribe's hands before again held it. She had ignored all of the questions about it and the curious glances toward her until then. Though the tribe members' eyes were wide as they passed the peculiar object around, many of them were still looking at her skeptically. They still didn't trust her.

Erkan approached her with the Panacea. She held it aloft.

"The Watcher gave this to me. It heals wounds almost instantly."

She put the Panacea back in her belt, withdrew the knife from it, and held it aloft.

"I know it's hard to believe. So watch." She slid the knife across her palm. The tribe gasped as crimson droplets fell to the ground. She handed Erkan the bloody knife and took the Panacea from her belt and held it over her palm. She thumbed the raised part. The effect was even more miraculous than she expected. The bleeding stopped in a matter of seconds, and the wound closed, leaving only a thin white line. Those closest to her gathered around, taking her hand in theirs, tentatively rubbing the scar.

"You see?" she said.

"That girl tells nothing but lies," a voice roared over the general confusion. Grashin. The crowd around her went silent and parted, and the frail-looking old man emerged.

She was surprised to see him. She thought that after his actions on the night she fled, after his violence, the tribe would have cast him out. Seeing him here, determined to frustrate her, in this time of peril, made her old anger bubble over. At both. *Grashin and the tribe. They were even more craven than she'd thought.*

Those nearest to her, sensing her rage, stepped away from her. Only Grashin stood staring at her, unflinching.

She reached for the Kaiinish weapon. But, with effort, she stopped herself. She looked directly at Grashin, and ground out her words.

"Be careful, old man. The Watcher told me things, things that you've been hiding for a long time in that cave of yours. Walk away now."

"You see?" he said, venomously. "She provokes me, she threatens me. You shouldn't listen to this girl, or her fantasies. She probably stole that stick from one of the silos. She's delirious. Probably feeling guilty about the deaths of all our brothers and sisters, that she was too late or too scared to prevent.

The words stung. She hadn't realized she was still capable of being hurt by this old man, but he had known exactly what to say to both deeply wound and enrage her. The impulse to use the Kaiinish weapon was almost overpowering.

Then Mori's face came to her, in a flash. She *had* to control herself. She forced a tight smile and said, "You don't have to listen to me. But I think this," she held up the Panacea, "gives me the right to be heard."

Grashin was about to speak, when Erkan stood up.

"Quiet, Grashin. Let her speak. Let her finish." Others muttered agreement.

Tian spoke quietly but earnestly. She explained how she had met Mori, about their journey, and some of the things Mori had told her—enough for them to understand Mori's motives, and to understand the danger they were in. She didn't tell them about the Kaiins, and didn't say much about the planet's or the tribe's histories. There wasn't time for that. But she tried to make clear how great a threat the Qah were. Most of the tribe cried when she came to the end of her story, and mentioned the silo, even though she said very little about it.

"So, we need to get everyone to the winter caves, and send out messengers to the other tribes."

"You're forgetting something, Tian," said an elder, Kalwarn. "We have almost no food. We don't even have enough to last us to the caves."

Tian realized Kalwarn was right. She faltered for a moment. She hadn't thought about the details at all; she'd been too wrapped up in grief and exhaustion.

"There is a way."

Grashin again. Tian held her tongue.

"The horses," he said, a malevolent grin spreading across his face.

"No!" Tian cried. A murmur rippled through the tribe. Tian could see what Grashin was thinking: *Nimsha'h.*

"You tell us these things and expect us to believe you? You say how urgently we need to leave. Well, what other choice do we have but to eat the horses? It will be hard, but their meat will be the only way we can survive the trip to the caves. If your story is true."

Tian's mind raced, trying to think of alternatives. But he'd cornered her again, outplayed her. The forest around was them was nearly bare, the stores almost empty. There was no other way.

"We'll need some of them to carry the tools and bedding," one of the tribe said. He'd waited a few seconds to see if Tian would say anything else, but she remained stony faced and silent, rage almost bursting through her chest.

"Oh, of course," Grashin said quickly. "We'll take the youngest, the freshest, with us." " Feigning sadness she wondered if he truly felt, he added, "We'll have to slaughter one now, so we can smoke the meat overnight."

Tian said nothing. Grashin had beaten her, again.

She silently watched them make the preparations for the

slaughter. She wouldn't allow herself to see which horse they'd choose; she couldn't bear to say the final goodbye if it was Nimsha'h. Instead, she simply sat in the Circle, turning her knife over and over in her hands.

The tribe worked quietly but quickly. Usually they would roll up the hides and readying everything they needed for the next village. This time, though, they couldn't carry everything they usually did. They focused on stripping the village of its most important things: tools, cooking and storage pots, crafting materials, and bedding.

A few of the villagers came up to Tian to talk to her. Some wanted to know whether she had seen their lovers or their birth-children at the silo. Although it pained her, she had to say "no." She didn't add that the corpses had been burned beyond recognition.

Others came up individually to welcome her back, to apologize for Grashin, or to ask more about the Watcher and the Panacea. Tian didn't feel like talking at all, but their warmth kept her talking well past secondmeal, despite her fatigue. Eventually, Erkan noticed she was beginning to lag, and asked her to go lie down and get some rest. She was so tired that she immediately fell into a deep, dreamless sleep.

When she awoke, it was still daylight and the tribe was packing. It was strange to see how little they were taking. They lived sparsely, but not this sparsely. Her thoughts drifted to Mori. The more Tian thought about the Confederation, at least the fragments Mori had told her about, the more this life, this world, seemed a farce, a shadow of real life. She thought of the lives and suffering that could have been saved by the Panacea, the freedom they could have had with the Cornucopia, the time and energy they could have had if they hadn't had to spend hour upon hour collecting firewood, scrubbing mud from roots, smashing nuts and gathering seeds. She had always wanted a better life for them, but Mori had given her a glimpse of a life that even Priash couldn't have imagined. As she looked at the weary, dirty faces of her tribe, she couldn't help but think of her.

If Priash, on that fateful night, had a Confederation weapon when she met the Qah, she might still be here now.

CHAPTER 5

The tribe left at dawn the next day. The villagers bore heavy loads, their packs full of provisions, tools, furs and jars. Tian's heart had leapt when she saw Nimsha'h, alive. She was eager go before anyone had second thoughts about leaving the village, and so many of the things their brothers and sisters would have taken, behind.

They set out quietly, the usual excitement that surrounded a move absent. Their thoughts of the missing and their heavy burdens weighed them down as they made their way along one of the hunting paths towards the mountains.

They were wary, too. They sent a small group of hunters ahead of them, bows and spears at the ready, with another group trailing them in case of a Qah ambush. All of them, even the youngest, were at home traveling in the forest. Still, the danger of the Qah made the familiar bushes and trees alien and frightening as they snaked single file through the forest.

They stopped at nightfall. Despite the dangers of the Qah spotting the smoke, they lit a fire. Everyone wanted the comfort of the fire, the songs, the stories.

"Perhaps we shouldn't have been so quick to leave," said Julla, the oldest of the tribe. She spoke very little. She was completely blind, her eyes a cloudy white, but her frail, bony hands were adept at fashioning intricate knots, which she took joy in teaching to the youngest of the children. "We didn't properly say goodbye to the others."

The tribes differed in their approach to death. All of them held ceremonies, but the particulars varied. Some tribes, particularly the nomadic plains tribes, burned their dead on funeral pyres or left them on raised platforms for the birds. Others held long feasts in celebration of the lives of the dead, and others held simple burials where loved ones told stories about the lives of the deceased. The coastal tribes left their dead on beaches for the rising tide to taketo be swept away at the rise of the tide, reflecting the Way's teachings about inaction, allowing nature to take its course.

Tian's tribe, as was the custom of many of the forest tribes, held a highly theatrical feast honoring the dead, with different villagers taking on the different roles. Those closest to the dead would act as celebrants. A smaller group would act as mourners. After the feast, consisting of simple foods eaten in silence, the mourners would begin to sing a long, sad lament that continued for some time.

After a while, someone in the celebrant group close to the deceased would stand up and begin to play an instrument, usually a drum with an animal hide head. They'd play slowly, barely audibly, at first. Others in the celebrant group would then begin to sing in time with the drummer. They would get louder and louder as more celebrants voices and other instruments joined in, until their song drowned out the mourners' lament, and the mourners joined the celebrants. The song would continue until everyone was exhausted, and a second feast would take place, where everyone would eat and drink delicacies. After the feast, the tribe would bury the dead at the edge of the Circle, a carved stone set flush with the earth marking the place. Occasionally, even though the tribe rarely used the same places for villages, they would find these markers when they erected new villages, and would place the Circle in the midst of the commemorative stones.

But they had never lost so many before. Ten seasons before, a branch had fallen and killed three sleeping hunters. Each had their own ceremony on consecutive nights; that had drained the tribe. To even contemplate holding ceremonies for all those lost to the Qah was exhausting. Yet Tian knew Julla was right. Everyone realized something needed to be said or done to remember and celebrate the lost, and restore the Way. But they were in too much of a hurry, now. Tian said nothing after Julla spoke, but she slept little that night.

Conversation buzzed at firstmeal the next day. It was clear they'd hold an ad hoc Circle. When they assembled in a crude Circle in a clearing. One of the tribe lit a small fire in the center, and the meeting began.

It didn't take long. They thought they were deep enough in the woods to avoid Qah patrols, and decided to hold a mass funeral ceremony that night.

They'd held ceremonies without bodies before, when a child had drowned, caught by a flash flood, and when the Qah took Priash. But they were concerned that they could not restore the Way in the face of such a devastating tragedy.

Despite their misgivings, they held the ceremony. The smoked horse meat was a poor substitute for the usual funeral feast foods, and the celebratory song much weaker than usual.

Mori was seven days hard traveling south of the silo, concentrating on getting through the close-packed trees and dense undergrowth in a heavy rain. It was difficult going, and Mori gave little thought to its nagging worries about the Qah, the Kaiins, and Tian. There were few animal tracks, and none of the tribes had been in this part of the forest for some time.

It was night when Mori nearly stumbled across a small camp; as Mori neared the camp, it smelled the distinctive aroma of roasting flesh. The camp was set up against the exposed roots of a massive tree, with dense cover all around, to give whoever had set it up some protection from the elements.

Mori stayed motionless in the undergrowth, trying to sense whether its approach had been heard, but the camp's occupants weren't stirring. Mori was used to staying perfectly still for hours at a time. Now, Mori, slipped into a near-meditative trance, yet retained its heightened observational senses as rain dripped down and ran off its shoulder blades.

After a time, Mori began, ever so slowly, moving closer to the camp. Then it paused again, head cocked and senses straining to detect any movement. Finally, it glimpsed them: three men. All Qah. All masked. They were all larger than the forest tribe people, but one of them was huge. The men Tian and Mori had killed at the silo were much smaller, just local bandits that had joined the Qah.

The fire was low, and the Qah spoke in low murmurs. Mori could see that they were heavily armed. Two of them had large axes, and Mori spied the distinctive, curved design of a Kaiinish weapon in the burliest man's belt.

Mori knew it was in no position to fight them, and as far as Mori knew there were no tribes or Qah bands in the area. The men could be here for only one purpose: scouting out the nearest silo. It had to be their destination. There was no other reason for them to be so deep in the forest, and in such a small group.

A Qah scouting group meant trouble for the Watchers inside the silo. Mori had no idea whether the men had already scouted the silo and were on their way back to their main band, or whether they were en route to the silo..

Finally, Mori tore itself away and circled around the group, trying to see if it could make out any tracks; but the rain had washed away any trace of their path. Mori decided to wait. If at dawn they headed north or east Mori would have plenty of time to warn the silo before Qah attacked it; if the Qah headed south or west, Mori could probably reach it first and warn any Watchers there, as well as trigger the emergency ansible broadcast. Either way, Mori wanted to eavesdrop on them.

Mori settled down in a tree about fifty meters from the camp. It had long ago gotten used to the unpleasant smells coming from the roast dead animal that was the Qah's meal, and welcomed the chance to rest for longer than an hour.

At first Mori tried to listen to what the men were saying, but their conversation was difficult to hear over the wind. After an hour or so, Mori saw the men retiring to their hammocks. When Mori was satisfied the men had fallen asleep, Mori nestled against the trunk, nervously anticipating what the morning would bring.

Mori awoke with a start. It was still pitch black, and clouds obscured the moons and the stars. Mori hadn't meant to sleep so long, but the journey had left it wearier than it thought. A strong feeling of uneasiness crept over Mori, as if something were standing right behind or above it. Mori looked toward the camp, but there were no lights, no fire. The rain started again. The drops made the leaves rustle and the undergrowth shake. Peering around the branches, Mori could see nothing. Mori jumped when a large drop fell on its face. Mori hadn"t slept properly for weeks, and the rain and nervous tension had made it skittish. With another glance toward the camp, Mori settled back against the trunk, turning its face away from the rain.

But something wasn't right.

Mori still had the distinct feeling that something was behind it. If Mori had hairs on its neck, they would have been raised. Mori switched to its infrared vision. The fire was a dull orange now, the embers all but extinguished by the rain. Mori could make out the bright white of the Qah's horses five meters to the south, and a few smudges in the surrounding forest that were probably nocturnal animals.

But the hammocks were empty.

Mori started again. Looking at the branches above, Mori fully expected to see a masked Qah warrior staring down. But the tree was empty. Mori swung its head around, searching frantically. The instinct to flee was strong, despite all of Mori's training. Its adrenaline levels were rocketing, but Mori was reluctant to move anything but its head for fear of revealing its position to unseen eyes.

Despite all of their training and adaptations, Watchers sometimes made mistakes. On a few occasions, the tribes had seen them. Living in such close proximity to a people that were deeply attuned to their natural surroundings, and indeed reliant on them for food and shelter, made it inevitable that the tribes would catch a glimpse sooner or later. On the plains and steppes, observation was especially difficult, almost impossible at times.

Of course, most of the first settlers knew exactly what the Watchers were, and told stories to their children as a way of distancing themselves from what they represented. The stories also created a sense a sense of danger that would discourage them from contacting a Watcher, should they see one; but the children were also aware on some level that the stories were fantasy, so when they grew older they thought of Watchers as nightmarish fairytale creatures. The reaction in the village to Tian's story about Mori was precisely what the first settlers had intended: a mixture of fear and disbelief.

Over the orbits, Mori had had a few brushes with discovery. Mori had ducked out of sight at the last moment when a hunter skipped along right below on a few occasions. Even when a villager did see Mori, it would only be a glimpse. Usually, the stories and legends about the Watchers would be enough to convince them Mori was a mirage or, for the more superstitiously inclined, a forest spirit or demon. Notwithstanding these occasional, inevitable lapses, the Watchers were hard to spot. Their black skin that made them stand out on the plains made it easy for them to slip away in the forest, and no Watcher Mori knew of had ever been spotted at night.

So, despite the potentially deadly situation Mori now found itself in, there was some comfort in knowing that it was almost surely invisible to the Qah warriors, even if they were staring up from right underneath the tree. Yet the rising sense of foreboding was hard to quell. It was possible that the men had heard Mori approaching the camp and had waited for Mori to settle down before closing in on it.

Mori waited for several long minutes. The tension was almost unbearable. Mori began to question whether its night vision was working correctly, and half-expected a Qah axe to come crashing down on its head. Finally Mori, too nervous to wait any longer, started to climb upward, hoping to get a better view of the camp from a higher branch. The moment it did so, a call came from below.

"Not another move, freak," the voice bellowed. Mori heard the mosquito whine of a coilgun charging up. "Get down here. Now."

Mori froze. The loud voice in such close proximity made Mori's heart race and stomach contract. The unmistakable sound of a coilgun here, in the forest, was chilling. But it was the command itself that left Mori light-headed and struggling to breathe.

It was in Kaiinish.

Part IV

Chapter 1

It had been a difficult journey. They'd had to butcher and eat another of the horses, and leave most of the supplies it carried by the side of the trail. Again, Tian couldn't bear to watch the slaughter. And again she almost broke down when she learned it wasn't Nimsha'h.

But the tribe finally reached the winter caves in a driving rain. Eeveryone was tired. Even with the few remaining horses taking the bulk of the load, the trek had been exhausting.

Along the way, Tian had spoken little. She'd focused on getting the tribe to the winter village, and the sadness and steely determination in her eyes were enough to deflect all but the most persistent from asking about the Watcher. When she'd replied to questioners, it was in monosyllables.

Once they arrived at the caves, she wasn't entirely sure what to expect; she couldn't remember what Mori had told her to do once the tribe got there. So she improvised, doing the best she could. With a few modifications, the caves could probably hold off a Qah assault for a short while. Tian didn't know how long Mori would be, or when—or if—the Confederation ships would arrive, but she urged the tribe to scavenge the surrounding foothills to augment the long-term stores in the caves.

By now, the tribe had accepted her story—at least most of it. If they had doubts, they no longer voiced them in front of her. They put up crude barricades at the entrances to the caves, and didn't object when she asked them to block several of the side passages. They spent most of their time foraging for berries and seeds—game being scarce—and chopping enough wood to last through the increasingly cold nights. They posted sentries on the steep approach path, and, after a heated discussion, once the main barricade was finished and the horses rested from their arduous trip, they sent messengers to the neighboring tribes.

Tian stayed with the tribe. She wasn't confident that the barrier they had erected would hold up against a concerted Qah assault for more than a day or two. She knew that if the Qah got inside it would be a massacre, just as it had been at the silo. Still, she was determined not to give up without a fight, and hoped that Mori would return before it came to that.

Being at the winter caves was peculiar. For one thing, the view was spectacular. Whenever Tian got a break from barricading the cave entrances or scavenging, she looked over the sprawling forest below; it was breathtaking, the thin air fresh and clear. The snow and wind in the winter season made spending any time outside the caves barely tolerable, and, despite the reason they were here early, many seemed to be enjoying the novelty of spending time outside the caves.

Tian had no idea whether the neighboring tribes would believe the riders they'd sent out. Despite what Mori had told her, she didn't expect more than the usual one or two tribes to actually make the trek to the caves. The closest ones might come, but she suspected those deeper in the forest would simply move farther west or south. If they did all come, feeding them would be a huge task; and at one of their hasty Circle one of the elders noted that gathering all of the forest tribes into one place, despite the concept of safety in numbers, might not be the wisest strategy for surviving concerted Qah raids.

Despite these doubts, three days after they arrived they finished work on the main barricade, and concealed or barricaded the smaller entrances; some of those would be easy enough to unblock in case of emergency. They had plenty of water from the springs inside the caves, and the long-term stores would allow them to survive, if barely, over the winter—if the Qah didn't massacre them first.

Once the main barricade was finished, Tian, Erkan, and a small band, went hunting. It was a clear day, and the heavy rain of the day before had filled the forest with a rich, earthy aroma. Erkan's eyes roamed the brush ahead for signs of prey. Tian and the others walked behind him, weaving through the trees on a narrow animal trail.

They had a surprisingly successful day hunting, and started back with carcasses slung across their backs. They made camp at dusk, not trusting their footing in the dark on the climb up to the caves. It was cold, and they gathered around the fire. Neither of the moons were out, and the forest was dark.

The tribe had mostly avoided asking Tian questions on the journey to the caves, and the hectic process of constructing the barricade had left them too weary for idle conversation since then. Now, the hunters had time to satisfy their curiosity. At first, they asked her about the Qah. They were especially interested in the men she had killed, something that Tian had revealed inadvertently during the feast for the dead. She'd regretted it the following morning, but thinking back now, she realized it was probably for the best. So she spoke plainly.

Knowing what had happened to their brothers and sisters, however horrifying or grisly, was better for the others than leaving them in the dark, their doubts and fears only prolonging the agony of loss. It was what she would have wanted. If someone could have told her what had happened to Priash, Tian thought she could have handled her death better, been able to move on.

After she'd answered the questions about the Qah, there was a heavy silence. Then three of Tian's brothers began singing a soft, rhythmic chant, taking turns singing the solo parts. The

familiar song lifted her spirits. After they finished the song and
the fire died down, though, the gloom returned, and they fell
asleep, or tried to. Tian soon heard a few soft snores as she lay
awake staring up at the stars.

She couldn't get comfortable, so she got up to stoke the fire.
She could tell some of the others were still awake, but they didn't
say anything. She was a reminder of the Qah to them, and she
also realized how much she'd withdrawn into herself. The others had picked up on it; they could sense the change in her. Even
though they were all around the same age, they'd begun treat-
ing her like an elder, listening a little closer to what she had to
say, the usual playfulness and teasing gone. She'd caught them
looking at her in an unusual way, with awe, maybe, or respect.
Whatever it was, it upset her. That look was just as unsettling
as their distance, but she didn't know what to do or say to get
them to stop. It bothered her that they seemed to be looking to
her for guidance.

Erkan came strolling casually back into the camp. His eyesight was astonishingly good, and he had no problem walking
in the thickest, most tangled forest even on the darkest nights.

"All done," he said, squatting next to her, reaching his hands
out to the warmth of the fire. Tian shifted. He'd sat a little too
close for comfort.

"Hmm?" she grunted, not looking up from the embers.

"Set the traps for the night. Should have a few catches tomorrow morning."

"Oh, right. Yes," she said. There was a long uncomfortable silence; they both fidgeted. It was the first time they'd really been
together since she'd left the tribe after the fight with Grashin.

"Erkan, are you happy here?"

"What?" he said, thinking he'd misheard.

"Are you happy in the forest, with the tribe?" she repeated.

He cocked his head, conscious of those listening in the dark.

"Happy? Yes, I guess. I'm not sure. I've never thought about
it." He paused.

"I just *am*. Just try to live every day, like we all do. I don't really think about whether I'm happy or not."

"I don't feel like I belong here any more, Erkan. Something has changed."

"We're still the same, Tian. I'm still the same."

Tian shook her head. "This place feels so small now. I used to think these woods were the entire world."

"We all did. It's normal. A few seasons with the coastal tribes cured me of that."

Tian looked at him in surprise. She'd forgotten that Erkan had spent some of his childhood on the coast. So much of the time before Priash and Mori seemed like another life to her, now.

"No, I mean . . . Oh, I don't know what I mean."

They sat silently for several moments, feeling more comfortable with each other. Finally Erkan asked, "What did the Watcher tell you?"

She looked over at him, saw the same curiosity she'd seen on all the other faces, and answered, "Everything. It made me realize how ignorant I am, how ignorant we all are. How we take things for granted, how we don't question things that we should."

Erkan paused to think about that. After a moment, he spoke, "We don't need to, Tian. The forest is full of game, the trees heavy with fruit, the ground filled with roots and berries. We still sing our songs and dance our dances, and listen to the stories and follow the Way. Why would we change any of that, when it has been so good to us?"

The others were sitting up now, the pretense that they were sleeping long gone.

"I've always felt... different. You're right. The forest has been good to us. But there's something missing. Something beyond all this. It feels like we're just existing, just getting by. Not really living. Does that make sense?"

"No, it doesn't. What about all the festivals, all the visitors, all the dances? All the hunts? Don't you remember them? Didn't you feel it again today? Don't tell me you don't get a warm feeling when we're setting up a new village or when we're sitting around the fire, surrounded by people who love us." He placed a hand on her shoulder. She shrugged it off.

"Yes, I feel all of that," she said, annoyed that he'd been able to get to her. "I mean, we're just happy to live like we've always lived. Never changing, never trying to make things better for ourselves, even when it'd be simple to do. I bet we're doing things that we've been doing for thousands of seasons, speaking and acting and dressing exactly like people did back then."

"Change isn't always good. The Way teaches that. And you haven't explained why we need to change. Like you said, we've been doing it for thousands of seasons. It works, doesn't it? Otherwise we wouldn't be sitting here talking now."

"I want to see new things. I want to make things better, try new things. Sure, some of the things we try might not work, or they might be dangerous or against the Way as Grashin always says. But being with that Watcher . . . That Panacea, for example . . . Never in a thousand seasons would we be able to make something like that. Think how much better our lives could have been if we had that? I bet they have hundreds of things like that. I'm just bored with everything having to be safe, Erkan. Always the same. Like we're settling for less than we're capable of. Tied down by stupid tenth- day rotation, collecting firewood or mashing roots or grinding nuts. Tired of being stuck in those stupid caves because we can't build warm huts out in the forest because it'd be against the Way. Tired of all the rules and traditions and customs that make no sense, that just seem to make life harder for no reason at all."

Erkan sighed, which hurt more than Tian wanted to admit.

"I don't know what to say, Tian. I'm just sorry you feel like that. But wherever you go there will be things like that. You've been to the plains, I've been to the coast. We've had people visit from all over. It's the same everywhere."

Tian didn't reply. Erkan placed his hand back on her shoulder. She ignored it. She had no wish to lie with him; she just stared into the fire.

After a while, he stood up and left.

Tian stayed up well into the night, before lying down and staring up at the cold, bright stars.

They rose early the next morning, eager to return to the safety and warmth of the caves. The climb was tough, laden as they were, but they reached the entrance just after the sun reached its zenith.

The clearing in front of the cave was full of people and animals. Tian and her hunting group yelled greetings. It was one of the neighboring forest tribes. They hadn't expected to see another tribe for at least a week.

Recognizing a familiar face in the throng, Tian rushed over towards an elderly man, whose long hair was woven intricately into elaborate knots. He sat on a faded, patterned blanket that looked as if it had seen too much sun.

"Yehla!" she cried, embracing him.

"Tian? I barely recognize you!" the man said, hugging her warmly.

"Here, I have yusha," she said pulling away, opening a pouch and taking out a pinch of the dark ribboned herb and dropping it into his open palm. She sat down next to him.

"Ah, you remembered," he said, his eyes wrinkling into a smile. "If there's anything I missed about our tribe it was this," he said, rubbing the yusha tenderly between his fingers. "Grashin always was the best at curing yusha."

Tian's smile faded momentarily, but she hid it by hugging the old man again.

"When did you arrive? Just now?" Tian asked, looking over Yehla's shoulder at the tribe around them. She pulled away from him, looking puzzled.

"Why are your sleeping things still out? Did you sleep here last night?"

"Well, yes..." he answered.

Tian looked around again. Erkan caught her glance; he looked worried.

"We're just a few paces from the caves. Why did you... has something happened?" Tian scrambled to her feet. "Are they all right?"

"Yes, Tian, they're fine," said Yehla.

Erkan walked over to them, giving Yehla a dark piece of cured meat by way of greeting. "I talked with Bal. He said the tribe wouldn't let them in, that they forced them to camp here."

Yehla's head dropped, his knotted hair falling across his face.

Looking from Yehla to Erkan, Tian's face hardened. She swung around and marched off toward the entrance to the caves.

"She'd changed so much, Yehla. I hardly know her any more."

The old man looked up at Erkan. "Your people told us some of what happened. The things she has seen. The things we've become capable of."

"They left you out here because they were scared, didn't they?" Erkan asked, softly.

Yehla nodded. "Who can blame them? They said they didn't have enough food. Then they started to argue amongst themselves. It got out of hand. They closed the entrance on us, brother. Some of them told us to leave."

"It is against the Way," said Erkan, sitting down next to Yehla.

"You have lost so many, so suddenly, so horribly," Yehla said, chewing on the yusha Tian had given him.

"All the more reason for us to help you. It is so dangerous out here."

Yehla said nothing for a while, looking toward the cave entrance where Tian was waving her arms around wildly, the sharp wind not completely able to drown out her shouted recriminations.

"I'm not sure I know any of us as I thought I did, brother," Yehla said, shaking his head. "The Way isn't always as clear to me as it once was."

* * *

The Kaiinish command barked out again. Mori flinched. The huge "man" had to be a Kaiin, an inherently aggressive species modified to be even more aggressive, with massive strength, incredibly sensitive hearing, and vision almost as acute as a Watcher's. No wonder it had so easily found Mori.

The huge "man" had to be a Kaiin, an inherently aggressive species modified to be even more aggressive, with massive strength, incredibly sensitive hearing, and vision almost as acute as a Watcher's. No wonder it had so easily found Mori.

The language matched the species. Kaiinish was a rough, guttural language, designed intended for shouting orders over the din of warfare and the screams of victims. Or so the more sensationalist of the holonovelists back in the Confederation liked to portray it. Mori knew this to be unlikely; Kaiinish warriors had hardwired neural tech and tended to use no verbal communication at all on the battlefield. Still, the rough voice coming out of the dark was unnerving. Mori could well imagine the impact that voice might have on other species.

Mori slowly crept down the tree, still trying to place the voice in the surrounding undergrowth.

"What are you doing here, Kaiin?" Mori said, its voice a whisper compared to the bellowed commands.

The coilgun went off. The sudden pulse was deafening. Mori cried out in pain at an appalling, burning sensation in its hip. Losing balance, Mori tumbled from the branch, hitting the forest floor in an awkward heap.

Disoriented and frightened, Mori tried to rise, but was unable to move its leg. Mori heard the whine of the coilgun charging up again. Mori pushed itself toward a low rocky outcrop. There was another sudden blast and an intense burning sensation engulfed its lower torso. Mori slumped, unconscious.

Blinking against the bright light, Mori awoke, its arms bound behind its back. Its left leg dangled limply from the table it was stretched out on, face down. Its jaw throbbed, and several of its front teeth were missing. Mori tried to run a diagnostic scan, but its internal neural systems and much of its bioware were offline. With a barely suppressed groan, Mori tried to roll over, but the pain was unbearable, and it slumped back onto its front with a grunt.

Mori's eyes began to adjust to the light. It was in the living area in one of the silos. Mori could see that most of the electronic displays were offline, and there was blood on the floor. Mori strained to listen for the Kaiin or anyone else, but could hear nothing but the rush of blood in its ears.

Something moved next to Mori. Warm skin brushed and then pushed against Mori's back.

"Hello?" said Mori quietly, half-expecting to hear the sound of of the coilgun charging in response.

"Query: status?" came a muffled voice.

"Yes? said Mori. "Who are you?"

"Designation: 4723.10.22-N5/578-ATIA-AO129," said the voice. It was a Watcher. Alive.

"I didn't recognize your vocalization. My neural network is damaged, I can only communicate verbally," said Mori, trying to turn over to look at 129. Mori had talked regularly to 129 on the infosphere, but they had only met in person a handful of times. "Can you unbind me?"

"Negative. Request: remain still. Captors return imminent."

"The Kaiins are still here? Where is 77?" Mori asked.

"Deceased. Surprise attack." 129's voice became a whisper. "Advanced weaponry. Designation 4722.05.44-N5/578-JELL-AO77 decapitated, terminated instantly."

Mori winced. 129's crude speech was harsh after spending so long with Tian. And low-information verbal communication was rare between Watchers. It was simply too slow, too limiting.

"Query: status?" asked 129.

Mori tried to look back, but couldn't see its wounds.

"I can't tell," Mori said. "It might be bad."

"Query: terminal?"

"Perhaps. Abdominal injury. I'm numb. The table is wet with blood, though . . . very wet. How long have I been lying here?"

"Unknown. Captors using crude sedatives."

"Are you injured?" asked Mori.

"Affirmative. Nonfatal. Right hand nonfunctional, right eye nonfunctional. Extensive burns, bruising and four broken ribs. Query: purpose?"

Mori smiled faintly, painfully.

"I came to get help. The Qah have massacred the forest tribe I was assigned to, killed AO57 and AO14 and destroyed the G15 silo. I haven't been able to log into the infosphere. I was hoping...." Mori's voice trailed off. "The Kaiins are here, aren't they?"

"Affirmative. Infosphere jammed. Advanced weaponry: Kaiinish. Query: assailant Kaiinish?"

"Yes."

"Identification confirmed. Query: next action?"

Mori tried to swallow, but its mouth was too dry. "We need to contact the Confederation. They need to know the Kaiins are here, that this might be the prelude to a full-scale invasion."

"Negative. Infosphere broadcast equipment destroyed, emergency ansible disabled, presume destroyed. Deliberately targeted. First console destroyed following 4722.05.44-N5/578-JELL-AO77's termination and own incapacitation."

Mori groaned.

The sound of approaching footsteps echoed from one of the corridors behind Mori. Mori felt 129 tense, as Mori lay still and tried to control its breathing.

Three humanoids came into the room. They were speaking Qahi, a terse dialect of the Dodonan language not far removed from the standard Confederation of their Feral ancestors. Mori guessed that only one of them, the near-giant it had seen in the camp was a Kaiin. The other two seemed to be Qah. They ignored the two injured Watchers, and they remained out of sight behind their prisoners. Mori strained to hear what they were saying, but couldn't make much out. The pain began to return, the burning sensation in Mori's abdomen rushing back. Mori's head started swimming, and, unable to suppress the pain chemically, Mori vomited. The voices and the bright lights above floated into the distance.

A painful tugging in its abdomen awoke Mori. Its mouth was dry, and it felt extremely nauseated. Mori tried to rise, but a firm hand held its shoulder down against the cold table.

"Request: remain still. Panacea treatment in progress." 129's speech was still stilted and unfamiliar, but seemed less harsh now.

Mori opened its eyes. Mori was on its back and could see 129 clearly. Its right eyelid and most of its nose were missing; the flesh on its face was scorched.

"Your face," Mori stammered.

"Affirmative. Panacea unable to restore features. Too much tissue destroyed. Right hand now functional. Query: pain?"

Mori shuffled on the table. Aside from the sensation from the Panacea, most of its body was numb. 129 had untied Mori's hands, and they tingled unpleasantly as blood flowed freely though them.

"No pain. Extent of damage?" asked Mori, slipping into 129"s speech patterns.

129 removed the Panacea, placing it on the table. "Analysis: terminal if untreated. Panacea ineffective. Damage extensive. Blood loss extreme, severe hemorrhaging. Requires medical bay. Silo medical bay offline. Query: mobility?"

Mori struggled to sit up with 129's assistance, and then looked down. Mori's torso was a scorched pulp.

Suppressing a grimace, Mori looked around the silo.

"Query... Where are they? Did they leave? How did you get free?" Mori asked.

"Captors gone. Restraint on arm loose. Return soon probable."

"What are they doing here? Why haven't they killed us?"

"Captive purpose: known. Primary mission: secure facility. Secondary mission: destroy broadcast equipment. Tertiary mission: subdue or terminate obstacles to mission completion."

"Yes, but what is the mission? Why are the Kaiins here in the first place? Why are they doing this so quietly? They could have just destroyed our silos from space."

"Captive's purpose clear."

Mori looked at 129 with surprise.

"What? You know why they are doing this? Did you hear something?"

"Captive's purpose clear: military occupation effective temporarily, long-term untenable. Reason: Confederation fleet technological superiority. Ulterior motive: propaganda. Locate marginalized group. Arm group. Stimulate internecine warfare. Result: genocide. Sow disunity within Confederation. Require intervention. Result: Confederation demoralization."

Mori followed 129 with growing dread. *Of course*, Mori thought. The Kaiins weren't interested in the Watchers or the silos at all. Controlling the silos was a precaution to stop the Watchers using the emergency beacons. Their real goal wasn't to provoke a conflict with the Confederation fleet, but to make Dodona's tribes destroy one another, leaving a fractured Confederation trying to pick up the pieces.

"That means the Kaiins aren't after the silos or after us, then," said Mori.

"Affirmative. Tribal population is primary target. Anthropologist population and Confederation observational facilities: secondary concern."

"Oh, no," said Mori, its voice faltering.

"Query: pain?"

"No. Oh, 129. I didn't know. I made contact with one of the tribes. I told them... They are going to the winter caves. They are *all* going to the winter caves. The Qah and Kaiins will slaughter them."

129 said nothing for a few seconds.

"Query: 'all'?"

"Yes. All. At least all of the forest and the southern river tribes. I told them to contact them all... I didn't know the Kaiins were here. I thought they'd be safe there, that the Qah alone couldn't dislodge them."

"Winter caves: no match for coilgun weaponry. Query: winter cave location known to Qah/Kaiins?"

"I... I don't know," faltered Mori, feeling weak, its body heavy..

"Assumption: probable. Request: infolink?"

Mori nodded weakly. 129 touched the inside of its arm to Mori's. Although Mori's neural network was offline and it couldn't authorize the transmission, 129 bypassed the damaged cells and began the memory transfer. The stored data took a while to transfer, 129 having to reboot many of the protocols to access the cached memory block.

"Emotion: concern. Opinion: incorrect procedure regarding Tian. Opinion: empathy, past events clouding rational judgment. Correct action: contact silo, noninterference."

Mori"s head dropped.

"You know why I couldn't leave that girl."

"Affirmative. Convey emotion: pity, understanding." 129 touched Mori's shoulder gently.

129's head snapped suddenly around to look as footsteps approached. Mori tried to lie back down on the table, looking around desperately for the restraints. 129 handed it something clumsily, but before Mori could see what it was the Qah and Kaiin were already inside.

The sound of the coilgun charging filled the room. 129 pushed Mori to the floor before turning to face the three men, placing itself between them Mori. The Kaiin raised the heavy weapon, pointing it directly at 129. He fired. The blast rocked the room, throwing Mori's prostrate body to the floor.

A loud ringing lingered in Mori's ears. Mori glanced across towards 129, who had been thrown backwards by the blast. Somehow, 129 was already climbing back to its feet. Astonishingly, it appeared unharmed. A metallic smell of ozone filled the room.

Only then did Mori realize what 129 had thrust into its hand: a shield generator. It had protected them from the energy weapon. Only the shockwave had made 129 lose its balance and fall to the floor.

The Kaiin, reeling from the blast, dropped the heavy coilgun. The two Qah flanking him lay prone on the floor, stunned. But the Kaiin began to stagger across the room toward where Mori lay.

"Command: stop!" shrieked 129 to the Kaiin, its voice high-pitched and barely comprehensible. He stopped in his tracks. 129 had to think of something, and fast. Once the Kaiin had his wits back, he could simply walk through the shield and break their necks.

The Kaiin shook his head, pulled off his mask, and leered. He let out a snort, revealing sharp teeth beneath matted facial hair. Elaborate tattoos covered his bare skull almost completely, and his bright yellow eyes stared wickedly at 129.

"I haven't got my trophies yet. I'll skin you alive," he spat in 129's direction.

129 said nothing. Although far taller than the Kaiin, the Watcher was much less powerfully built. With the two Qah struggling to their feet, the situation looked hopeless.

"Well? Are you going to fight back?"

"Command: leave. Confederation fleet: notified. Conclusion: mission failure."

The Kaiin looked puzzled momentarily, then he grinned revealing his fangs. He reached into his belt and removed a long, curved blade from a concealed scabbard.

"That won't stop me slicing your guts."

Mori was transfixed by 129's apparent tranquility. The Kaiin and Qah were advancing on 129, weapons raised, Mori temporarily forgotten on the floor. 129 had only seconds to live. Mori was paralyzed. Helpless. Iit would be forced to watch the Kaiin butcher 129, before it was butchered, too.

When the Kaiin was less than five meters away, 129 threw a spherical object, similar to the shield generators, to the floor. The Kaiin, demonstrating remarkably quick reflexes, leaped behind a nearby console. The two Qah weren't as fast. They watched dumbly as the metallic object came to a stop at their feet. The ball exploded into a cloud of smoke, and they slumped to the floor.

"You and your infant's toys," came the Kaiin's voice through the mask he had pulled over his mouth and nose. He rose from behind the computing console and advanced toward 129, kicking one of the prone Qah as he passed him.

"You should learn how to fight like men," he roared. "Maybe then we'd respect you more." Sweating and shaking, he walked toward 129, raising his blade over his left shoulder.

Even in the face of this powerful creature barreling toward him, 129 remained calm. Then it said to Mori: "Request: scream, maximum. Ultrasound."

Mori and 129 screamed together at a bone-piercing pitch, even as the Kaiin's blow penetrated the shield field and sliced clean through 129's upraised forearm. Mori thought it was over, that 129 was done. Then blood streamed from the Kaiin's ears, ands he his next swing was blind, missing 129's head by a hair. Disoriented by the ultrasound, the Kaiin staggered around the room, striking out wildly. In his wild thrashing, he nearly decapitated one of the Qah and deeply slashed the other's abdomen. The Watchers stopped screaming only when the Kaiin fell to the floor, convulsing.

* * *

The Circle lasted well into the afternoon. The tribe had allowed the hunting party to enter the caves, but not the other tribe. There had been a great deal of excitement when the lookouts first spotted the other tribe, but this was soon replaced by anxiety about food supplies. How much did the other tribe have with them? If it wasn't much, would the long-term stores be enough to last the winter?

At first, the tribe hadn't wanted to make a decision without Tian, who had been the prime advocate for uniting with the other tribes in the caves. When Tian heard this she was ready to shout at them, appalled by their docility and abdication of responsibility, their need for a decision-maker, a leader. This upset her even more than the danger to which their behavior had subjected the other tribe.

In her absence, while out with the hunting party, they'd turned to Grashin. Grashin and his small cohort of elders had talked at length in the Circle about the dangers of the Qah. Grashin had also spoken on the tribe's history and the Way, arguing that the tribe was acting justly in refusing access when they were faced with immediate peril. He said they'd been manipulated by Tian into inviting the other tribes, and that they shouldn't be bound by a decision made under duress. But several members of the tribe had blocked his motion to send the other tribe away. Likewise, Grashin and his followers had blocked motions to honor the tribe's invitation and allow the other tribe in. The deadlock had lasted for hours.

Now that Tian and the rest of the hunting party were back, the tribe called another Circle. They were still deadlocked. Every new motion was blocked, and the decision about the tribe outside in limbo.

Tian was astonished at how quickly many of her brothers and sisters had reverted back into their insularity, at their willingness to acquiesce to Grashin. Most of those at the Circle knew or were related in some way to those in the other tribe, yet they were still seriously considering leaving them outside or sending them back into the forest for the Qah to hunt down.

Erkan drew her aside during another long harangue.

"They feel vulnerable, Tian. I told you that. Forgive them."

"Bah!" Tian spluttered. "Mori was right. The Way is old fashioned, useless to us. You see how easily they manipulate it for their own ends, to save their own skins," she said, pointing at Grashin's clique. "We've been gone for one nightfall, and they're already spinning their tales. The Way is stupid. A fairytale."

"No. Like I said yesterday, we've lived by it for generations—"

"No, you listen. I know what they're doing here; this whole system is a bunch of lies and... What do you know, anyway? I've seen the histories, I've spoken to a Watcher, I've been inside the silos. What would you know about it, about anything? You're just as ignorant as they are."

Erkan reeled back. Tian stared at him, unrepentant.

"What are you really angry about, Tian? That the tribe out there is in danger," he said, pointing to the barricade, "or that the tribe in here aren't doing what you want them to do?"

He turned and walked away, out of the cave, before she could answer. Tian watched him for a moment. She didn't want to think about what Erkan had just said. She allowed the speaker a few seconds longer before she stood up and began shouting again, drowning out whatever he was trying to say.

Outside, Erkan sat apart from the other tribe, smoking in silence. He took long draughts from his pipe, savoring the thick, aromatic smoke that engulfed him.

"You shouldn't draw so fast. The yusha will get too hot. It impairs the flavor." Yehla sat down next to him, crossing his bony legs. "This stone is cold. You should come sit with us."

"I'm not sure I'd be welcome," Erkan said with a sad smile.

"Why? Oh, but of course you would. Many of them understand what is going on. They certainly don't hold it against you personally. But between you and me, the longer we're out here, the easier the Qah will have finding this place." He winked at Erkan.

"It's terrible in there. I haven't seen them talk to each like that for, well, ever. They're just shouting at one another, calling each other egoists, traitors. I think what happened at the silo made them... they"ve all forgotten the Way, brother."

"The Way is sometimes complicated. How is Tian?" asked Yehla.

"She's the loudest. Ever since she met that Watcher she's been saying things, horrible things about the tribes, about our ways. Even about me."

Yehla sighed. It was a clear, chilly afternoon, and the forest stretched out below them for kilometers. The moons were beginning to rise, their pitted surfaces bright even in the late afternoon light.

"She says that the Watchers are from the stars. She says our ancestors are the same, and that we used to live up there," Erkan said, nodding looking upwards. "Do you believe that?"

"Tian always did have an imagination. Who knows? I've seen some of the histories, some of it doesn't really make a lot of sense to me. I don't think it really matters anyway. What matters is what is happening right now, right here. Still...Tian..."

They said nothing for a while, each occasionally pulling on their pipes or fidgeting on the cold, hard ground.

"Before I forget. Here," Yehla said, offering Erkan a small beaded bracelet. "I never returned your greeting earlier."

Erkan took the pipe from his mouth and examined the gift.

"Thank you, brother," he said, slipping it over his knuckles.

"Not everyone has forgotten the Way," Yehla said, with another wink.

CHAPTER 2

129 sat on the table while Mori ran the Panacea over the stump of its arm. The Panacea could only repair tissue damage, and 129 would need days in the medical bay at another silo to generate another arm; the bay at this silo was severely damaged. They hadn't been able to get the AI back online, either.

They discussed killing the Kaiin. Neither of them felt comfortable about killing their captive in cold blood, even though the crazed Kaiin had maimed both of them, Mori perhaps fatally. In the end, they couldn't bring themselves to do it. Instead, 129 injected him with a coma-inducing sedative and tied him to a pillar.

"They'll come looking for that Kaiin, if he hasn't called for help already," said Mori after they finished securing the restraints.

"Affirmative. No other course of action presents itself at this time, Mori."

129's complete sentence, and its addressing Mori by Tian's nickname, made Mori do a double take. With the infosphere down, and unable to use the proxisphere, Mori had no idea what 129 was actually thinking, whether 129 was being serious, attempting levity, was in shock from the assault, or was passing judgment on Mori's relationship with Tian.

"Is there any way we can get my neural network back online?" Mori asked. "I'm feeling lost without it."

"Perhaps. But dangerous. Primary and secondary energy cells damaged, emergency functions keeping you alive. Barely Dangerous to reboot without endangering vital systems."

"We need to discuss this, and I can't do it by talking," Mori said. "There is too much to be said, and too little time."

"Affirmative. Request: lean down, will attempt direct link."

Mori did as 129 asked, and felt a burning in the back of its head as 129 placed its arm on the back of Mori's neck, establishing a physical link between their neural implants, patching into Mori's damaged biowareneural network manually.

"Bandwidth still low. What is your status?" asked Mori.

"Mild shock, significant damage to lungs and eardrums from auditory distress. Panacea sufficient to repair."

"You must have been shouting louder than I was then, 129."

"Yes. I was experiencing physical trauma at the time."

Mori looked at 129 again. It appeared to be joking.

There was a sudden, blinding light; they were connected, the familiar rush of emotions and thoughts swirling around their heads.

"What now?" asked Mori.

"You require urgent medical care. Suggest travel to silo G22."

It was refreshing to hear 129 like this, to communicate properly again after being so long without the infosphere.

"What about the tribes? If the Kaiins and Qah know where they are, they'll kill them all."

129's reply approximated a curt shake of the head.

"Look, 129, I can't let anything happen to them. I know I crossed the line, I shouldn't have breached the agreement, but it's too late now. If I don't help them, I couldn't live with myself. I can't see Tian end up..." Mori winced with pain.

"The downloaded memories indicate you fear that news of Qah violence might spread to the Confederation," 129 sent. "As I said earlier, that seems a reasonable prediction given recent events and knowing the Kaiins are here. However, I do not see why that is a concern."

Mori frowned. "There will be some in the Confederation who will see how the Qah have evolved into a hierarchical and violent tribe as a justification for greater secrecy and military escalation. You know that. There are some who have been clamoring for for borders and centralization. I've even heard that there is a fringe group demanding the creation of a strong political authority as a temporary emergency measure. It would be devastating if the Confederation found out about the Qah uprising. It would justify all of that."

129 frowned. "I am not sure I follow your reasoning. Just because we have identified the likely course of events, and perhaps the Kaiins' motivation for instigating the violence, it does not mean that the Confederation will react in the way that you suggest. But again, why do you care, even if they did?"

"*What!?*" sent Mori.

"Why do you care how the news is received in the Confederation? Our mission here is to observe. No more."

THE WATCHER ♦ 171

Mori swallowed, the shooting pain making it difficult to con-
centrate on the fast exchange. "It's clear that the Kaiins have
made contact and contaminated the tribes with their ideologies
and technologies, perhaps many seasons ago. It only took one
tribe, living in relative hardship, marginalized from the wider
continental community to welcome the strangers and their
weaponry, and kill their own people. If it can happen here, it
could happen anywhere in the Confederation."

"I disagree," sent 129. "The Kaiins only stoked the fire under
what was already a hot situation, and the Qah might have struck
against the southern forest tribes and their quasi-religious, ossi-
fied way of life even without them."

"Exactly. Don't you see? If the Qah were always going to
act like this, then the Kaiins would have been right all along.
It would be a huge victory for them. Besides, this world offers
them a backdoor, a stepping stone into Confederation space.
Even if the propaganda victory of the tribes descending into
violence doesn't splinter the Confederation, the planet itself
will be hostage to the Kaiins."

129 emitted a burst of emotion. "You don't give the Confederation enough credit. It doesn't follow that an upsurge in
violence here undermines the foundations of our entire civilization, or tells us something we didn't already know about
humanoid civilization. The Qah simply demonstrate that humans can behave in a manner similar to the dead civilization
we found the remnants of in orbit, and, latterly, the Kaiins, in
extreme situations. The war proved that long ago."

"What has the war got to do with the Qah?" Mori sent.

"A hundred orbits ago almost no one believed the Confederation would ever need to fight to protect its values, let alone its
people. Now huge ships fitted with advanced weaponry patrol
every population hub, and heavily armed militias are mobilized
across Confederation space. Do you really think the events oc-
curring here involving a few thousand settlers will undermine a
civilization, a culture, that has existed for millennia?"

"Have you not accessed the recent reports on the Kaiins, on the war?" Mori transmitted.

"Of course I have," snapped 129.

"Well you know what they're capable of. They know our reluctance to authorize military operations, especially when there might be loss of civilian life. They exploit this."

"What is your point? I know the history of the conflict." 129 sent a databurst to Mori, a summary of the major battles, assassinations and acts of terror of the long war, as if to prove it.

"My point is that the Kaiins would have no qualms about doing the same here. The thought of Kaiinish cities here, on this pristine world—doesn't it horrify you? We know they will stop at nothing. They have no boundaries. They will destroy the ecosystem, pollute the atmosphere, and probably wipe out the sentient marine life for sport. Even if you're right, and the Confederation isn't thrown onto turmoil by news of the Qah violence, the loss of this world to the Kaiins... I cannot bear it, 129."

"So it is the loss of life, rather than a concern for Confederation values or wider strategic worries that troubles you now?"

Mori winced again. "Not just a loss of life. I've seen that before. But this is different. It's a complete loss of a way of life, something that is worth protecting against the Qah and the Kaiins. We can't just stand by and hide behind the settlement agreement. These tribes deserve protection. They are innocent. This is not their war."

129 was quiet for a moment. Mori could feel 129's mind working, contemplating Mori's words.

"Perhaps you are right."

With that, 129 broke the link. They had been connected for just seconds. 129 rose and went into one of the corridors. It returned a moment later with a small satchel, offering it to Mori.

"Medical supplies. Basic analgesics." 129's voice was strange again, distant, devoid of nuance. "Travel to G22. Make contact with Confederation with working emergency ansible. I will go to caves and warn the tribes, as you wish."

Mori shook its head. "No, 129, I can't let you go alone—"

"There is no alternative. G22 is ten days travel. Unlikely to last much longer than that in your condition. Winter caves at least fifteen days at sprint, probably longer. No other alternative. Request: do not worry about Confederation. Knowledge of Kaiinish presence in this sector important, but do not worry about propaganda nonsense. Confederation: stronger than you think. War changed them. Confederation no longer so naïve as once were. Grown resilient, adapted."

"Thank you, 129." Mori looked at 129, noticing again the extent of its burns. "But wait, no. You are injured too, 129. Come with me to G22, then we'll go to the caves together."

"Negative. The Qah and the Kaiins will move to destroy all the tribes when this one fails to report," said 129, gesturing toward the bound Kaiin, "if they haven't begun already."

Mori frowned. Mori wasn't sure it could make the trip to the other silo, let alone a long trek through the forest to the caves. But to leave Tian, to leave 129 alone...

"I will be vigilant, Mori. Request: depart." 129 turned to go.

"Wait, 129. Take this." Mori, picked up the coilgun from the floor where the Kaiin had dropped it. "It will slow you down, but if the Qah are already there you'll need it."

129 looked down at the gun, its remaining black hand taking it from Mori hesitantly. Then, with a nod, it slung the gun over its shoulder and walked out of the room, giving a final glance 129 gave to one corner where the headless body of AO77 lay covered by a bloody sheet. Mori hadn't noticed it before, and a lump formed in its throat as it watched 129 momentarily pause before heading down one of the dark corridors, toward the winter caves, and Tian.

* * *

The shuttle touched down with a discernible bump. Its occupants stepped out into a clearing, met by a faint breeze and the smell of burnt grass. The shuttle engines powered down.

The surrounding trees rocked in the wind. The creak and rustle of living things was strange after so long on the transport. They stood motionless listening to the alien sounds.

It was the first time Mori had ever been outside without a suit on, the first time it had ever seen a tree, breathed anything but recycled air, or seen the sky through anything but a visor or a dome. Mori was thrilled, and could see the experience was having a similar effect on the others. They'd all spent thousands of hours in simulators, but knowing that this was authentic, not a trick by an AI, was overwhelming. Mori wiggled its toes in the muddy ground, felt the tug of the unfamiliar gravity, squinted in the alien light that seemed to give everything a greenish hue.

The forest was surprising, too. For twenty meters there was nothing but short grass, and then a seemingly impenetrable wall of brush and trees burst from the ground. Mori switched wavelengths, marveling at how much life was behind that wall, how compact and interwoven it all was. It was like nothing on Namir or the other two planets it had visited. This was too real, too unmanaged, too untouched. Too wild.

The proxisphere was momentarily quiet as they stood and looked, but it was soon again active as the minds around Mori tested the unfamiliar planetary infosphere, probing for hotspots and synchronizing with it. This took most of their neural processing capacity, so Mori and the others just stood, staring in wonder at the forest while the links were established.

A thrill of excitement passed through Mori. *I'm finally here.* After all the orbits, after all the obstacles and frustration, after it looked like the whole program might be shut down when the Namir facility was opened to scrutiny, Mori had made it. Out of the hundred or so genetically altered children liberated from the facility, sixty-three had chosen to make this final journey, the last candidates to join the now autonomous DSE program on Dodona. They were free to live out their lives as they were meant to be lived. To study the tribes in this paradise. They would be the last. There would be no more Watchers coming.

They were joining the hundred anthropologists already here, sent in two previous waves by the DSE. A Confederation committee had given them a mandate to carry on the program until the last of them left or died. After that, the Dodonan observations would be scaled back and automated.

Knowing that they might be the last outsiders to step on this world for thousands, perhaps tens of thousands, of orbits gave this moment extra poignancy. Not only was this the culmination of all of their training, they were the last of their kind. They felt both pride and sorrow.

The synchronization completed. They blinked and looked around as if awaking from a trance, the full capacity of their neural processors reasserting itself in a split second. Then they went into action.

There wasn't much to unload from the shuttle. The largest thing aboard was a replacement medical bay for one of the northern silos, but the shuttle would drop that off later. Besides a few small pieces of equipment, the anthropologists had little to carry. They were in a remote area hundreds of kilometers from any of the tribes. This was standard DSE practice to ensure that newly transferred Watchers could acclimatize without fear of disturbing the locals. That some of them were barely out of early childhood was an even greater reason for such caution. They'd disperse to the silos scattered across the continent, where they'd spend time catching up on local tribes' developments before going into the field.

For now, though, they had their freedom, and the long-awaited opportunity to stretch their legs on this lush planet. There were smiles and a good deal of nervous energy as they approached the dark forest. If anyone from the tribes had stumbled upon the scene, they would have been startled, but perhaps a bit amused, at the sight of so many naked, fearsome-looking monsters hovering nervously at the edge of the forest. With a final chattering on the infosphere and some more exchanged glances, they stepped into trees.

Mori was among the last to leave. The butterflies in its stomach were almost unbearable. With one last look back at the shuttle, and with a small frown at the four scorch marks below its raised frame, Mori turned and strode after the others, the forest engulfing its tall black body.

Mori was home.

* * *

Mori awoke feeling faint and nauseated. It had passed out shortly after 129 left, the blood loss too much for its struggling bioware to compensate for. It tried to stand, but its head spun violently and it lurched towards a chair, grasping it for balance. Mori hadn't examined the wound in its abdomen properly yet, but knew that it was probably fatal. 129 had told Mori as much, and Mori didn't hold much hope of reaching the other silo alone; it only hoped that 129 would reach Tian in time. But it might be able to get the AI operational and, perhaps the medical bay...

A laugh startled Mori, and it fell to the floor. It was the Kaiin. His mask removed, his chin and beard dripping with blood, he wore a maniacal grin on his face. He had somehow managed to slip from his restraints.

"You should have given me a bit more of your sedative, Watcher," he said. He laughed again. "So, they're all hiding in the mountain caves. How convenient."

Mori watched in horror as the Kaiin bought his wrist up to his mouth and spoke guttural words into what had to be a transmitter.

"Yes, you definitely should have killed me, you cowards. Now all your precious test subjects are going to end up roasting on a Qah fire."

Mori dry retched, a violent lurch convulsing its entire body.

"You are a weak species. But some of you can be trained fairly well," the Kaiin said, pointing to the two Qahs. "Now I'll finish what I started. My inner ears are shattered, and you can scream all you like this time. I won't even hear it."

The Kaiin lied. Mori screamed and the Kaiin staggered and fell to his knees. Then he lurched toward his blade next to the decapitated Qah.

The last thing the Mori saw was the glint of the steel, its razor edge cutting through the air as it descended toward Mori"s face.

* * *

Tian awoke with a start. The sleeping furs were empty, the other pillow cold. She rose, brushing sleep from her eyes. The smell of a fire prickled her nostrils, the sweet aroma of yusha lingering in the hut, the sound of soft snoring barely audible over the morning birdsong.

"Priash?" Tian whispered. Someone mumbled a complaint at the disturbance. "Priash?" she whispered again, a little louder. This time a shoe came flying across the room toward her. Getting the hint, she clambered out of bed, the chilly air making her shiver. She dressed quickly and tiptoed out of the hut as quietly as she could.

Outside, the village was empty. It was still dark, the first light from the approaching dawn in the east, the earliest birds already singing. Neither of the moons were out, and it took a little time for her eyes to adjust to the dim light. Only the embers of the previous night's fire remained. She walked to the kitchen and found some shelled nuts. She ate them hungrily, throwing a few to the braver birds who had ventured down to the kitchen to investigate the early riser.

Her hunger satisfied, she wandered over to the stables in the morning twilight. Nimsha'h trotted over and rubbed her nose against Tian's shoulder, knowing she could expect a treat.

"She must have spent the rest of the night with Yuri, the little traitor," Tian said to Nimsha'h. She was more than a little hurt that Priash had left to lie with someone else after her, something she had never done before.

Nimsha'h nuzzled her, and soon got the piece of dried fruit she was expecting.

"The other horses must get jealous, Nimsha'h," said Tian, patting her on the nose. "I should stop giving you treats. You'll get fat and have to stay home when I go out hunting. I'll still love you though, Tian said, smiling at the horse, who was nuzzling her for more fruit.

She heard a noise from the forest, the snap of a twig and the rustling of leaves. She stopped smiling. One of the boys said he had seen a lone wolf a few kilometers to the south of the village, and they had sent parties out in search of the predator, who might easily take one of the smaller children or a foal if they strayed too far from the safety of the camp.

The dogs were silent. Nimsha'h's ears flicked back at the noise, but she didn't seem perturbed. Even so, Tian remained quiet, wondering who or what might be out in the forest so early.

She ducked behind Nimsha'h just as a figure stepped out of the trees. She glimpsed Grashin's unmistakable gait when she peered over Nimsha'h's back.

Grashin? What was that old fool doing wandering around at night? She smiled at the thought of him being taken by the wolf. Then she heard a voice that froze her blood.

"Show it to me. You promised."

"Quiet! I can't show you now, everyone will be getting up soon."

"I did what you asked. Now show it to me," said the voice, getting louder.

"Shut up now or you'll never see it, child."

"No, show it to me now, or I'll scream."

"If you scream, Tian will find out."

Tian took a sharp breath. The voices went quiet for a few seconds, then Grashin resumed.

"I'm sure she'd understand. Going down on your knees for the old shitstool just for a peek at some old books and knowledge from the ancients. She'll be fine with it, I'm sure."

Tian gripped Nimsha'h hard, the horse's ears alert now, its posture more upright, sensing Tian's tension.

"Maybe we'll come out again tomorrow morning, and I might show you something," Grashin hissed. "If we don't, it would be a shame if Tian found out."

"You promised, you promised..." the voice said, meekly.

"Stupid girl."

Tian heard the old man shuffle away. After some time, she risked a glance. Priash sat in the darkness, her head in her hands, her hair and back covered in leaves and twigs, weeping silently, her shoulders heaving. This was why she'd given up so easily at the Circle after demanding the library be opened up. She'd cut a deal with Grashin. *Grashin!*

Tian silently backed away from Nimsha'h. Sthe she circled around through the woods to the sleeping quarters. No one else was awake, and the village was quiet, the sky still only hinting at dawn. She crept into the hut and climbed into the cold bed, pulling the blankets all the way over her head. She bit down hard on her knuckles.

After a few minutes, she heard someone walking into the hut. The blankets lifted gently and a gust of chilly air hit Tian's bare legs. Priash slipped quietly in beside her, her cold feet brushing against Tian's legs under the thick blankets. Tian pulled them away, and curled up, not wanting to give herself away and not wanting to touch Priash. She heard Priash sigh and roll over.

Neither of them slept, and neither said a word when they rose. But every morning after that, Tian would wake before dawn to an empty bed.

Two weeks later Priash was dead.

Chapter 3

Tian slept poorly the night after she returned from the hunt. Grashin had regained much of his confidence now that he was back in the winter caves with his library, and had been strident in his arguments against allowing the other tribe entry.

The next morning they were back at it. Tian knew that the longer the meeting went on, the more likely Grashin and his cronies would concede, but they wouldn't give up without a fight. Gone was his pleasant, bumbling demeanor; the Circle saw him in full force. They saw the Grashin that Tian had been trying to warn them about for so long. Still, he managed to keep the meeting deadlocked for two days, and Tian had no idea what would happen when another tribe arrived seeking shelter.

Fighting Grashin was debilitating. His arguments were intricate, complicated, and often supported by direct quotations from the Way that the tribe recognised from his many stories. Grashin knew when to appeal to emotion, to talk about the dead, to talk about the old ways, and how to press home his advantage when a speaker was tired or when a proposal became long-winded or confused.

Tian hadn't been alone in fighting him in the Ccircle, but she had shouldered most of the burden in refuting his claims. All the while Yehla and the other tribe sat outside, completely unprotected from the Qah. Grashin had the situation in hand. That was, until Tian demanded to see the library.

"Show me where it says that, Grashin," she interrupted him. Etiquette in the Circle had broken down hours before.

Grashin faltered. He'd gotten carried away discussing a specific maxim that the Way supposedly laid out concerning the treatment of the sick in times of famine.

"You question Grashin's integrity?" asked Bal. Grashin threw him a quick scowl, not wanting to be sidetracked by a debate about his character.

Grashin thundered at him, "Don't interrupt! The obligation to care for the moderately sick is clearly distinct from the practice of mutual aid. The duty of rescue simply doesn't apply to those outside the tribe who are not in immediate danger, which those outside clearly are not. Therefore we are under no obligation to render them hospitality, even assuming that doing so might or might not contradict the duty we have to ourselves of self-protection and the preservation of the Way."

Haroon replied, "You are going around in circles. First you say we don't have to help them because they're not in any danger, and then you say we can't help them because we might endanger ourselves by doing so. You're leading us around in circles."

Grashin allowed himself a small smile, pleased that he'd been able to steer the debate back into a convoluted discussion of ethics, where he could muddy the water, and not the library or his personal integrity.

"Not at all. I'm simply reporting what the Way says—" he broke off, realizing he was opening himself up again to interruption from Tian. "The duties are complex, but must be adhered to even in times of crisis. They are the only way our society can continue to function in accordance with the Way."

Tian stood up again. Grashin continued more loudly, hoping to drown out anything she might say.

"If we assume then that our duties under the mutual aid principle are thus negated by the fact the tribe outside are in no immediate danger, we are thus under no moral duty of rescue and, instead, have a moral duty of self-protection, then, as it is written, specifically concerning the responsibilities laid out under the provisos for protecting against banditry, we are impelled to withdraw..."

Tian snorted with contempt at the nonsensical spiel. "Show

us where these things are written down, show us the library, the complete library, Grashin. If you can't or won't, what you're saying is just boarshit and we'll ignore it. If you can show us where it says that we should abandon our friends to be butchered, then we cannot live the Way any longer. Make your choice, Grashin. Show us where it says that, or allow them entry."

Grashin frowned. "You dare to question the Way? … Fine, allow them entry. But there will be consequences." He waved away a few objections and walked away toward his library.

They ate well that night, the cave filled with laughter and shouts from the smaller children. The huge barrier that blocked the entrance and their bolstered numbers gave them a feeling of security; the anger and outbursts were gone, and in their place big appetites and triumphant dancing. The drums played well into the night, and the fires were mere embers when the last revelers made their way to the beds.

The next morning Tian awoke exhausted, the Panacea gone from her belt. At first she thought she might have left it somewhere in all the excitement and drinking last night. But no. She knew she hadn't smoked that much yusha and could clearly remember everything about the night. She searched through the blankets. Suddenly she had a thought. *Grashin*. He had abruptly given up last night. Too easily. She glanced across the cave to where Grashin usually slept. He sat on a thick blanket, looking at her. He turned away, pretending to look for something in one of the small bags that lay around him, but Tian knew he had been watching her. How dare he! The familiar rage boiled over. She leapt up, determined to confront him and take back the Panacea.

A hand caught her by the shoulder. She turned around, expecting Erkan, ready to snap at him. Instead she saw Yehla, a concerned look on his face.

"Come with me, Tian," he said, quietly. A few others had

turned to look at her, wondering what the commotion was about. When they saw Yehla intervene, they turned away, their instinct for peaceful coexistence, honed by years of communal living, being far greater than their curiosity.

Tian started to protest, but Yehla gave her a look that brooked no response other than to follow him meekly into one of the narrow passageways. The stone was cold on her bare feet. She had barely had time to dress before noticing the small device was missing, and she was beginning to regret her haste.

"You've developed quite a temper," said Yehla. He sat down on a small ledge jutting from the wall, pushing the stub of a candle to one side to make room for his narrow frame.

"You're no longer the meek young girl I remember, who would turn pink whenever she was asked to speak in the Circle."

Tian stood impatiently, but didn't dare say anything in case she would regret it later. She clenched her fists tightly, a burning sensation radiating from where her nails dug into her palms.

"Erkan told me a bit about what has been going on with Grashin, and the rest I heard about last night. It sounds like you had quite a fight over us in the Circle." He paused to look at her. "Has this been going on for a long time?"

Tian nodded, still not trusting her tongue.

"Since Priash?"

Tian turned away from him toward the wall Neither said anything as Yehla slowly packed his pipe with more yusha.

He finished, rose, and said "Come. Let's go for a walk. I need some fresh air."

Yehla walked away, leaving Tian to follow. With one last look down the corridor toward the sleeping cave, she turned and followed him, cursing how young he made her feel.

They wandered down the narrow passages, Yehla's pipe leaving a trail of thick, aromatic smoke in their wake, heading for one of the two smaller entrances that hadn't been blocked. Tian didn't like that they were still open. Still, the tribe wasn't taking any chances; both entrances were very narrow, had steep dropoffs, and the tribe could block them in a matter of minutes if the Qah attacked. At least that was what Tian hoped.

They walked silently for about ten minutes, single file, Yehla taking a leisurely pace. The passage became narrower and more more winding, and a faint breeze and a steep decline signaled that they were nearing the exit.

They clambered out of the opening and then down a steep path to a ledge from where they could just see the main cave entrance below them. The morning was chilly, and Tian regretted again her lack of suitable footwear. The first snow was evident on the taller peaks, and there was a stiff breeze.

They silently contemplated one another for few moments. They had the same eyes and cheekbones, but Tian was a few shades darker than Yehla. Everyone assumed that Yehla was her bloodfather, but it didn't really matter to anyone, and Yehla and Tian had never spoken about it. He had left the tribe when she was about forty-five seasons old, soon after the incident at the silo where he'd been forced to kill the bandits. He had since traveled widely with the southern tribes, and they had only seen one another once in the caves since that incident.

"Tell me what happened with Priash."

Tian sighed. She didn't want to be out here, with Yehla, let alone talking about Priash. She wanted to get the Panacea back. She felt strangely attached to it, even though it wasn't hers to begin with. She realized that she was being childish about it, even an egoist, but she didn't care. Mori had given it to her. It was from the Confederation, from another world. She should be getting it back, not talking to this old man about her dead lover.

She tried to say as much, rising to make her way back into the caves. Yehla put his hand on her shoulder, stopping her.

"Sit, Tian. She knew about the histories, didn't she? About what Grashin and the others have been hiding all these seasons?"

Tian sat down heavily. She managed a nod.

"Not many of the elders know what's been going on, but

some of us do. You have to understand, it started long before Grashin was even born."

Tian didn't fully understand what Yehla was telling, but she kept quiet.

"Things had been getting bad. Tribes were beginning to fracture, they had lost a lot of the hatred toward the Confederation, lost a lot of the knowledge of why it was so bad. So *evil*. There was talk about planting crops, about permanent settlements. There had even been some violence, too; one tribe stole some horses from another. A small group even walked into a silo and asked to return to the Confederation. Most of the people still knew the stories the original settlers had told them about the Confederation, and for some of them it began to sound a lot more attractive than what they saw as the tedium and hardship of living in the forest. Where the original settlers saw Confederation culture and technology as morally wrong, their children's children were more forgiving. Admiring, even. They were wrong, of course. Something needed to be done, but they had almost nothing to guide them. They had the settlement agreement—I'm sure Priash told you about that—and a few battered old books that the settlers had bought with them, but nothing else."

"So they began to write new books," interrupted Tian, thinking of the vast corridors full of documents and parchments.

"Yes. But they didn't even know what the books they still had really meant. Most of what was left was just fragments, and no one knows what the Way actually was. I'm not even sure what it was called originally. The books talked of cities and technology and science, and our ancestors were here living in huts in the forest and on the plains. It was completely alien. So they improvised. They interpreted. They kept a lot of the language, and used some of the old phrases, and they began writing a new Way, one that we could actually fit our lives around here. They kept the parts that seemed to make sense, like the consensus Circles, and left out the rest. The confusing bits."

"So they made everyone believe the Watchers were evil, and erased all the records about the settlers and the Confederation and the original Way and replaced it with their own version?" asked Tian bitterly. "And Grashin is just repeating the lie."

"No," protested Yehla. "You must understand. Our entire way of life was in danger of collapse. They were—and still are—trying to protect what we have here, this paradise, this freedom. They thought it was worth it. I agree with them, Tian. This is the way we're meant to live, the way we're born to live. Yes, it might be hard sometimes. But I know we're not meant to live the way the Watchers do, the way they do in the Confederation. That isn't a life that I want to live, as part of some hive, where no one's voice means a damn thing over all that noise."

Tian lit up. "But they have tools that can mend wounds! Produce heat and light and fire whenever they need it! Make as much food and medicine and—"

"No! That isn't any way to live, Tian. Look out there," he said, with a sweeping gesture to the forest below. "This is our home. We hunt here, we live here, we love here, we die here. We have the tribes and nature. We have everything we ever need. We don't need space ships or machines or people whispering in our minds to be happy here. We have the Way, and that keeps us together. Keeps us alive."

Yehla's speech had moved her; it was easy to forget the things that she loved about these woods and the tribes, because of everything she was discovering about the past. But she wasn't going to give up that easily.

"We weren't supposed to need weapons, either." Tian couldn't help herself, and knew it was unfair to the old man. "The Way didn't stop that."

"You're right," Yehla said. "Our ancestors thought that if we followed the Way we'd never come to this. I think they were right, too. If the Qah followed the Way then they would never—"

"Why should they follow it anway? We made it up. Maybe they're shunned because they didn"t stick with our stupid set of rules," she said, remembering what Mori had told her. A lot of the cryptic things the Watcher had told her in the woods were beginning to make sense, now.

Yehla shook his head, frowning.

"Whatever you might say about how it started, the Way is not stupid. I bet if your Watcher were here now he'd agree with me. It might not be perfect, but it has lasted a long time, and it gives us good and just morals for the way we live here. Some of our recent interpretations might be mistaken..."

Tian pulled a face. "You say the Watcher would agree with the Way? Perhaps some of it. It said as much when I was with it. But it would never have agreed with the way it was created or about how we decide it applies. Mori would never have agreed that it was right to let Grashin alone have access to the histories and to change whatever he wants." Tian was fishing here, hoping to get a reaction from Yehla to confirm her suspicions. He flinched visibly, the accusation hitting home.

Tian went on, "He uses it for his own ends, and has done so for a long time. How many others down the seasons have done the same thing? We"re clinging to a bunch of old fairytales cooked up in secret, and we don't have a say in any of them, and we kick out or shun anyone who strays from the only path that we allow. They tried to kick me out when I proposed that we plant a few herbs. How long has that been forbidden? Why is it even against the Way? Because someone like Grashin didn't like it a hundred seasons ago? It doesn't make any sense. Don't try to defend it, Yehla."

He sighed. "I'm sorry, Tian. I"m sorry that you don't understand."

"I understand perfectly. Grashin and his friends have been growing herbs for seasons and seasons. Who knows what else they"re doing? I bet he's even changed some of the histories so if anyone looks the Way will say those herbs of his are fine. Maybe it'll say that leaving other tribes to be massacred is fine. Maybe—"

"The Way is *necessary*. Without it, we'd be lost. We would be machines, automatons; we would be slaves to civilization, to technology."

Something had changed in Yehla's voice. He was talking almost mechanically, as if reciting from a sacred text. "That Watcher lied to you. Their culture is dangerous. It is full of liars and bandits, full of polluters and egoists. They have no limits, no boundaries, no morals."

"Yehla, what are you talking about? What are you doing?"

Yehla had stood up, and had walked to the edge of the sheer cliff. He looked down at the forest far below.

"Come away from there!" she said, suddenly concerned.

"We've followed the Way for generations. It's true that we kicked out the Qah a few generations ago. They were dangerous. They'd abandoned the Way."

Tian gasped. Yehla had taken the Panacea out from his jacket and flung it down the cliff.

"No! What are you doing!?" shouted Tian, lunging toward the edge, catching a glimpse of the Panacea as it smashed against an outcrop of rocks. She slipped and barely caught herself from falling over the edge. "Yehla! Have you lost—"

"The Way doesn't apply to traitors. To those who encourage others to abandon the Way. Like *Priash*. Like *you*."

Yehla caught her by surprise, kicking her hard in the back of the knee, causing her to fall to the ground, twisting her ankle.

"See, Tian? Technology. It will destroy us. See what the Qah have become with it. See what *you* have become with it. You've only had it for a matter of days and you're ready to throw yourself off a mountain to keep it."

He kicked her again in the stomach. Bringing his leg up almost to his chest, he stamped down hard on Tian's head, catching her behind the jawline. She cried out in pain. Yehla aimed another hard kick to her back, and Tian could feel ribs snap. Dizzy, she flailed at him, but he easily avoided her blows, and kicked her twice more in her side.

Yehla stood over her, panting. Another figure stepped onto the ledge. She risked a glance, hoping desperately that it was Erkan, or Mori.

It was Grashin.

* * *

129 made good progress, despite the lack of its right forearm and the encumbrance of the Kaiinish weapon. It was fairly confident that it could outpace any pursuer. Watchers were designed for speed and stamina, both of which the Kaiin lacked in favor of brute strength.

It reached the mountains in good time, having stopped only for short rests. 129 had decided that if it beat the Qah to the caves, it would simply ask that they send out runners to any tribes that might be approaching to warn them off, and would hand over the coilgun to the most reasonable looking of the tribe, before returning to the nearest silo. 129 felt some discomfort at the prospect of interfering in the tribes' affairs, and especially at the idea of revealing itself, but knowledge of the Kaiinish threat diminished the feeling.

Something was troubling 129, though, something it had seen when it had downloaded Mori's memories. Mori had tried to suppress it, but during the short time that they were physically linked the memory kept resurfacing, however hard 129 tried to ignore it. Mori had strong emotional associations with it that had crossed over to 129, now, whenever it thought about Tian and her tribe. Feelings of guilt, of helplessness. 129 had so far managed to resist the urge to access these sensitive memories that Mori had tried so hard to hide, but it was becoming impossible, and they were starting to encroach on 129's other, conscious thoughts. 129 couldn't think about Tian without a prickly sensation emerging from this latent, unintended memory transfer. With a last twinge of regret, 129 let the nagging story play out.

129 had seen many orbits worth of feeds from other Watchers, but none had such a profound emotional effect as this one. It was always unsettling to see the world through another's eyes, even a specially trained, scientifically detached pair of eyes. There was always a residue of thought, of opinions, of feelings embedded in the feeds. Usually 129 could filter this out, leaving only the raw observational data.

But this time the emotion was too strong; 129 could not filter out this memory. It was as if 129 was there, living the memory as Mori had done, seeing the events play out from Mori's eyes. It forced 129 to sit down, to catch its breath.

The memory was just as vivid as the feelings tied up with it. Mori had retained every single detail of the recording, and 129 had to close its eyes to ensure it didn't lose its balance. 129 could feel the wind as if it were running over its own body, smell the odors of the forest, taste the meal Mori had just eaten, and hear Mori's thoughts as if they were its own.

It was a windy night, and Mori was following a small group of villagers as they struggled through the forest into the gale. They reached a valley with a small lake, and Mori circled around downwind of them when they settled in for the night. It wasn't clear to 129 when this recording was made. It had been stripped of all identifying metadata, and the stars were hidden by clouds, but 129 recognised a few of the faces from Tian's tribe and figured it was only a few seasons old.

Then 129 saw the girl, and felt the slight flutter deep in Mori as her face came into view, her hair wild in the wind. 129 knew the face immediately from the reports Mori had sent. Priash.

It looked like she was heading back into the forest. But instead of moving off as it should have done, following normal procedure, Mori remained in the trees, even though the girl was heading directly towards it. This was unsettling. Had Mori made contact with Priash? Was there something going on between them?

But the girl passed under the tree, close enough for Mori and 129 to see the details of her face in stark detail, but she didn't look up. Mori watched her go, heading back down the trail, its thoughts a confused tangle.

It was clear to 129 that Mori had unusual feelings for Priash, something that went beyond the usual feelings that Watchers developed toward the tribes they spent so long watching. This accounted for some of Mori's peculiar behavior in the silo, and towards Tian.

The playback continued, skipping ahead an hour. The wind hadn't abated, and Mori hadn't moved from its perch. Mori was semi-dozing. Not fully asleep, but still observing, its mind ticking over much more slowly than usual. 129 knew the feeling well. It was a sort of hibernation, essential for the long nights when the tribes were asleep and there was little to record.

Mori roused at a noise from the camp. 129 felt Mori attempt to amplify and filter the sounds to hear over the wind. A few minutes later a figure emerged from the camp on the path that Priash had taken. He was on horseback, and although his face was covered against the wind, Mori and 129 knew who it was. Grashin.

129 felt Mori's flood of memories about Grashin and Priash. The memories of Priash's muffled cries back in the forest around near the village before dawn. Mori hesitated, but not for long. It followed Grashin, carefully, at a distance.

Grashin soon came to where Priash had made a makeshift camp, by a large felled tree. Grashin's horse's ears began flicking around nervously. Mori stopped. When it was clear that the horse was just unnerved by the wind, Mori approached, settling into a tree above, and watched the scene play out.

"You can't just run off like that, child. We have an arrangement, remember?" Grashin's voice was loud, startling 129.

"I'd have been back before dawn," Priash replied.

"Of course you would. I hope you're not having second-thoughts, child? After all, in a few days time you'll be able to see the whole library. Just think about all those books you haven't read yet."

Priash attempted a smile, but her body language made it clear that she was deeply uncomfortable.

"What is it?" Grashin asked.

"Nothing. Only, are you . . . you promise you'll show me everything I asked for?"

Grashin removed his scarf and smiled his unpleasant grin. 129 could feel Mori's disgust rise up like bile.

"Of course. Like I said. You've kept your end of the agreement. I'll keep mine."

"What about the Way?"

Grashin"s smile faded at once. "What?"

"The Way. Will you show me that, too?"

"That wasn't part of our deal."

"No, bu—"

"Listen Priash. You've already caused enough trouble. Just be happy that you'll get to see your stupid herbalist books. Don't test my patience." Grashin approached her now and patted her on the head like he might a dog or an infant. "Just forget the Way, and be content with what you're getting. Not many your age get to see these books, and most never see them at all."

The horse was becoming increasingly nervous. Grashin turned to look at it, and Priash took the opportunity to pull her head away from his patronizing caress. He whirled back around. Mori could see the fury in his eyes.

"Now now, child," he said, grabbing her chin and squeezing it. "I think we should make up for your little unannounced departure before I go back." He pushed her to the ground.

She didn't resist.

129 felt something in Mori snap. Whatever it was, the sound of Priash's muffled sobs, the ripped belt, or the disgusting grunts coming from Grashin, Mori was unable to stop itself. Mori had no plan, no idea of what it would do. It started down the tree. But no sooner had Mori moved, than Priash opened her eyes. She was lying on her back looking straight up, Grashin banging away on top of her. She saw Mori. 129 felt the shame, felt the

anger, felt the despair in Priash's eyes. Mori shrank back at the look, but not before she flinched violently.

Grashin thought she was struggling. He hit her hard in the face. She pulled her hand up to her bloody noise, but accidentally caught Grashin as she did so, giving him a slight cuff behind the ear. This enraged him further. He hit her again, then again. He seemed to be enjoying it, and he began goading her, whispering into her ear.

"You don't really think I'm going to take you into the library, do you? You idiot child. When we get back I'm going to tell Tian all about this. Does she know about our dawn meetings?" He laughed at her whimpers. "You might have a hard time explaining them to her. She doesn't seem the brightest child."

Priash kneed him, causing him to roll off. He bellowed at her, this frail old man filled with strength by his lust and anger. She got up and started to stagger away, toward the trees. He caught her by the hair, threw her to the ground, and reached into his belt.

She looked up again at Mori as the knife went in. Mori heard her scream over the wind. Grashing stabbed her again, and again.

He stood up and looked down at Priash's dying body. "It is a shame; I thought I might get a couple more fucks out of you before I had to do this," he said.

She died with her eyes open, staring up at Mori.

Mori hadn't moved a muscle.

Tears filled 129's/Mori's eyes as it watched Grashin heave the body onto the horse. He scuffed dirt over Priash's blood on the ground, and scuffed some on his bloodied tunic before he led the horse around the area repeatedly. He went about it calmly, like he would any tenth day task, the anger and turmoil of a moment before erased in a heartbeat.

Mori remained motionless as Grashin finally left, taking Priash's body out into the deep forest.

Mori's guilt and grief made 129 feel physically sick, and it took a long time for 129 to recover after accessing the memory. But before 129 could even begin to try to process it, the infosphere burst into life. It was deafening after so long in silence. Massive quantities of data streamed through. 129 pinged Mori, hoping for verification that it had reached the silo and had made the distress call to the Confederation. There was no response. 129 promptly requested a trace of Mori, concerned that Mori might be lying out in the forest somewhere, desperately needing medical attention. The response came back quickly. Too quickly. Mori was still at the silo 129 had left.

With a horrible feeling in the pit of its stomach, 129 requested the feed.

Mori's body lay on the floor, its head split open. 129 turned off the feed in horror. It sent a burst of data to the Dodonan infosphere, including everything it knew about the Qah and the Kaiins, and requested an immediate emergency ansible broadcast. Two seconds later, 129 lost the connection.

129 took a deep breath and began the steep climb to the winter caves.

Chapter 4

"Just kick her over the edge. I'm not letting her ruin anything else," said Grashin. "Kick her over. The Qah could be here soon."

"You still plan to cut a deal with them?"

"Of course, what else is there to do? Our only choice is to deal with them, let them take the horses and a few slaves. Let them know we won't resist. We have to protect the library at all costs, Yehla. They mustn't get their hands on it, it would destroy our cultural heritage, destroy the Way. We'd descend into chaos."

Tian snorted, tasting blood in the back of her throat, but managed to say, "You seriously think they'll leave you alone, shitstool? They'll do what they did to the others. They'll massacre anyone that can't work or can't fuck."

Grashin aimed a half-hearted kick at her. His toe caught her on a fractured rib and her face screwed up in pain.

Yehla turned to Grashin. "Are you absolutely sure you can reason with them, especially if what she says about these aliens is true?"

"She's delusional. Since when do the Watchers help us? Come on, Yehla, be done with it. It's freezing out here."

Yehla stood staring at Grashin, motionless.

"Fine then, give that here." Yehla handed Grashin the Kaiinish weapon. Grashin fumbled with it. Tian gasped when she recognized it. She had forgotten all about it; Yehla must have taken it when he took the Panacea.

"Don't do this," said Tian.

"Oh shut up."

Tain snarled at them, "How are you going to explain this to the rest of them? You won't be able to cover this up, Erkan will know."

Grashin smirked. "It was a tragic accident. You stumbled over the edge after smoking too much yusha. And if that little shit Erkan starts making trouble, we can arrange for him to have an accident, too."

Grashin fiddled with the Kaiinish weapon. He smiled, a vicious, triumphant smile, as a light flashed on its stock. It was armed.

"Yehla, help me!" Tian screamed. Yehla looked at her contemptuously, and Grashin raised the weapon, but didn't fire immediately. He was clearly relishing tormenting her in her final moments.

Tian closed her eyes and thought of Priash.

There was a short whine, then an enormous blast shook the rocks. Tian flinched violently, expecting sudden pain. None came. Grashin was falling to the ground, a gaping, smoking hole in his abdomen, a look of complete bewilderment on his face. He began thrashing, clutching at the hole in his stomach.

The peculiar whine sounded again, and Tian froze as she saw a black figure emerge from the rock-face behind Grashin.

Yehla bent down toward Grashin's writhing body. Tian tried to gain her footing, but cried out and fell when she put weight on her twisted ankle.

"Mori!" she cried as she stumbled. Yehla turned around, following her gaze. He stared at the tall black figure for a moment, then at the weapon it held.

"Demand: surrender."

The loud, melodic voice made both Yehla and Tian jump.

"Mori?" asked Tian.

Yehla stared open mouthed at the huge Watcher as it approached him, at its horrible scarred face and frightful yellow eye.

Yehla turned and leapt from the cliff.

He landed on a rocky outcrop far below, his back snapping. Tian looked away. The Watcher approached Grashin's shuddering body, kicking the weapon he'd dropped away from him.

"Query: injured badly?"

"Mori? Oh, Mori! Your face! Your hand!" cried Tian, seeing the Watcher's injuries.

"Tian. Clarification: I am not Mori. I am AO129."

"What? Who— Where is Mori?" demanded Tian.

"Mori is dead. Convey emotion: sorrow."

Tian stared blankly at this alien creature before her, barely understanding it.

"What? Why are you speaking like that? What is happening? Oh, Mori! And Yehla!" Tian crumpled into a heap, the pain and the shock overwhelming her. "How could he…"

129 stood, saying nothing, unsure how to proceed. It felt nauseous again. The scene it had stumbled upon here had left it horribly conflicted. Seeing the girl, Tian, seeing what the elders were doing to her, hearing what they planned to do to the tribe, was too much; something had snapped. Whether it was Mori"s

memories, so fresh in 129's mind, or the sight of Mori's body in the silo all those kilometers away, or the overwhelming desire to protect this vulnerable girl that overrode years of genetically and emotionally suppressed empathy, 129 would never know. But the desire to act was so compelling that 129 had pulled the trigger.

Grashin thrashed and began a horrible, keening moan.

"Prognosis: death. Panacea ineffective. . . Probably deserves. Raped. Murdered Priash."

"*What!?*"

"Affirmative. Rape. Murder."

Tian understood. Even half-prone on the ground, she managed to kicked Grashin's wound as hard as she could with her one good foot. He screamed. She kicked again. He screamed and made a gagging noise, clutching at his guts, his hands slippery with blood. She felt a hand on her shoulder.

"Request: stop."

She shook the hand off and scrambled the two meters to the Kaiinish weapon that Grashin had dropped and 129 had kicked away. She pointed the weapon at Grashin's terrified eyes, her finger hovering over the trigger, her mind filled with memories: the countless Circles he'd manipulated; his egoizing; ilyup; whispered threats; the flood; and his and Yehla's revelations.

Then Tian remembered Priash's face. She pulled the trigger, and Grashin screamed no more.

129 had had a hand in taking one the man's life, and had caused another to end his own from sheer fright. 129 had interfered in the tribe's internal affairs, ignored its overriding moral imperative, all to save one girl. 129 suffered in that moment the intense pain Mori must have felt in the woods all those seasons ago when it saw Grashin rape and kill Priash.

And 129 understood.

129 crouched next to Tian, attempting to comfort her. "Tian, request . . . Please listen to me. I am sorry about Mori. Died try-

ing to save you and your tribe. Please, Tian, look at me."

Tian looked up, her face twisted with grief and anger.

"The Qah are coming here. With Kaiins. You leave the caves, spread out across the forest. Dangerous for you to all be in one place. They have strong weapons, many, like these. You not match. You must warn others, tell them—"

"Tian?" came a voice from behind them, Erkan's. 129 stood up to face the boy. Erkan took several steps back toward the cave at the sight of the monster.

"Request: go back inside. You need to leave caves. Qah are coming. Go tell everyone to leave, now."

"Tian? What is going on? Fuck! What happened to Grashin? What happened to *you*?" Erkan advanced towards 129, his fists clenched.

"Erkan, go. Grashin tried to kill me. The Watcheris saved me," said Tian.

"What? Wait, I don't understand, Tian. Come inside, explain what—"

"Command: Go! Gather supplies and leave caves, now! The Qah come!" bellowed 129, its voice a deep bass that Tian felt reverberate through the stone ledge they were standing on, the same horrifying expression on the Watcher's face as she'd seen on Mori's at the silo. She recoiled, and Erkan turned and fled into the caves.

"Sorry, Tian. I suspect the Qah come soon. The one who killed Mori may be close behind." 129 glanced around, half-expecting the Kaiin to jump out from behind a rock. How fast could a Kaiin travel? 129 didn't want to find out. It slung the coilgun over its back, and took out a Panacea from its belt, and placed it over Tian's swollen ankle.

129 was worried. It had already inflicted enough damage because of its and Mori's emotions, and needed to make sure Tian and Erkan warned the tribe without any more interference than was strictly necessary.

Tian was talking to herself under her breath, unable to look away from Grashin's corpse. "He killed Priash, Mori. He killed my Priash. That shitstool took her, they did things to her, and then killed her. I always knew. I always knew he lied to me, that he did it. I always thought Grashin gave her to the Qah, but to do that... I hate them all. I never want to see any of them again.

"Take me away Mori. I want to leave, I want to go to the Confederation with you. I hate this place. I hate these people and their *Way*. Take me to the Confederation, Mori. I want to see the infosphere and the cities and the stars and Priash again."

129 paused. Tian had stopped crying now, and was looking intently into 129's face.

"What about your brothers and sisters? They need you."

"No, they don't. I'm turning into one of *them*," she said, kicking Grashin's body. "If I go back in there now, they'll expect me to lead them. They'll want me to make the decisions. I'll turn into him, if I haven't already."

And Erkan?"

Tian's eyes shone with tears. The Panacea stopped flashing. 129 bought it up to Tian's face, touching her cheek gently with its long fingers.

"He doesn't need me. I'll never... After Priash... I can't stay here. Please, don't make me stay."

129 had no idea what to do. It was still half-expecting the Kaiin to appear at any second. It also knew that if it entered the caves with Tian, any chance at the tribe's returning to a normal existence was all but gone, if it wasn't already. And, like every Watcher, it knew that the settlement agreement stipulated that any member of the tribe that requested help, including repatriation to Confederation space, could not be refused assistance.

But the Kaiin needed to be stopped, now. That was clear.

"Tian, I am not Mori. I realize I look and sound like Mori, but I am not Mori. I am AO129. Mori is dead. I need you to understand that. Do you?" Tian nodded.

"I also need you to understand that, if you come with me, you'll probably never see your tribe again. Including Erkan. You can change your mind along the way, but once you leave this planet, you can never come back. Do you understand that?"

"Yes."

"Your tribe is in great peril. A Kaiin has tracked me here, probably. He killed Mori. If he gets here before the tribes leave, he'll kill many of them, maybe all. We need to stop him."

Tian nodded numbly.

"You understand? You can go to the Confederation, but we need to stop this Kaiin first. Hopefully, once we've done that, the tribes will should be scattered enough that the fleet will get here before the Qah track them all down."

"How do you know the Kaiin is coming here?" asked Tian.

129 looked at her, still not sure whether she was fully cognizant yet.

"I don't know. But I strongly suspect it. Now come, we must leave before Erkan returns."

129 hoisted the coilgun, resting it on the stump of its missing hand

"Let's go," Tian said, a cold look in her eyes.

* * *

Erkan evidently had succeeded. Gods knew what he had told them. That Tian had killed Grashin and Yehla? That he'd seen a monster? That the Qah were coming with powerful weapons? Maybe just the sight of Grashin's mangled body was enough.

Tian and 129 watched the tribes file out the caves' main entrance, and saw them send out runners on horseback, presumably to warn the other tribes to stay away. Tian nearly broke down when she recognized all those familiar figures walking out of the caves down into the trees, but when 129 raised an enquiring eyebrow at her she just frowned.

Erkan searched the mountain for hours, looking for Tian. The sun was setting when he headed off into the forest. He didn't look back.

When they were sure the tribes were gone, Tian and 129 entered through one of the side entrances. The caves were deserted. Fires still smoldered and dirty dishes lay scattered about. Tian grabbed a pair of shoes, some blankets, a small bag of smoked horsemeat, and a knife and a bow they'd overlooked in their haste to leave. Tian had the urge to go to the histories and burn them, but knew she couldn't waste the time.

129 hurried her outside, and they found a small cave that gave them a good view of the main entrance and the approach. The Kaiin, when he did come, would have difficulty sneaking up on them in the daylight and, 129 hoped, the thick cave walls would shelter them at night from any infrared spotting devices.

The infosphere crackled on three times while they were waiting, but it dropped out in less than a second, leaving 129 unable to establish more than a basic connection. Still, it gave 129 some hope. It would be far easier to coordinate a response to a Qah attack or Kaiinish incursion with the planetary infosphere operational.

They didn't talk while they waited. Tian was still nearly in shock, and 129 had no interest in talking when there was potentially a Kaiin around. 129 still had the coilgun and the Kaiin''s hand weapon. 129 had also taken the last four shields from the silo before it left, but the Kaiin might have taken the one from Mori's body if he was smart, and 129 had no reason to assume he wasn't. 129 gave two of the shields to Tian, explaining briefly how they worked. After that, they waited.

129 was startled by the Kaiin's brazenness. He had waited until morning, probably camped in the trees at the foot of the mountain. 129 watched him climb slowly, in full view, with no attempt at stealth.

129 had no wish to engage him inside the caves; the farther away he was, the better. 129 judged the coilgun to have an effective range of about fifty meters, and the hand weapon even less, so once they were closer 129 and Tian probably had a couple of

202 ♦ N<small>ICHOLAS</small> P. O<small>AKLEY</small>

shots before the Kaiin would be close enough to do real damage to them, assuming he had no weapon of his own beyond his sword.

As the Kaiin climbed the path to the cave entrance, 129 told Tian, "Stay hidden, up here. I'm going to try to get a shot at him before he goes into the cave. If he doesn't go down at first shot, run away." Grasping the coilgun in its hand, it snuck along a ledge to about thirty meters from the cave entrance, where it had a clear shot. 129 placed the unwieldy gun's barrel between two large rocks, that concealed 129's body and everything but the gun's muzzle. Then 129 waited.

The Kaiin climbed the final three or four hundred meters, to and stopped about a hundred meters from the cave entrance. He stood there motionless, scanning the entrance and the area around it.

Despite the cold 129 was dry mouthed and sweating, as the Kaiin remained motionless. When he started walking again, and was with forty meters of the cave entrance, 129 yelled, "Kaiin! Surrender!"

The Kaiin looked up, almost nonchalantly.

"Did they all leave? What a shame," his voice boomed.

Where did they—" he didn't bother to finish his sentence. Instead, he began running at full speed up the rocky path, his acceleration startling.

129 pressed the trigger of the coilgun, its whine barely audible over the Kaiin's battle cry. The Kaiin kept running, the shimmer and crackle of an energy shield forming and disappearing around him as it absorbed the blast. The gun whined again, and 129 fired again as the Kaiin was within ten meters of him. Again, the shield absorbed the blast.

The Kaiin was nearly in striking distance now, his blade raised to slash 129.

129 saw the Kaiin look up at the last second, just as Tian's arrow plunged through his shoulder. He roared, nearly losing his footing, but lurched toward 129 anyway, swinging wildly,

his blade striking bare rock and sending sparks flying. Another arrow hit the flailing warrior under his outstretched arm. He roared again as he landed, driving the arrow deeper into his side.

The Kaiin stumbled, blood pouring from his wounds. as 129 rolled away, grabbing the coil gun as it retreated. But then the Kaiin was up again, his combat augments fully kicking in; adrenaline pumped through his body, his heart beat ferociously, veins stood out on his arms and neck. He let out another deafening roar.

Tian loosed another arrow. It missed his head by centimeters.

The Kaiin grinned and turned on 129, who was desperately trying to scramble away and recharge the coilgun, the barrel burning its hand, red lights flashing on its display.

129 turned and fired just as the Kaiin raised his blade for the final blow.

This time there was no shimmer.

The Kaiin stopped dead, his entire shoulder and right arm blown away. The shield generator had finally run out of power. He collapsed to the ground with a thud, like a tree toppled by lightning. The glimmer in his terrifying eyes was already beginning to fade as Tian approached his still-twitching body. She pulled out the final arrow from her quiver, took a deep breath, and drew back the bowstring. She looked down at Mori's killer. The monster responsible for all of this, for the deaths of so many of her tribe. She released the arrow from point blank range into the Kaiin's open, bloody mouth

Long after the sun had set, they began descending toward the forest below. They didn't say anything at all as they began the trek to the nearest silo, each lost deep in their own thoughts.

* * *

"Are you still sure you want to leave this place, Tian?" 129 asked several days into their trek. Snow fell as the sun went down, the temperature creeping down low enough for the fragile flakes to begin forming patches on the forest floor. The infosphere had been flickering on and off all day, and 129 had managed to communicate a few times with the other Watchers, telling them that the Qah were heading to the caves.

Tian looked up at 129, seeing Mori for the thousandth time towering over her. She smiled.

"Yes, sister," she said. "I'm ready to leave."

PART V

CHAPTER 1

The ribbondrives disengaged with the slightest tremble, and the expeditionary fleet slid into orbit around the planet. The cruiser was the nearest thing the Confederation Navy had to a dedicated war vessel. Its three companions were former civilian ships retrofitted for battle.

The blue-green glow of Dodona was startling. Nobody in the fleet had ever seen another world so similar to the Confederation origin world.

They tried to establish contact with the planetary infosphere, to no avail. There was interference with the fleet's own communications, too. The source of the jamming became clear almost immediately. The Testa's sensors located it low orbit. Kaiinish. But just a single vessel.

The Testa's combat began to run simulations as the fleet's infosphere lit up with chatter.

"Is it a scout ship or war vessel?"

"The AI indicates a troop dropship."

"That means there's probably a Kaiinish force on the surface."

"Can it block the infosphere?"

"On the planet, yes. Within the fleet, probably not."

"It hasn't made any communications since we arrived, either to the surface or beyond."

"I suggest we try to make contact with them, however unlikely a reasonable response. They might have hostages on the surface."

"Or they might use the opportunity to take hostages. One of the AI recommendations is a surprise attack."

There was a surge of distaste across the fleet infosphere.

"It hasn't detected us?"

"The AI indicates that it hasn't. Its jamming must be interfering with its own detectors. It would have begun attacking if it had seen us."

"Against four warships with better shields and weapons?"

"Affirmative. The AI lists 322 examples of unprovoked Kaiinish attacks against heavy odds."

"Looks like this will be 323. The ship is moving out of orbit, coming toward us fast."

The AI cut in. Rather than explaining and discussing, it simply showed. The infosphere went quiet for a brief moment as the crew members processed the different scenarios.

"Consensus on scenario two?"

"Consensus," came the collective reply.

The Testa's weapons charged and fired, ripping into the rear of the Kaiinish vessel. It looked for a moment like the hostile ship would fly apart, but it didn't; the AI's calculations had been accurate. The Kaiinish ship began to tumble.

The smaller ships had fired simultaneously with the Testa, destroying the ship's weapons systems and both the communications and /jamming devices. The AI calculated several dozen Kaiinish deaths.

"How long have the rest got?"

"Not more than a few hours. Sensors indicate a significant loss of internal temperature, and hull breaches on several levels."

"Volunteers for rescue?"

There were thirty.

"Can we further disable the crew?"

"One conscious Kaiin could take out five of us in such a confined space."

"AI indicates high probability of violent resistance to rescue."

The AI flashed a new series of scenarios. The first was simply destroying the Kaiinish vessel without attempting rescue. The second involved boarding, with potential heavy losses among the rescuers.

"Consensus on scenario one?"

"Consensus failed. Have the AI run different incursion strategies."

"Bots with sonic or gas weapons seem our best choice."

"Agreed."

"Preparing the medical bay for survivors. Initiating production of sedatives."

"Do we have suitable holding areas?"

"Request: details of Kaiinish physiology."

"How long before we can send a force down to the planet?"

"Planetary infosphere rebooting, estimated uptime two minutes."

"Can we expect significant planetary casualties?"

The Testa's engines pushed it toward the stricken Kaiinish vessel. Her hostile occupants were already suiting up and grabbing their weapons.

* * *

The silo was too confining for Tian. It reminded her of the winter caves. 129 and the other two Watchers made her feel welcome, but it was difficult living amongst them. For one, they were extraordinarily quiet. Even though they tried to talk aloud as much as possible when she was around, their awkward speech patterns made prolonged conversation difficult. It was weird to see these three lanky people sitting around the silo clearly engaging in conversation, even gesticulating to one another, without actually making a sound. Tian could never shake the unpleasant feeling that they were talking about her.

Fortunately, she'd managed to persuade them to switch off the gas around the silo, so she could spend as much time above ground as she liked. She spent a lot of time up there doing nothing, simply sitting in the clearing near the silo entrance.

129 had told her what it knew about Mori, and even about Priash. Finally knowing, after all these seasons, gave her something to hold onto. Knowing that the tribe was free from Grashin's tyranny and the immediate threat of the Qah brought her some consolation, too. She couldn't be mad at Mori, either; they shared a lot. If only they"d talked more before Mori was killed.

. . .

129 had asked her a number of times since they'd arrived at the silo whether she wanted to return to the tribe, but Tian knew that Dodona, was no longer her home. There were too many bitter memories. She couldn't bear to see the faces of the tribe again. But she would miss these woods, miss this place.

The Watchers had answered all of her questions about the Confederation. They had shown her things that took her breath away. It would take a long time for her to get used to the Confederation, but she knew she had to. She had to get away from the memories of Priash, Mori, Yehla, the tribe. Start again somewhere else.

She wanted the implants, too. They would enable her to remember Priash, remember Mori, even if they were not her own memories. Sitting on the cold ground outside the silo, looking up at the sky, she returned to that thought over and over. She'd give anything to hear their voices, smell them again, touch them again. 129 had told her to let them go, but she couldn't. Not yet.

A breeze blew from the south, bringing with it the cold mountain air. Tian shivered. She'd spent most of the day inside the silo talking to the Watchers. It was as hard as ever to keep up with their conversation. Even their spoken words were sometimes too fast to understand. It was as if their thoughts raced faster than their mouths, forcing them to utter contracted, barely comprehensible sentences. She wondered why Mori had never been like that. Mori had always talked slowly to her. These three seemed nearly incapable of doing so. But then she wondered a lot of other things about Mori, too. Whatever the reason, the Watchers' attempts to converse with her had given her a headache, and she excused herself to go outside to sit in the fresh air.

She wondered whether there was anywhere on the Confederation worlds like this. Mori had told her that most people in Confederation culture lived in cities or under domes, where there were only oases of vegetation. She'd asked 129 to show her these places on the display, and had marveled at them, hardly believing they could be real. She hoped she could live somewhere close to one, even if it was just a faint imitation of the forest.

It was a cloudy day, and at first she thought the distant rumble was thunder. But it went on for too long, and just kept getting louder. She looked up. An enormous black object emerged from the high clouds. Shiny, like the silo behind her, but bigger. Far bigger. Over the rumble she heard someone shouting at her.

"Tian, they're here! They've arrived!" 129 said, stating the obvious.

The flying silo slowed to a crawl, hovering like a monstrous hummingbird over Tian in the clearing, then beginning its final descent.

"Unable to contact. Something still wrong with infosphere," 129 shouted over the din. Tian's heart jumped. 129 saw her look.

"No, not the Qah, or the Kaiins. The relays are malfunctioning. Instigated reboot of entire system. Ansible beacon sent from this location, explains their landing here."

Tian looked at the shuttle in wonder. Five suited people emerged from it and began walking toward them. As they approached, she could see their faces behind their visors, and could see their smiles. Even so, she moved closer to 129.

"Hello," came a voice from a helmet; it sounded like the AI. She didn't respond. The man in the suit took off his helmet. Tian looked at his face. It was so familiar, yet so alien. He had closely cropped hair, but no hair on his cheeks, chin or neck. His ears were odd, and he wasn't wearing any necklaces or earrings; alongside the lack of hair, that made him look naked. His teeth were bright white, as white as Mori's had been, no stains from the twigs the tribes chewed to clean their teeth.

He reached out a heavily clad hand to her. She looked down at it, and he followed her look. As if realizing a mistake, he took off the bulky glove and extended his hand again. She kept looking at it, unsure what she was supposed to do. She took off one of the bracelets she wore and put it on his bare wrist. He smiled and looked at 129. Tian knew that look from her time with the Watchers. They were talking with their minds. A few seconds later he looked back at her.

"Hello Tian. I'm Yor. Let me introduce everyone else here." The other four suited people came forward, having lingered back when they saw Tian, not wanting to crowd her. The man introduced them, and she smiled at them each in turn. Even the women had short hair, and she couldn't tell if one was male or female until he spoke, the masculine jaw hairless, and the bulky suit concealing any telling curves.

"The Qah..." she started to say, but one of the women interrupted her.

"We know, Tian. 129 just told us everything."

"We're going to do everything we can to stop them hurting any more of the tribes," said one of the others.

"What will you do with the Qah and the Kaiins, if there are more of them here?" Tian asked.

"We'll find them, then attempt to incapacitate them. We've

already captured their starship. Without orbital support, the rest won't be any trouble."

"But what will you do with them?"

129 had spent a long time, much longer than Mori had, explaining how the Confederation worked, including how most of its planets and autonomous regions treated murderers and deviants. Still, Tian's mind reeled at the likelihood that they weren't going to kill the Qah or the Kaiins.

"I mean, you aren't going to just let them go!? You're not going to take them back to the Confederation, are you? I'm not sure if 129 told you but they killed... I want to come back to Consensus with you but not if—"

One of the women held up her hand.

"No, Tian, calm down. We're going to stop them. That's our main priority. I know the Watchers have avoided interfering as much as possible, but we will. We won't protect murderers or slavers. If we find any more Kaiins on the planet, we'll going to put them into cryo and send them back to Kaiinish space eventually."

"If it's any consolation, they'll almost certainly be executed for cowardice when they get there," said Taj, the beardless man. Four heads turned toward him, eyes wide. "Well, it's true," he said, shrugging his shoulders.

"What about the Qah?" Tian asked.

"When we find them, which won't take long, we'll attempt to rehabilitate them here on Dodona. We're fairly sure that the Kaiins conditioned at least some of them. We'll keep them under observation—secure observation—while our medical team assesses them. Then, we'll use behavioral modification, positive reinforcement. We'll eventually let the ones go who we think aren't dangerous anymore."

"But what about the others? What will you do if they stay the same horrible Qah that they always were?"

Taj half-smiled and asked, "Did Mori or 129 ever tell you about the other continents on Dodona?" Tian nodded. "So you know there's a whole empty continent where we can send those beyond help."

Tian tried to imagine what it would be like to live alone on a vast continent, without a tribe or another person to talk to, to sleep with, to love or laugh with. It instantly made her think of her own tribe, and sent a chill down her spine.

"I wouldn't wish that on anybody," she said.

"No. But hopefully it won't come to that. Our medical teams are pretty good. And the tribes might take in some of the less seriously affected."

"What about the tribes, then?"

The five stirred simultaneously, as if they"d heard something that she hadn"t.

"Listen, Tian, we can discuss this on the shuttle. We need to find the Qah before they attack any more silos or other tribes."

"You want me to come with you, on *that*?" Tian said, pointing at the shuttle.

"Yes. 129 says you're thinking about leaving this place and returning with us to the Confederation. If you want to do that, you'll have to get on a shuttle at some point."

"Are we leaving now?"

"No, we're not going anywhere yet. You can still change your mind."

"What about you?" She turned to look at 129. "Are you coming?"

"Negative, my place: here. Much work to do. Go Tian."

Things seemed to be moving too fast. She was worried that she"d never see 129 again, and 129 was the closest thing she'd had to a friend since Mori left her.

129 seemed to read her mind. "Do not be concerned. We will communicate again before you depart for the Confederation worlds. But really you must go now. You still have many questions. These people can answer them. I already explained everything to them. Request: go."

129 turned away and walked into the silo. Tian watched it

go. The five suited people were already turning back toward the shuttle, beckoning for her to come with them.

The excitement got the better of Tian, and she soon forgot her worries. Even the lurch in her stomach as they lifted off was more exciting than nauseating, and she watched in wonder as the trees and then the clouds flew by.

The shuttle was nicer than the silos, more comfortable. They left her on the observation deck at the front of the shuttle, explaining that they needed to discuss things with the fleet and possibly prepare for a strike against the Qah. Moving at the rate they were, Tian was surprised that they hadn't already found them, but she didn't say anything, just looked around curiously.

A few minutes later the ship began to descend. As it penetrated the thick blanket of cloud, she could see that they were still above the forest, but she had no idea where. Ora, one of the crew, came to talk to her.

"We've found them," she said.

"The Qah?" asked Tian.

"Yes. There are Kaiins there, too."

Even though her heart was beating fast, remembering what the Qah and Kaiin had done to the tribe and Mori, Tian asked, "Can I come with you?"

"No. You'd just get in the way. You can stay here and watch." She pointed to a display screen, similar to the ones Tian had seen in the silo.

Tian turned to look at the display, which had suddenly burst into life. It showed that they were hovering over a sprawling camp. She let out a gasp when she saw the size of it; there had to be at least five hundred people down there. Qah. She could see upturned brown faces, and thought she heard the sound of dogs barking. There were bright flashes. A few of them were shooting Kaiinish weapons at the shuttle. Tian looked at the woman beside her in alarm, but Ora was placid, unconcerned.

"Aren't you going down with the others?" Tian asked.

"No, I'm not trained for it. Some of us specialize in certain areas. Like you are trained in hunting. You do it all the time, you've had a lot of practice, and you're good at it. I could do what the others are about to do, but I'm much better at healing than I am at shooting," she said.

"Like Priash," Tian murmured, looking back at the display.

There was a lot of confusion below them. She could see people running away into the forest in panic.

"But they're getting away."

"Don"t worry." Almost as soon as these words left Ora's mouth, there was a dull thudding sound that lasted about ten seconds. Tian saw almost everyone on the ground freeze and look up at the sky. A few started running toward the forest. Nothing happened for what felt like minutes. .

Then there was a bright flash, followed by a tremendous blast of noise that rolled on and on. Even inside the ship, it was the loudest sound that Tian had ever heard. On the display, people fell over in droves.

Then, just as suddenly as it started, the noise ended. The display started to flicker, a strobing light somewhere out of view flashing upon the forest below like lightning. Just seeing it made Tian feel sick, and she looked away.

"What's happening?" she asked Ora.

"Some of them are wearing Kaiinish masks. The gas we dropped to incapacitate the rest wasn't having any effect on them. We had to use less pleasant means."

"Will it kill them?" Tian risked a glance at the screen, at the fallen figures in the strobing light, and quickly looked away, again.

"Are they dead?"

"No, but they'll feel pretty bad for a while."

"What about the animals? The slaves? There are innocent people down there."

"We know, Tian, but the alternatives are much worse. They might start killing hostages, and we'd have to use lethal force.

The effects of the weapons are temporary, and it's much better than getting into a firefight where people would be killed."

The flashing ended. The display showed small black objects falling from the shuttle, landing in small clusters amongst the Qah. Tian realizsed with shock that these were people. They must be the crew. They had just jumped from the shuttle and landed on the forest floor a hundred meters below, apparently unhurt, as if they were made of nothing more than feathers. She watched as they made their way speedily through the forest, stopping over each prostrate Qah before moving on.

Tian could see two moving figures to the north of the camp. The display had highlighted the crew that had jumped from the shuttle in green. These two figures, though, were glowing red.

"Kaiins," Ora said.

The two red figures began to run toward a clearing where a small cluster of green shapes were checking bodies. Ora told Tian that the crew were tagging the Qah, and administering a sedative. The green cluster didn't appear to react to the on-coming threat, and kept crouching down amongst the bodies, seemingly unaware. Tian looked at Ora, but she had the same unconcerned expression as before.

The red shapes were around fifty meters away from the green ones when another bright light flashed from the shuttle. Instead of bathing the entire forest, though, it isolated the small area around the two red figures. It didn't flicker, either; the beam just seemed to pulse. The two red figures stopped in their tracks.

Ora looked uncomfortable. "Our newest and most unpleasant weapon," she said.

"What is it?" Tian asked, her voice almost a whisper.

"It disrupts the neurotransmitters in the brain, and destroys their implants. We only use it in extreme situations."

"Won't that kill them?"

"No, but they"ll need lengthy treatment and weeks of re-habilitation. If there was any other way... Unfortunately, we've been around them for far too long. They never surrender. It would be dishonorable. They'd rather die. And they can be very, very dangerous, even when they're badly injured. As you know. You were remarkably fortunate to survive your own encounter."

"So you never kill them?"

"We try to avoid it, unless lives are at immediate risk."

"But how will you ever win your fight with them, your war?" asked Tian.

Ora smiled. "Obviously we'd prefer to avoid fighting them. But we'd rather fight the same Kaiin a thousand times than kill them in cold blood. For us, that would be losing the war. We return them to Kaiinish space. We've heard that the Kaiins kill them, but we can't control what the Kaiins do to them. We *can* control what we do to them. We don't kill prisoners."

Tian thought that sounded specious, but on the verge of seeing the wonders Mori had described to her, she wasn't going to argue.

Ora continued, "Nobody really ever really wins a war, Tian. And you certainly don't win wars by abandoning your values. We learned that a long time ago."

Chapter 2

Tian followed the progress of the small green figures on the display for some time. She watched as they picked up the still inert Qah and placed them on flat surfaces that looked to Tian a lot like the beds in the village. It was hard to tell though from this angle. She found herself squinting, almost frowning, at the display, involuntarily turning her head to one side to get a better view. Ora's hand reached over and pointed to something on the display. It looked like a small green eye. The woman indicated that she should press it, so she did. The display changed, making Tian back away. The screen was suddenly full of activity. The overhead view was replaced by fifteen or so small boxes. Tian's eyes scanned them all, trying to take everything in. Ora told her to press one of them, any one, and she picked one of the top ones. Her fingers barely touched the surface when the picture enlarged, displacing all of the others.

A Qah face came into sharp focus. Her eyes were shut, and the mask had fallen from her face revealing a strong nose and full, slightly flared lips. Even though she was a Qah, it was hard to hate such a graceful, handsome face, as much as Tian hated to admit it. She scowled, mostly at herself. Then the face was gone, and the body placed gently on what looked like a padded hammock by a pair of suited hands.

"What are they doing?"

But Ora didn't answer. She didn't need to. The platform the Qah woman was on started to move, change. The edges curled around her, tightening like a snake around prey. Tian saw the woman's arms compacted against her sides, and her bare legs pressed together, before she was engulfed, wrapped up like a spider would a fly. Before Tian could see what happened next, the man had turned his head away.

Tian continued to watch as the man approached other prone figures. He placed a small stick on each of their necks and waited for a light to flash. Most of them looked peaceful, like the first woman Tian had seen, but a few had blood beneath their noses, and one had a deep cut above his eye.

"Don't worry, they're perfectly safe," said Ora.

"Are we going to go down there? The shuttle, I mean?"

"Once they've secured everyone, yes. We need to pick up the Kaiins, then we'll work out who is who down there. They seem to have a number of slaves. We'll set up a medical facility here, and start processing them."

"You'll let the slaves go, though? Back to the tribes?" Tian was trying not to think about her tribe, and the fact that there might be some of her own people down there amongst all those Qah.

"Depending on how the Qah have treated them, we hope so, yes."

218 • NICHOLAS P. OAKLEY

"But what will you tell them? Mori said you wanted to avoid contacting the tribes, that it might ruin things here."

"I think we're going to have to take a serious look at the way we operate here, Tian. And I think the Kaiins and Qah have already changed things, don't you?"

"You're not worried about the settlement agreement?"

Ora laughed. "No, Tian. You've been hanging around with those anthropologists for too long. We're not as concerned as they are about rules and etiquette, especially with everything that's happened. Of course, we'll try to avoid too much 'contamination,' as they like to call it, but things will have to change."

Tian shifted, uncomfortably. She had reconciled herself to the fact that she'd be leaving this world behind. Deep down, she knew that she couldn't live here any longer, knowing what she knew about the Confederation, the Way, and Grashin. She felt as if she were somehow protecting the tribe from that knowledge, what it represented, by leaving. To hear Ora speak, it seemed that the tribe's whole way of life would end anyway, whether she went or not. Tian sighed and looked downward.

Ora looked closely at her and said, "Tian, surely you of all people see that restricting knowledge in some sort of noble desire to protect others is simply untenable. It leads to divisions. Exploitation, even. None of those people down there chose this life. A group of idealists chose it for them many, many orbits ago. Why should they have to live the life their ancestors wanted? Why should they die in childbirth, freeze to death in poorly made huts, toil for hours collecting roots, spend days searching for food and water, unless they want to? That might have been the life the Ferals wanted, that they chose, but you never chose that, did you?"

"No," said Tian. She'd turned back to the display, watching the progress of the man securing the Qah. If the tribes, the Qah, had been given a choice, would any of this have happened?

As if reading her mind, the woman continued. "They thought the only way they could protect their culture, their way of life, was to hide the past away, or make up scary stories to help enforce their beliefs. To take that choice away from everyone else, and construct rules and customs to keep things the same, to stop questions, to stop development that strayed from their narrow ideology. All that they achieved was to make life here harder and more unpleasant, with far fewer choices."

An anxious expression passed over Tian's face. "So what do you plan to do? Most of them love it here. You're not going to make them leave, go back to the Confederation, are you?"

"No, of course not. But we think it's time we stopped being so worried about 'contaminating' them. We've been discussing it. We'd certainly like to hear your views."

"We?" Tian asked, looking around the room.

"Yes, the Confederation. We'd talk to you once you're linked intoon the infosphere, as a kind of delegate of Dodona. It's much easier."

"Surely we can do it like this, just talking?"

"Well, yes, but—"

"So what are you planning?" Tianshe asked, firmly.

Ora paused for a split second. Tian suddenly had the feeling that they were no longer having this discussion between just the two of them. Tian tried not to think about how many people were seeing her face through this woman"s eyes.

"First of all, we plan to contact every tribe. We'll do it as unobtrusively as we can. Certainly no shuttles or light shows, or even Watchers."

Tian smiled at that.

Ora continued, "It's clear that we'll need to maintain a greater presence than previously."

"The Kaiins," said Tian.

"Yes. We'd like to prevent any further Kaiinish presence here. We're not planning to build settlements, but we'll probably put a few observation satellites in orbit, and some automated weapons bots. We're also thinking about removing the limits on silo usage, as well as the gas that discourages abuse. It appears that a lot of the hostility here stemmed from what was, basically, a territory dispute. The Qah were pushed away from areas that could support them comfortably, to marginal areas that could only support a subsistence-level existence. We think the silos can mitigate need or hunger as an instigator of conflict. Obviously those who don't want to use the silos won't have to, but we'd like to make them available for everyone. The tribes are not children. They can make their own decisions."

"Sounds... reasonable. Though I'm not sure what the Way would say about that."

"That's the next thing. We'd like to distribute something like these." Oraq pulled out what looked like a piece of paper from one of her pockets and handed it to Tian. It was light and flexible, made of an unfamiliar material. "A few of the tribes held a lot of power because of what they knew. Yours was one of them. Not just about the Way. About a lot of things. Herbs, ways of making things, the histories. When only a few people have access to information, it gives them power, control over those who don't. Do you see what I mean?"

"Yes. You're talking about Grashin and the Way, aren't you? Leaders."

Ora nodded. "Yes, but not just that. It seems quite possible, probable in fact, that the Qah saw how Grashin and others like him in other tribes used their knowledge to control behavior, restrict choices, rather than help others. And they took that to its logical conclusion, violence and slavery."

"They really did that, didn't they? I don't know why no one ever saw it before." Tears sprang to Tian"s eyes. "That's why Mori got so upset with me: Mori knew all along. What happened with the Qah was our fault, just like Mori said it was, but I just couldn't believe it"

"You had no reason to suspect." Ora placed a hand on Tian"s shoulder. "To try to avoid anything like that happening again, we're proposing to give each tribe, maybe each individual, one of these." She reached over and made a small gesture in the center of the paper, and it filled with writing and symbols. "It holds a lot of knowledge. Some very simple, some not so simple. And look," she said, knocking it out of Tian's hand suddenly, "it's very sturdy, too." It landed on the floor and seemed to bounce, apparently undamaged.

"You think that this will stop another Grashin?" asked Tian, stooping to pick up the paper.

"We hope so."

"But if you give them this... if they learn about all these things, . . . won't they all want to leave?"

"I don't think so. You said yourself that most of them are happy here, that they wouldn't dream of changing most things in their lives. And why would they? If Priash and Grashin hadn't been in your life, you'd probably feel the same, too."

"Maybe," Tian admitted reluctantly.

"It might make them more critical of their current way of doing things. It might push them too far in that direction. Maybe it'll change their culture profoundly, maybe they"ll abandon the Way. But it'll be their choice. The things in that," she pointed to the strange paper that Tian had picked up off the floor, "are only the kind of things in Grashin's library. If it gets to the point where the tribes want to know more, the silos can tell them everything they want to know."

And you'll let them leave?"

"Yes. That was always part of the agreement, only it was forgotten long ago or suppressed by those who feared change or wanted power over others. We're just letting people choose for themselves again, Tian."

"What about the Panacea?"

Ora let out a sigh. "We've thought a lot about that. There's a general consensus on the other things. Consensus on everything except that one. What do you think?"

Tian stopped to think. The display was still showing the view from the man's eyes below them. It looked like he was taking a break.

"My only concern is that, well, Mori once told me that your Confederation relies on technology for everything. That you can't survive without it. Mori also told me that when things break they're difficult to replace without more technology. Is that true?"

"Yes, I suppose that's fair."

"If we had a Panacea, then we might forget how to mix herbs or make ointments, and if it ever stopped working, we'd be lost."

Ora smiled. "That's the way some of us feel about it, too."

"There's another thing. I only had a Panacea for a few days, but it was, well… it's hard to describe. But the look on the others' faces when I used it. I can see it having the same effect as Grashin's library. Whoever knew how to use it would be looked up to. I only had it for a few weeks, but it was so valuable, so important, I felt like I couldn't trust anyone else with it. Even people I lived with my entire life. I've never felt like that about anything ever before, and I can see it changing people. And if someone like Grashin got their hands on it . . ."

"We could get around that by giving everyone one though, couldn't we?"

"Yes, I suppose." Tian paused, deep in thought. "But where would it stop? I've seen things on this ship and in the silos that are so incredible that they would completely change our way of life. If you gave everyone a Panacea, why not give them all implants, or any of the other extraordinary things, technologies, that you have? I bet there are a hundred things on this ship alone that the tribes could use to make their lives better. And I think that's what unsettles me about it. It isn't anything about destroying a way of life or anything like that. I just think there's a big difference between this paper and the silos, where people have the choice to use them, and things like the Panacea where everyone would need one. Life just wouldn't be the same without it. That reliance… I'm not sure I like that, or the tribes would, either. As much as I hate to admit it, knowing and what this thing can do, I think the Panacea is just a step too far."

"You don't think the tribes should decide that for themselves?"

"Maybe. I guess it depends on what you want. If you want to make sure everyone has as much informed choice as possible, then you should ask them all. Show them the options, give them the choice. But if you want to stop another Qah, or let the tribes live independently, without relying on you and all of your technology, then I'd say no. But then you'd still be making a choice for them by withholding information.

"We've actually thought of a third way. Let me share it with you and, see what you think.... As I said, we're as conflicted as you are, for both the reasons you express and a great deal more that I won't go into. Essentially, we'd like to give everyone an informed choice. We'd like to show them the Panacea, and some of the other things the Confederations has to offer. But we won't distribute any technology except the 'paper.' If anyone wants the other things, they'll have to leave Dodona and go to one of the Confederation worlds. How does that sound?"

"I'm not sure. A bit unfair, I suppose," Tian said. "Like telling someone a story and then stopping before the end. Or showing a dog a piece of meat and then snatching it away just as she opens her jaws. How could they refuse if you show them things like the Panacea, or the shuttles, or the Cornucopia, but tell them that they can only have them if they leave?"

"Well, we there's something else to think of. Remember, we want to give everyone a choice. But we have a duty to this planet, too. We're committed to protecting this ecosystem, the biodiversity of the forest and the plains, the oceans and the sentient life there. There is a price for living here, in such a paradise. You're right that once we start to disseminate advanced technologies we risk all of that. There are already a very vocal few who are arguing, as we speak, that removing the limits on the silos will cause a population boom that is unsustainable. That it will lead to cities, and that we'll have to intervene in a few generations anyway."

"Do you think they're right?" asked Tian.

"We're hoping that the knowledge from that 'paper' will off-set some of that. "If we give the tribes an understanding of their place here, the reasons behind their unique culture and way of life, we're hoping that will be enough. If people choose to leave, fine. But if they choose to stay, and we think most of them will, then they should be given the opportunity to understand why and how it is that they came to be here, the privileges and duties that arise from living here."

"But what about those who don't want to leave, but who re-fuse to accept those ethics, those duties?"

"You underestimate them. You won't like me saying this, but it's the way they've lived for a long time. Most of what they learn won't be foreign to the tribes at all; they'll already feel it intui-tively after living here in the forest all of their lives. If you strip away all the self-serving nonsense, all the archaic language, in-terpretations and rituals and so on from the Way, what do you get, what values? Respect for nature, harmony, sharing, only taking what you need and giving back as much as you can, mu-tual aid, hospitality, cooperation, solidarity. These are all values that work well for a reason. They make the tribes' lives easier, but also allow them to live here generation after generation. They couldn't survive here without those values. A few things that they learn from us might make that easier, like better ways to store food, or to cultivate medicinal herbs, but these can be done sensibly, where everyone understands the needs and lim-its of such practices.

"You'll always have some who, for whatever reason, refuse to live peaceably in the tribes, or who disregard their values. Egoizers, as you call them. Hopefully there will be fewer of them if they can choose to leave if they choose, but we think the majority of the people here will carry on the way they've been living for a long time."

"I think it will change them," said Tian. Ora had almost con-vinced her, but she was still reluctant to admit it.

"We're not imposing anything on them. We're giving them what every single Feral settler who came here had: choice. They'll know what Grashin and a few others always knew. They'll know that if they aren't happy here they can leave, rather than rebel or fight, and they'll know how important their role here is, how unique and special their lives are, what a privilege it is to live here. I'm sure most of them feel that way alredy. But they deserve to have that knowledge, and make their own decisions."

Tian's eyes roamed back to the display. The man was up again, his short break over, busying himself with checking another body. He turned over a Qah who had fallen face down. Tian let out a gasp. She recognized him. He was from one of the plains tribes she'd spent a few seasons with after Priash disappeared. But he wore Qah clothes, and had Qah beads in his ears and notches in his beard. Tian remembered him distinctly, though, despite how much he'd changed. He was always quiet, a bit solitary. After Priash's disappearance, she'd been quiet and solitary, too, and had struck up a friendship with him because of that. He was an outsider, like her, and he never asked her questions or spoke about himself. At the time, still in mourning for Priash, Tian had appreciated that, and appreciated his company and a warm body to lie next to at night. To see him now, so changed. A Qah. What could have happened to him? Had he been captured? Was he a slave? Or had he joined them voluntarily? Her mind reeled. Meanwhile, he disappeared into one of the platforms, swallowed whole by the strange device.

Tian turned back to Ora, who had been watching Tian's reaction to the display with interest. With a long look into Ora's eyes, behind which countless others were watching, Tian finally gave a firm nod.

"You're right. Give them the choice," she said.

* * *

As the shuttle soared toward the stars, Tian marveled at the way the land below fell away, losing its detail, turning into a mass of green, brown, and then blue that extended beyond the horizon. Then she'd seen the curve, and the blackness above them. And then the starship.

Tian awoke. A hand pressed down on her chest as she tried to rise. Her head felt sore, and she was groggy, like she'd smoked too much yusha or drunk too much of Haroon's yeasty beer. She forced her eyes open. The room was too bright and she mumbled a protest.

She must have fallen back asleep, because when she tried to open her eyes again the room was dark. She could still feel the hand on her chest, though, and she couldn't sit up. She reached up to push the hand away, but it wasn't a hand. It was a belt strapping her to the bed.

Then she remembered where she was.

Her hands found a clasp and the belt retracted into the bed below her, freeing her upper body. She sat up, her head still thick. With a sudden flutter of fear, she realizsed she couldn't hear anything. There was nobody in her head; she was still alone. The operation had failed, the implants weren't working. She cried out, realizing that she would never clearly remember Priash or Mori, that she'd never be part of the Confederation.

Her cry brought a short man bustling into the room as the lights came up. He was dressed entirely in white. He held his hands up in an attempt to calm her down.

"They're not working!" she shouted.

"I know, I know. Calm down," he said, taking her hand. "We explained this, don't you remember? They don't work right away; you have to get used to them. You have to wait for all of the connections to establish themselves. That takes some time. Remember?"

Tian tried to think. It hurt, but she thought she could remember some of the things the man was saying.

"Ugh," she groaned. "I feel . . . "

Her head swam. She lay back down and went to sleep again, dreaming she was being engulfed one of those strange platforms.

CHAPTER 3

Tian awoke to a gentle tap on her shoulder. Her head was clear now, and the lights less harsh on her eyes.

"Tian? Wake up. We need to talk to you."

She mumbled something and tried to sit up. "What? Did something go wrong?"

"No, it went fine."

"But I *still* can't hear anything?"

"You will shortly. The neural implants have started to come online, started to connect, and the bioware is integrating into your body. It's a bit daunting at first, but you'll be fine. It was a success. But listen, something has happened. We're going to have to leave here sooner than we expected."

That brought things into sharper focus. "What do you mean?" Tian asked.

"We received a message from the Confederation. There's been an attack. A big one. The Kaiins have landed troops on two worlds. We're needed back there right away."

"Now?"

"Yes. We've recalled almost everyone from the surface."

"But, what about the tribes? What about the Qah?"

"We're going to leave a small group here to start to implement the changes we discussed. But this is a warship, and the war is being fought right now, very far from here."

"I can't go yet. I need to say goodby to the Watchers, to 129."

"Tian, you have two choices. You can either leave now, with us, or we'll take you back down to the surface."

"How long would I have to stay?"

"We think it'll take about four seasons before the Qah are fully reintegrated or resettled. We'll schedule a transport to arrive then to pick up the remaining crew and anyone from the tribes who wants to leave."

"Four seasons?"

"Four seasons, give or take."

Tian's head began to hurt.

"Will I have the infosphere?"

"Yes, but only the planetary infosphere."

"But I thought we were going to visit the oceanic stations, see the marine life. You were going to show me the other continents. We have to visit the tribes, give them all paper—"

"We don't have time for that now. The Watchers and the team we leave behind will sort all of that out."

"We never talked about what will happen to them, the Watchers. Will you let them stay here?"

"It isn't a matter of us letting them or not. They want to stay here, so they will stay here. This is their home too."

"Yes, but will they still watch the tribes?"

"From a distance, yes. Like they've always done. They are anthropologists, after all. It's what they live for. We'd never stop them doing that, if that's what they want."

Tian stood up. Her head was pounding, and she desperately wanted more time to think. To leave now, so suddenly, without saying goodbye . . . But the alternative, to sit in one of the silos for four seasons waiting to leave, seemed just as unbearable.

"I don't know... What should I do?"

"Either way, you need to sit down. The bioimplants could activate at any time, and it's better if you're asleep when that happens. It's easier."

"But you woke me!" Tian said in protest.

"I know, but we had to find out what you wanted to do before we left. I know it's sudden, Tian, but we need a decision."

"Right now?"

"Yes. We're ready to leave now."

"Let me see it," said Tian. "Dodona. Let me see it, show it to me it. I can't decide until I've seen it."

The doctor sighed and then took her by the hand. "Come on then, but let's make it quick. If you start to feel sick or your vision starts to get fuzzy, let me know."

"Will that mean the implants are starting to work?" She was already feeling unwell, and the room had been spinning for a while.

"Yes. Come on," he said, helping her up from the bed. "Let's go."

Tian hobbled to the door. They walked down a narrow corridor, as Tian concentrated on placing one foot after another. At last they walked into a big empty room.

The door closed behind them, and then the far wall started to retract upward into the ceiling. A blue-green orb against a black background began to spread out before them. The wall continued to rise. The view took Tian"s breath away.

The whole of Dodona: a perfect blue-green globe, dotted with white specks of clouds and the brown masses of continents. She sat there for a long time staring at it.

A few moments later there was a rumbling somewhere deep below them. The doctor, who she'd completely forgotten about, stirred at the sound.

"Tian, we're ready."

His voice sounded strange, distant. The room was spinning, and she felt light headed. "Will the memories from down there be back in the Confederation, too?"

The doctor paused for a fraction of a second. "Yes, of course," he said, fending off a hundred queries over the infosphere asking what the delay was.

"Okay. Let's go," Tian said finally. "I'm ready. Goodbye Mori," she whispered.

As the words left her lips her head was filled with a thousand, a million voices, colors, thoughts, emotions. It was as if she was walking out of the deepest, darkest cave into a forest filled with birdsong, bright colors, smells and light. The sensation was overwhelming, but beautiful. Incredibly beautiful. One minute she was alone, the next she wasn't. The doctor said something, and she heard it in her mind too, but it was so much clearer, so much more detailed, had so much more depth to it than the words he spoke aloud.

"Hello Tian," said a thousand different voices.

Then, in an instant, the planet that had filled the wall but a second before vanished, falling away in the blink of an eye.